LITTLE FACE
AND OTHER STORIES

LITTLE FACE

AND OTHER STORIES BY JEAN THOMPSON

A GROLIER COMPANY

FRANKLIN WATTS / 1984
NEW YORK / LONDON / TORONTO / SYDNEY

Library of Congress Cataloging in Publication Data

Thompson, Jean, 1950–
Little Face and other stories.

I. Title.
PS3570.H625L5   1984   813'.54   84-7578
ISBN 0-531-09760-9

"Foreigners" was first published in
Southwest Review, Winter, 1981

"Having Words" was first published in
Chicago, December, 1981

"Remembering Sonny" was first published in
Kansas Quarterly, Vol. 13, no. 1, Winter, 1981

"Sex Life of the Sponge" was originally published in
The Banyan Anthology, 1982

"Little Face" was first published in
Mademoiselle, August, 1983, under the title
"Lessons from an Older Man"

C∅NTENTS

LITTLE FACE
AND OTHER STORIES

FOREIGNERS

There were many foreign students at the university, which was famous everywhere for its laboratories and solemn libraries and its island of handsome gray buildings in the middle of the battered city. In post offices or banks, clerks grew used to explaining, then repeating the explanations, then again, a little more loudly each time, until the still-baffled foreigner grew conscious of standing there too long. Winter somehow managed to make these students look even more isolated, more like exiles. Most of them were unused to the cold of this northern city, where the wind was a steady glacial blast, impersonal and humiliating, where one might go two weeks at a time without seeing the sun. Perhaps from lack of experience, the foreign students bought the kind of winter coats that you never saw elsewhere. They might be lined with matted gray fiber, or fastened with little wooden barrels, or made of hulking plaids, or else they were shapeless black old-lady coats which flapped like sails in the wind. It was monumentally sad to see an Indian woman, her feet in sandals and white wool socks, picking her way through the winter-filthy street, a scarf tied babushka-style around her head, a yard of thin bright sari, turquoise or gold or green, fluttering below such a coat. On the face of the woman would be a look of intense, unseeing concentration, her dark eyes measuring some distance known only to herself, as if panic could only be warded off by this resolute inward turning. One January, in fact, an Arab student had chained himself to the bed in his dormitory cubicle and set the mattress on fire.

Paul saw a number of such students, and their families, from the windows of the bookstore where he worked: Japanese, Africans, Latins. Many of them lived in the hideous tracts of apartments nearby. They were a part of the life that streamed past him on the other side of the glass, tantalizing and unknowable. After a time he could pick out the less conspicuous ones, the Slavs or the Greeks, say. They all had that same unseeing stare, that determined inwardness, and once you learned to recognize it, it was as unmistakable as a badge.

He had lots of time to look out the window, because the bookstore had few customers. It was a small place, relying heavily on atmosphere, losing ground in perceptible but undramatic ways. A film of dust marked those shelves no one could easily reach, like the timberline on a mountaintop. The plants hanging in the window quivered in the currents of drying air. The table of unsold "specials" grew ominously. Paul ordered the books he wanted to read and spent whole hours buried in them at his desk, startled out of his trance by the sudden consciousness of silence. Or sometimes, at the end of the day, when he tugged the heavy iron grating across the windows, the sound of the dull metal made his heart drop in his chest, as if he were locking himself not out, but in.

Les, who owned the store, was scornful of any booksellers who stocked bridge tallies or birthday cards or Gothic romances or comics, and while Paul agreed in principle, he was beginning to suspect that principles, in isolation, did nobody any good. The store was on the fringe of campus, a precarious frontier post about to be engulfed by slums. Les came in a couple times a week to check up on things. He no longer pretended that business was not bad, but he attributed it to the decline of literacy: Do they read? My sweet ass. Picture books about space ships and rock stars. Poetry is what comes in a Hallmark card. Art, that's an electric guitar. By "they" it was understood that he meant youth, punks. Paul always wondered, uncomfortably, what deficiency in himself made Les set him apart.

Paul thought about other jobs. But the store was comfortable, he was willing to settle for little money in exchange for little work, and he had only vague ideas about the sort of job he might want instead. He was twenty-three, no longer in school himself. Yet he had gravitated to the university because he still loved the atmosphere of study, of seriousness and purpose. And he still thought of himself as a student, with plenty of time until his real future began. He was going to be a writer, and he had come to the city to write. He wanted to know more about life; the only way he could think to learn was by placing himself in proximity to it. A combination of shyness and impatience had always made it hard for him to go about things more directly. He wanted to absorb experience; he wanted to live intensely.

At his desk in the store, or at night in his rented room, he labored over his writing. So much time spent simply staring at the page! But he knew that frustration was part of the experience he sought, that it could even be considered suffering, and therefore valuable. He would write about his childhood. It had been like everyone else's. He would invent a character who had had a strange and brutal childhood. His pen tapped the paper. Smoke from his cigarette curled effortlessly, an intricate blue tendril. He would write about vital things, about suffering, and need. He would write only thin pretentious imitations of what he had read. When these thoughts grew unbearable, he rose and walked to the window and leaned his head against the cold glass. Beyond it would be the city night, its secrets, its promise of gaudiness and violence. Mocking him, the glass threw back his own reflection. A pale smooth face, the forehead high and exposed, dark oversensitive eyes. A puppy's face, he thought in a fit of self-disgust.

He walked for hours through the city's early darkness or its rare blue days, gathering the faces he saw, gathering men in bars, old women on buses. Walking along railroad tracks and sidewalks, his white breath a kind of secret speech, breathing out all the things he could not say. He lay on his drooping mattress and the city revolved around him, or perhaps he himself revolved, a space traveler sealed in his own smooth bubble of skin. He was sick with longing, and with waiting for his life to begin, and with terrible unreasoning joy.

It was November, and Les had already hung dozens of glossy Christmas ornaments from a complicated network of ceiling wires. Paul kept brushing them irritably out of his hair. All day he had been fighting sleep. The night before he had gone to a movie on campus, a grainy, flickering film with subtitles and lots of moody close-ups, shown in the basement of the law building. He yawned, squeezing tears from the corners of his eyes. A man's face appeared against the glass, disembodied, a balloon on a string. Then it vanished.

Objects in Paul's vision went instantly black, as if a flashbulb had gone off in front of him. Frost in the corners of the window obscured everything but the man's revolving shadow. He was pacing in front of the store, hesitating, wheeling, pacing again. Paul had imagined it over and over, such a moment, such a face. It was a holdup. It had happened at the grocery down the street, just like this, in broad daylight. Casual big-city meaningless death. Paul had a vision of himself on his knees behind the desk, his fingers groping for the holes the bullets made, blood pumping out of him in spurts, like hiccups. The man had stopped pacing and was standing, hands jammed deep in his coat pockets, before the door. There was no one else in the store, no one in sight on the street. If he leapt up now, he could throw the bolt, or dash out the back way. Too late; the jingle bells on the doorknob crashed against the glass.

He was tall, young, hatless, and he wore a gray nubby overcoat that seemed to pinch his shoulders. He glanced at Paul, then quickly away. The man's nervousness terrified Paul; he was sure he was right. The cash register held only thirty-three dollars, he remembered. The man picked up a book, put it down, and once again faced Paul. Please, he said.

What? said Paul. What.

Please, would you allow, the man began. His voice was rather high for his size, and a little wavering. In your window. I have these . . .

And he drew from beneath his coat a stack of damp-looking, blue-inked papers. Paul stared, then craned to read upside down. He saw DEATH and FREEDOM. Quickly the man turned them around.

THE SHAH IS A U.S. PUPPET!
SUPPORT FREEDOM—JUSTICE
DEATH TO TYRANTS AND AMERICAN IMPERIALISTS!
ALL WELCOME

It was a notice of a meeting, sponsored by the Iranian Students' Association. I see, said Paul. He felt weak, hilarious. You know, he said, for a minute there I thought you had a gun. The student's chin jerked upward. His thick black eyebrows and mustache were like what a child might draw with a crayon, three heavy, wavering lines. The rest of the face seemed to exist is a different plane, curiously detached from them, a young, narrow, small-boned face. Everything about him, in fact, seemed slightly out of proportion, or maybe joined together too hastily. Now he was staring at Paul with enormous mistrustful black eyes. Paul sobered himself, hoping the student would think it all some inexplicable American slang.

Please, said the student. If you would allow.

Les wouldn't like it. Les would probably never see it. Paul continued to frown, just to steady himself, though he'd already decided to say yes.

I have tape, the student said with an air of triumph, as if this was a clinching argument. And he pulled, from the same recess beneath his coat, a roll of brittle yellow tape. He set it down on the desk and began picking at it, coaxing it to unroll. Bent over, he seemed even more awkward, tensely mobile, all elbows and big chapped hands.

OK, said Paul. Let's find a spot. Trying to feel purposeful, he got up from his desk and leaned over the window.

No, said the student. The center more, please.

He was right. The frost in the corners would hide the words. Shrugging, Paul centered the paper. It obscured one of Les's gold foil stars and a copy of *Beloved Christmas Tales*.

OK? Paul said again. The student nodded formally and coughed. The black lines across his face arched themselves. Paul realized he was preparing for speech.

An important meeting, he said. About the American crimes.

Hopefully, he watched Paul for some reaction. Paul kept his face in the expression of mild interest that he reserved for people who talked to him on subways. The student coughed and tried again.

The Shah is a criminal. He must be overthrown. American government is a criminal because they need oil, they are the Shah's great friend. Can you deny it?

I really wouldn't know, said Paul.

There is torture, there is no freedom, the student went on, a little flatly now, as if he needed more argument to keep himself going. In my country, one can be imprisoned seven years just for reading Jack London.

Paul nodded. He didn't care much for Jack London himself, he could have said, but he knew better. He cared even less for politics. He wished the man would leave.

An important meeting, he repeated insistently. Very important. It seems the language was making him clumsy, trapping his thoughts in some fine constricting web so that only the smallest squeezed through. He gazed out over the massed books, then turned once again to Paul. Perhaps you will come to our meeting, he said. Very important, to learn.

Perhaps, said Paul, not knowing what else to say. This time the man bowed, a quick dipping of his pinched shoulders. He thrust his bare hands into his pockets, and left the shop.

It depressed Paul to think of this meeting, which he imagined no one would attend, announced in this window, which no one ever looked at. But on that night Paul found himself strolling on campus. The lights of the auditorium were bright beads in the distance. Walking closer, his feet scuffing slightly on the cleared pavement. The door was propped open. This is probably a mistake, he thought as he entered.

In fact there were quite a few people there, and Paul was able to be as inconspicuous as he wished. An Iranian, a young man, made a speech at the whistling microphone. He thanked them all for coming; he said that they were here to inform and educate the American people about their government's complicity in the Shah's crimes. A beautiful young woman with long black hair stood up and said no, who cared about education, they were here to mobilize support for the revolution. She spoke passionately, and well. Was this where one met such girls, Paul wondered? He imagined her carrying a rifle.

The lines had been drawn for the evening's debate. All around him people were leaning forward in their seats, nodding or disagreeing, wanting to be heard. Paul watched their faces, intent, absorbed, animated by urgency or anger. He felt he had discovered a new world, one in which people grew larger than themselves, breathed some charged air, spoke to each other in a grave language of shared knowledge. As for what they said, he believed it. The Shah was a bastard. Americans were dolts. He had not been told before. It was as simple as that.

The meeting lasted almost two hours. Paul loitered in the doorway among the little knots of people still talking, hoping to see the girl with the long hair again. Instead he found himself standing before the looming, narrow-shouldered figure of the student who had come into the bookstore.

Paul ducked his head, hoping to pretend he hadn't recognized him. It was one of his shy, prickly habits, this involuntary shrinking. But the student's face was going through identical furtive movements; the black crayon slashes of hair squirmed, then went limp, trapped. Uneasily, they acknowledged each other. So, the student said, pinching his mouth into a smile, so, you have come.

It was very absorbing. Very informative.

Around them voices rose, still arguing, insisting. Their own silence lengthened and they regarded the air with interest. Paul was about to make some excuse and leave, when the student extended his hand. I am called Sahel, he said. Sahel—and here followed the barrage of sound that Paul would never learn to pronounce, let alone spell.

Paul announced his own name and took the hand, which was cold and sharply boned and seemed to struggle briefly in Paul's grip.

You are sympathetic, Sahel said after another pause, to the struggle of the Iranian people?

He had a nervous habit of raising his voice with every phrase, or perhaps it was just his skirmish with the language. Paul said something about not knowing that much, of course, but oh yes, he was sympathetic. A weak, idiotic nonopinion, but Sahel beamed. You see, he said, already it begins. The revolution, the struggle. Soon, very soon. Perhaps you will like to come with us tonight. We go to talk more.

Why not. Sure, Paul heard himself saying. Half curious, half afraid to detach himself from anything that might finally be happening to him. He sat with them at a grime-blackened table in a coffee house. The long-haired girl wasn't there, of course. Sahel sat beside him. There were half a dozen others, introduced so rapidly that all he caught was a heap of extravagant names: Davood, Ahmed, Huishman, Sudi, Reza.

Their dark heads nodded; they seemed a little amused at his presence. Then they forgot about him. Homeland, freedon, liberation, truth: their words bounced and cracked around his head like brightly colored, explosive balls. When he couldn't understand them, he watched their faces. The same scorn, or sadness, or impatience seemed to travel from one to the other in turn, as if they drew from some shared pool of feeling. He felt melancholy, and tender; he wished some larger purpose could envelop him also, he wished for some circle of faith. Yet at the same time he knew it could not be so. He was meant to be a solitary, an observer of himself as well as others; it would be both his weakness and his strength. For a moment more he sat watching, loving them for their reckless expense of feeling. Then he reached for his coat.

Ah, my friend. It was Sahel, bending toward him in his chair, his narrow face bobbing above Paul. He seemed drunk, and perhaps he was, on words, on sentiment. Even his voice was huskier. Ah yes, we have not even begun to discuss. We will talk more, there is much to talk . . .

Paul wondered what test or ritual he had undergone, to be so addressed, so appropriated. Later he decided it had been missionary zeal. He was Sahel's convert, his tame American. It is early, so early, you do not leave, Sahel insisted. He clapped Paul on the back, pinning him, and Paul gave up the fight. He imagined himself falling asleep on his crossed arms, revived at intervals to join in another round of toasts and table-banging, like the dormouse in *Alice in Wonderland*.

But Sahel moved his chair a little distance from the table, so that they sat apart from the discussion: Pa-ool. Say better? Pa-ool. You must tell me. We must discuss. The greed of American capitalists, this is the cause of all problems. My country is to be made a factory, an endless gasoline pump, the Shah, he is to be given his new toys, his missiles and his guns, the atom bomb too. Can you deny it? American people deny complicity?

There was much of this sort of talk, and more that was personal. Paul made the mistake of admitting he was a writer.

Write? Sahel exclaimed. You are writer?

Paul was forced to confirm it. His face was stiffening into the gloomy, brooding expression that was his only defense against embarrassment.

What books, where can I buy them?

Paul hurried to explain. He was just starting out, he hadn't published anything yet.

Oh yes, oh yes. More nodding. And what, Sahel went on in the same dangerous, enthusiastic tone, what is it you write about?

Stories, said Paul briefly. Fiction.

No, no, write about? What kind of stories?

Sweat bloomed freshly in Paul's pores. Irritated, he wondered how one went about explaining that people shouldn't ask those kinds of questions. He said, They aren't about anything in particular. Just . . . what I feel, you know.

He was reddening like an oaf. He decided that from now on he would tell people he couldn't talk about his writing, it was too personal. I will read your stories sometime, Sahel declared. When you have books, I will buy them all. Weakly, Paul muttered that he hadn't really finished any stories yet, that is, he wasn't happy with them himself. But Sahel had dismissed the matter. Now we talk about the revolution, he said.

And they did, for another hour. Once more, Paul lost track of their discussion. It righted old wrongs, it swept away the present corruption and replaced it with a new order of peace and equity. His ears rang as if they'd been battered with trumpets, and in truth he was battered, by their eagerness, their heat. At last he struggled to his feet and shook hands around the table. Pa-ool, said Sahel, practicing. Pa-ool. He emerged onto the street to find the world transformed by new snow and the air alive with light.

He hadn't really expected to see any of them again. But Sahel appeared at the bookstore two days later, clutching his old gray overcoat to him. It was this huddling against the cold, Paul realized, that made him look so furtive. They greeted each other with formal inquiries about each other's well-being. For a moment they stood silent, smiling vaguely. Then Paul grasped that this was a social visit, and he hurried to brew them a cup of Les's herb tea. They sat comfortably in old leather chairs, facing the street. Snow pecked at the glass, shaken loose from the bedraggled sky. The heater bathed them in warm air. Sahel stretched his legs and sighed. I am sad today, Pa-ool. It is too cold, I am too far from home. I wish to see my family again. I have pains in my feet. Very sad, I am.

I'm sorry, Paul said, still wondering why he had been selected, even seized on, for this sort of confidence. If you're cold, you know, you should get yourself a hat and gloves. And some better shoes, he added, examining the stretched, boatlike loafers that loosely encased Sahel's feet.

The cold is in my heart. It is because my home is far away. Again he sighed gustily, as a kind of supplement to communication, Paul imagined. Then he turned to Paul. You should write a story about the sadness of being far from home. I will tell you all about it, you will write it down.

Paul laughed. It doesn't work that way. If it's your story, you write it.

I have not the words, Sahel said earnestly. It needs beautiful words, and much skill, much heart. True? I can tell you what I feel, and you will make it the right words.

I'm beginning to think you're serious.

Serious important. Listen more. You can write also about the revolution. That would be very good, Pa-ool, to write of the struggle, of our hope. Two, three books you could make. Put in everything. Put in—and Sahel gave a quick, startling imitation of a hanged man, with rolling tongue and capsized eyes. Then he righted himself and looked expectantly at Paul.

I still don't understand. Are you trying to hire a publicist?

You will explain, please.

Somebody to write commercials. Slogans. Marching songs.

No! To write poetry, to inspire. To speak to the world! You talk about silliness and little songs, like the dancing hot dogs on the television. I am disappointed, Pa-ool.

All I meant was, I can't write like that. I have to write what I feel.

Oh, excuse me! Excuse me please! You have the so much important feelings, everything else is dancing hot dogs!

Where in the world did you get those dancing hot dogs? Calm down.

But it was too late. It was a mistake, Paul was to discover, to give Sahel an excuse for argument. He geared up for oratory with dangerous speed. Even his English grew sleeker, shedding many of its peculiar arabesques and flourishes: You do not understand. Americans are so innocent. So innocent foolish. And ignorant, Pa-ool, yes, you are ignorant. How can you understand our struggle? Life is so comfortable for you. So soft. You know only what you see on the television, and you will not look farther.

That's right. It's too hard to get up and switch channels.

Oh, make fun, make fun. I am afraid you are a frivolous person, Pa-ool. You do not know enough. You close your eyes, the world is only in your head, so neat and tidy, you will write tidy little books. You eat a corner of life, like a mouse with a cheese, and you think because you are full you have consumed it. If you know more, you will write books better.

You know, said Paul, trying to pretend his anger was from safely impersonal causes, I don't understand. Why are you wasting your time screaming at me? Go take your gripes to the government.

Then you admit, said Sahel triumphantly, that American government is wrong?

I don't know. I don't care. Probably.

You admit crimes? Conspiracies?

I didn't say that. What does it matter what I say, anyway?

Important to understand the American imperialism.

Damn the American imperialism.

Oh, very good, very good. Sahel had recovered his good humor; he seemed very near to clapping Paul on the back again. The three black crayon lines danced. Very good to discuss. I feel better now. I have hope. I will return for many more good talks. I like to talk with you, Pa-ool. I will help you with your books.

It's Paul. For God's sake, Paul.

Pool. I will practice saying. Pool.

How he came to dread those visits. Several times a week Sahel would appear at the bookstore, sauntering, nonchalant, pretending he had come for a book. They argued in the store, or on those occasions when Sahel followed him out the door, oblivious to Paul's stolid attempts to ignore him, over the clatter of silverware at lunch counters. They argued about American decadence, and politics, and Paul usually got the worst of it. Come with me tonight, Sahel would say. Another meeting, very important.

You know, said Paul, listening to your friends is like Italian opera. I can't really understand what's going on, but every so often there's an absolutely terrific aria.

That is because you are not a serious person, Pool. All day you sit in your little store, all night you sit and scribble. A wasteful life.

How else do you expect artists to work?

Artists must live first. Be men of action. Must suffer. Where is it you suffer?

My ears. From listening to you constantly.

Very not funny. You make me sad. I give a brother's advice. You are part of decadent civilization. I worry for you.

Christmas came and went. Its colored lights melted together in slick puddles, in the glass expanse of store windows. The city's saw-toothed concrete horizon was veiled in snow, softened and diffused. Sahel added to his ensemble a drooping muffler in painful shades of red and purple. Did he ever study or attend classes? Paul wondered. He was unsuccessful at discovering even what subject Sahel was supposedly working in. Sometimes he said engineering, at others, computer science. It was not so much dishonesty, Paul decided, as love of mystery. Sahel was full of dark hints: there were spies everywhere, here too, there was danger, he might never be able to return home.

Paul was puzzled. Just exactly what have you done, to be so persecuted?

I am officer in revolutionary student group.

And?

We bring the revolution.

But how?

Very secret. Cannot say more.

If it's so secret, persisted Paul, why are you telling me about it?

Because I trust you, Pool. Even to say so much, it is to trust you with my life.

Man of action, my foot. You know what your revolutionary students remind me of? Secret clubhouses I had when I was a kid, making up codes and passwords for things nobody else wanted to know anyway.

So very funny. So many jokes to make, while others spill their blood.

Poetry.

It was hard for Paul to imagine the malice of an entire government focused on the gangling and theatrical figure of Sahel. But he had to admit there was more to his feelings than that. There was also envy of those who could claim any credentials in a more vital world than his own. He envied them and something mean-spirited in him made him want to belittle it.

Things might have gone on that way, at least until Paul became a better or less tolerant debater. But one morning, on a day of blue sky and cold crystal air, Paul's reading was interrupted by a rush of wind as the bookstore door opened. Papers on his desk billowed, and he lunged for them. The man who had entered smiled apologetically. Sorry. He tiptoed, with elaborate caution, around the corner of the shelves. Ten minutes later he appeared, bearing a copy of the latest diet and exercise guide, smiling another apology. Excuse me, he said. Would you be able to recommend this book?

I haven't read it. A lot of people like it, Paul said truthfully. In fact he loathed all such self-improvement tomes.

No matter, said the man. I only want something to read on a plane. Diet and exercise, I don't take them too seriously. He slapped at his ribs, a fat man's comfortable gesture, and laughed.

Three ninety-five plus tax, Paul told him, but the man remained with his hand resting on the book cover.

It's such a long flight. I may need several books. Very long, very boring.

Where are you traveling? asked Paul, resigning himself to being polite.

/11/

To Iran. A very long way.

For the first time, Paul examined him. A thick-bodied, prosperous-looking man with a pink, well-groomed face. He spoke without accent and only a certain unconvincing extravagance about his clothes might have marked him as a foreigner. The hand on the book displayed a square gold ring, like an oversized tooth. He wore a furry peaked Russian-style hat, and a silk print scarf at the neck of his overcoat. It was the sort of scarf that Paul had, up to now, seen only in folded stacks on the counters of men's stores. It was a revelation to find that people actually wore them.

It certainly is a long way to travel, said Paul. Still the man made no move to pay.

Perhaps you know some of my countrymen. There are many here, completing their education at your fine university. Perhaps they come into your store. The fat gold of the ring twinkled.

They might, I suppose, Paul said. Sighing inwardly, he released the thumb that marked his place in the book.

Forgive my curiosity. I am a stranger here. Perhaps someone I know, some friend of my family's, is here.

Well, but if you're leaving town, it doesn't much matter, does it?

I'm not certain when I leave. Maybe not for quite a while. When I leave, who knows, I may come back. My business is like that.

He waited for Paul to ask him about his business. I'm in import-export, he said after a pause. Lots of travel, you see. He smiled, again with that undercurrent of apology. So I will be back. I like your store. I like to read. Books are windows to the world, true?

Of course, said Paul, prodded into conversation.

I will return many times. I would very much like news of my countrymen. Any news is welcome. I am surprised that you are not more familiar with them. A young person like yourself must have many opportunities to meet at parties, gatherings. He rummaged in a breast pocket, drew forth a number of cards, which he shuffled. Here are some of my friends. He laid a grainy black-and-white photograph, much enlarged, on the desk. You know him? Paul shook his head. Or this one? Or this? Sahel's face, a smudged profile, appeared on the top of the pile.

Paul looked up. The man's pink lips were set in a pouting smile. His eyes were surrounded by tiny lines, laugh crinkles, but the eyes themselves were remote. Who are you anyway? said Paul.

Young people on their own, the man said, young people in a strange place often need guidance. They become confused with strange ideas, they fall under the wrong influences. I am a father myself, you see. I think of my own children.

You'd better leave now, Paul told him.

From his back pocket the man produced his wallet, an over-sized slab of biscuit-colored leather. Perhaps, he said, by the time I return, you will have some news for me. He rummaged through a thick fan of bills, extracted a twenty. Here you are. No, don't bother. Keep it, on account, as you say. I will be back.

And, smiling wistfully, he touched his hand to his hat and left.

It had all happened too quickly, too matter-of-factly, even. It was ten in the morning, and the glittering sun still shone. He wanted very strongly to dismiss it all as some sort of clumsy joke or mistake. If there were such things as spies, secret agents, and he supposed you had to admit there were, somewhere in the world, they did not come marching up to one waving fistfuls of money. Or did they? How would he know? He thought of going to find Sahel, but he had no way of doing so. It occurred to Paul that he knew nothing of where he lived. All day time passed as slowly as honey dripping from a spoon, all day he waited for Sahel to appear, making one of his usual rounds, or for the man to return. Two middle-aged women came in, looking for cookbooks. An old man spent the afternoon coughing into a copy of Emily Dickinson. At five o'clock Paul shut the store. Darkness blotted the sky like ink, and the wind, which had been steady all day, seemed to gather a new whistling force. The sidewalks were heaped with petrified snow and the streets were emptying rapidly as people hurried to get home. Paul realized, after a few minutes, that he had no idea of where he was going. Then, at the end of the block, in a little knot of people waiting for the light to change, he had a miraculous glimpse of red and purple wool.

It took him another block to draw near to those bobbing colors and another to determine it was indeed Sahel. He ran awkwardly, wheezing, colliding with Sahel, who turned, startled and peered down at him. The folds of the muffler made his neck seem strangely elongated. So, Pool, we play football? Wheezing, Paul stood and tried to catch his breath. Suddenly he felt melodramatic and embarrassed. The morning's episode seemed diminished, unworthy of all this effort, something he had spooked himself with. Still, he did not have any choice but to follow through.

I have to talk to you, he said. Not here. And, steering Sahel by the elbow, he piloted them across the street to a bar. It was a loud, expensive place, inhabited by well-dressed men and slim, impossible girls. It contained, among other things, great quantities of stained glass, a stuffed moosehead, a popcorn machine, electronic games, a jukebox ornamented with winking, convulsive pink lights, enormous mirrors, and an old wagon wheel suspended from the ceiling. American decadence, Paul supposed. An impassive waitress appeared to take their order. Two brandy Alexanders, said Paul. They were the only thing he could drink.

So, Pool, we talk? Very good. An interesting place, this. We can discuss the waste and sick pleasure-hunger of capitalist society.

Listen to me. Again Paul felt that tide of embarrassment, of melodrama, which had to be thrust forcibly away. Why would a man come into the bookstore asking about you? With pictures of you.

Just then the waitress arrived with their drinks in grotesque, urn-shaped glasses. Sahel studied the creamy surface, gave the glass half a turn and watched the little molten waves.

Did you hear me? Paul demanded. Who was he?

When Sahel looked up, his skin was mottled, chalk and ochre. This man, he hissed, what did you tell him?

Nothing, Paul said, startled. He might have expected any reaction but this. Nothing at all. I told him to leave.

Names, perhaps. You let a name come out. Easy to do. You must tell me. A fool, a fool I am, to tell you anything.

Will you listen to me? I didn't say a thing. What's wrong?

Sahel passed his hands over his face. I am sorry. I believe you. But this is terrible, very bad. I must think. Again he rubbed his eyes.

Who is he? Can I help you?

Sahel shook his head and gave a purely muscular smile. No help. It is too late. You see, Pool, all my talk, where it gets me. You are right, I am all talk. Not a very important person, I am. Finally someone listens, the wrong someone. All a game, all nice words, until now. You and I, you see, we have the same problem after all.

What? said Paul. What do you mean? He felt a hand on his shoulder, saw a blur of gold from the corner of his eye.

Hello again, the man said pleasantly. He still wore his fur hat and his snugly buttoned overcoat, though the room was horribly warm. How nice to see you again. Perhaps I could join you.

I don't think so, said Paul, as the man drew up a chair and adjusted the skirts of his coat.

Sahel was staring dully at the man, his arms folded. Paul couldn't catch his eye.

You should introduce us, the man said. No? I'll introduce myself. Muhammed Armajani. Very pleased to meet you. What are you drinking?

Listen, said Paul. I don't know who the hell you are, but you're not welcome.

I have had the real pleasure, Muhammed Armajani murmured, of acquainting myself with many of our young people in my travels. I am always happy to hear of their little problems, to help, as I told you, with anything I can.

We don't want your help.

Your friend, though, he needs my help, I am afraid. He must come with me.

I'll get a cop, said Paul. Listen, where do you think you are? There are laws here.

Yes, laws. Very regrettable, but necessary. Laws about the visas, technicalities, unfortunate mistakes. Perhaps some small problems. I have no wish to alarm you. It is your friend and I, we have so much in common, lots to discuss, these little problems. Not here, I think. Much too crowded.

Muhammed Armajani stood up and gave a hitch to his overcoat. Sahel stood too. He looked sleepy, though Paul realized that was only because his eyes were narrowed in some kind of stupor of fear. Paul tugged at his sleeve. You don't have to go with him. You don't have to. Should I go for help?

Muhammed Armajani smiled. Such distress. I am sorry to disturb your evening. He raised his pink, gold-winking hand and cupped Sahel's elbow from behind. Begging your pardon. They moved forward between the rows of drinkers.

Your coat, Paul called after Sahel, but they were already gone.

He drained his drink and ordered another. He finished Sahel's as well as his own, and the sweet liquor taste flooded his head, like choking on perfume. When he stood up the room seemed to tip, its lights and motion sliding away from him. He folded the coat over his arm and left. It was so long that even doubled over it slapped against the ground. Once outside, he draped it over his own coat, walking clumsily, as if he were dragging a body.

The night was bitter, the wind shrieking. Pellets of ice were beginning to glaze the streets. He had to walk six blocks to a bus stop, and by the time he reached home his face felt frozen, transformed into glass, perhaps, as liable to shatter as to thaw. Unaccountably, it was only seven o'clock.

He lay down and was instantly submerged in some state stranger than sleep, half drunkenness, half dream, in which the storm outside was crying to be let in. No, he kept saying, but it persisted, it would not be stilled. He felt the walls shake as if they were living flesh, smooth muscle clenching. And all the while he knew it was useless to resist, that the wind had torn some gap in him that he could not ignore, no, he could ignore neither grief nor guilt nor fear, nor hold himself aloof, for the wind was all around him.

Sometime after midnight he awoke. Ice as thick as paste whitened his windows. He felt weak and parched. A strange humped shadow loomed up at him from the corner of the room and he emitted a strangled squawk. But it was only the frayed gray coat and muffler hanging on his closet door. A shaggy icon, which he might keep to remind himself of warmth, he who would now wander naked in the storms of the world.

HAVING WORDS

It was only her second gin and tonic. "Tim thinks all my ideas are—ah, nebulous. That's the word. I'm not sure what it means." She cocked her head and smiled, to show us it was meant to be funny. The rest of us had been talking about politics.

"Of or relating to a nebula," someone suggested.

"It must mean dull. Isn't that what you meant, Tim? Go on, you can say it. I'm dull."

"Enigmatic, baby," said Tim. "I said you were enigmatic. Like the Mona Lisa. Like Orientals."

"Orientals are inscrutable," somebody corrected.

"I certainly wouldn't call you dull, Marianne," somebody else said. "More of an unclassifiable. *Sui generis.*"

"Thank you," said Marianne. "Thank you very much." She sat back in her chair, smiling ironically. Having disturbed us by saying too much, she would now say too little. After a moment the conversation returned to the elections.

I stood up to refill drinks. She thrust her glass out, straight-armed. Gin and tonics were all she liked. Even now, in October, she drank them. I used to do that, years ago when I was first learning to drink, except I drank rum and Cokes. I was very glad to be done with that phase, I can tell you. Marianne's red hair was beginning to form darker, damp little tendrils along her forehead and neck. "Another?" I asked.

"Please." Then she laughed, breezily, for no real cause. Except that I always make her nervous, either nervous or sullen, for reasons I can half guess. And she was one of those people for whom liquor floats everything up to the surface, words and little stray impulses. She wasn't looking at me; she had taken refuge, as usual, behind her cloud of hair.

It was always hard for me to admit that I rather enjoyed the mistrust between us, the obscure rivalry. I enjoyed it because I always came off better in it. One tries to like one's own sex, on principle. It seems mean-minded and unfashionable to be catty, and especially to glory in it. But every time I saw her I fell into that pose of rivalry, that unworthy pleasure. We were not friends, this woman and I, though we were forced by circumstances to be cordial. We had long ago worn through our little stock of politenesses, and it was always a chore to produce some new vapidness for conversations. Perhaps it was only the strain of trying that had made us something close to enemies.

This evening, though, I was not too concerned with Marianne. My friends were arguing in the lazy, comfortable way we all enjoy. There was a fire in the fireplace, the first of the season, a little live beast confined by the brass grate. Blue autumn twilight pressed in at the windows. Two brown-glazed pottery bowls of walnuts and purple grapes stood on the table before the fire. The firelight dazzled glass and buried itself beneath the surface of the wood so that everything in the room, my room, seemed burnished and harmonious. I felt as one does when one's own efforts are able to produce and control such pleasures.

In the kitchen I poured out drinks. Even the look of the liquor pleased me, ice-clear or golden in its bottles of dimpled and quilted glass. Without turning around I sensed that Tim had followed me. So there would be this scene, too.

He stood in the doorway, scowling at me. He had the kind of face that looks its best scowling, a dark creased face, all eyebrows. He waited for me to say something, but I wasn't going to make it that easy for him. "I'm so sick of this," he said finally.

"Of what?" Though I knew very well.

"Of her stupid stunt, her little party trick, the going after me in public. And then pretending it's amusing. Why the hell does she do it?"

I didn't say, Because it gets your attention. I didn't point out that Marianne's method was to disparage him by first disparaging herself. I said, "*Did* you tell her she was nebulous?"

"No. I don't know. I guess so. But not just flat-out and nasty. I mean, it's not like I came home from work one day and started screaming she was nebulous. We weren't even arguing. We were talking about nuclear *power*, for Christ's sake." He seemed to think the topic was too impersonal for insult.

"And what did she say about it then?"

"Nothing. Nothing at all."

Tim looked at me as if trying to gauge the extent of my sympathy. He was the sort of man, impatient and assured, who liked to think he was above complaining about his own wife; he wanted me to do it for him. As a matter of fact, I found myself rooting for Marianne, who was using the only weapons she could against this man who would always patronize her. In a slightly different vein, I felt that Tim deserved anything he got for saddling himself with such a dreary woman. I said, "Every couple has their disagreements." Which hardly helped him.

"She has a mind like a puddle. Things fall in and float around in it and she fishes them up later when they've gotten soggy."

He closed his eyes and rested his head against the door. It looked massive and statuelike, that head. Whenever I look at Tim I find myself searching anxiously for signs of age. The skin under the eyes was getting parched and grainy. We had long ago used up all our jokes about gray hair. Flesh was beginning to sink closer toward bone. Somehow the weathering of this still-handsome man wounded my vanity more than my own aging did. So I was thinking as he stood there massaging his eyes. The problem is, of course, that at this very moment Marianne believes that Tim and I are either arranging a tryst or reminiscing fondly over our past affair. If I were married to Tim I'm sure I'd have the same thoughts. "Go back in," I told him. "Go back in and be nice to her. Kill her with kindness. It's an approach you haven't tried yet."

He gave me one of his glowering looks, which I just smiled at. Then he laughed and put his hands on my hips. "Dear old Em. You always know what's best for me, don't you?"

But he was still angry, and this embrace, this thrusting of his body against mine, was only another angry gesture. "Always, always," I said levelly. "Run along, now." I didn't want to seem either intimidated or attracted. It would be better if he went back to Marianne not looking too cheered up.

But when I returned to the living room they both seemed subdued, even placid. They did not look like a couple who would have words once they got home. Tim was listening to somebody's story of travel in the Soviet Union. "Drab? Even the food comes in black and white and shades of gray. Like a forties movie." Everyone laughed. Marianne was fiddling with her gold wedding band, sliding it back and forth along her knuckle. She had a child's nervous habits. Indeed, she seemed to exist in a state of perpetual surprise at finding herself an adult, at owning a real car, living in a real house of her own, and so on. Of course she was so much younger than the rest of us. That's one of the things we all marveled at when they married. It was all very well to choose one's bed partners so, but what would they *talk* about? Marianne seemed a woman of quite ordinary small bitchiness and insecurities, and

/19/

of little imagination. One almost felt sorry for her on occasions like this, when she was as out of place as a habited nun would have been, when everyone was polite to her but no one was kind. That is, one felt sorry for her until she made one of her peculiar, belligerent remarks. Among her own friends, she must have been talkative and outgoing, a manner she tried to retain here, but with no very good results. Often I would see Marianne regarding us all with baffled, suspicious looks, as if wondering how people she thought so boring could so intimidate her. Marianne worked in the medical records department of a hospital, one of those pretty, too sharply dressed girls who decorate offices. I pictured her surrounded by neat little green cards detailing malignancy, paralysis, infection, and death, tranquilly poking them into the right spots, pausing now and then to earnestly regard her fingernails.

When they left, Tim had his arm draped around her shoulders. He was yawning and not making any particular effort to stifle it. "Thanks, Em," he said. "I expect I'll be seeing you around the office in the next few days." Tim does a lot of freelance work for the magazine. I asked him about his next project, and we stood in the doorway a moment more, talking. "This one's going to be a pain, I can tell. You people are going to look at it and ask me why it isn't more *readable,* and more *sprightly.* Why does everything have to have the light touch?"

He was making little irritable, fly-swatting gestures with both hands. Marianne was twisting a button on her coat. She looked slack, either from the liquor or her own perpetual sense of powerlessness. And I did feel sorry for her then, especially since Tim was taking no notice of her. He needn't so automatically turn vivacious and animated the moment he forgot about her. I am not entirely spiteful. I said, meaning to draw her in, "Marianne, do you enjoy reading Tim's work? Or is it bad enough having to hear about it all the time?"

She had one of those unfortunate complexions, the kind redheads are always stuck with, opaque and white, like paint. When she lifted her face to stare at me, the few freckles on her nose looked muddy. "I read everything I can get my hands on. It's like homework back in school. I have to study and study before I understand anything."

They left after that. "Goodbye now," I called after them as they receded into the darkness. There was a curious scorched smell in the air, as if my little fire had escaped to fill the whole sky. I remember they walked very quickly and I was left talking to the empty space where they'd been. "Thanks for coming. See you soon, Tim."

In fact I didn't see Tim for two weeks, not until he poked his head unexpectedly into my office and suggested lunch. We walked the six blocks to the restaurant, down an avenue lined with city trees and sun-warmed, rosy brick housefronts. It was one of the last fine days that could still be called fall; the yellow leaves swam through the air as silently as fish. I remember feeling contented, or more than that, a sensation of being exactly where I wished to be. I was pleased to have come from my office, whose very untidiness somehow suggested the importance of my work, pleased to be walking through the fine weather with an attractive man, even looking forward to the too-elaborate meal I would waste my money on. A cruel, self-satisfied contentment, I suppose, since it shuts out all those who don't share it. In any case, it was a while before I asked Tim, "Why so quiet?"

He shrugged. "To keep from saying anything dour, I suppose."

I knew then that he had come to me just so he could talk. How many years had we known each other? Enough to have passed through more stages than I cared to think about. At the very beginning of our friendship we had talked about what we meant to accomplish in the world, he with his writing, I with my quickness and ambition. And neither of us had done too badly, as the world measures such things, but over the years we had been forced to regard our early hopes with a certain wryness and humor; that is, we were forced to betray them.

We had talked about sleeping together back then, which may be why we never did it. Somehow we had fallen into a pattern of archness, of teasing conversation, which quite effectively forestalled any real attempts. I never understood it, for each of us surely slept with people we liked less, and with far less deliberation. We talked over drinks, and standing in doorways late at night, and always something kept us from acting. Sometimes, if a silence came over us, we might look into the other's face and see there the long uncertainty of love, the possibility of it. The next moment one of us would always veer the conversation back to lightness, and the possibility was gone, deflected into speech.

Some cowardice it was, a reluctance to abandon those humorous, detached selves we had always been in each other's presence. Or perhaps we were afraid that here too we would not be able to live up to everything we thought we should. "We're too much alike, you know," Tim said to me once, after our absurd courtship had long passed. "Don't you think we would have wound up hating each other? Or is that just chicken-shit hindsight?" Instead we had fallen into the comfortable pose of old lovers who had forgiven each other everything, a pose made up equally of cynicism and affection. We did it so well that people might be forgiven for imagining it was the real thing.

When we were seated at the table and had been presented with drinks, Tim began. "It's like this. A man, a bachelor, middle-aged— no, don't shake your head, that's what I'd become, a good gray bachelor—anyway, this man finally marries, much to the amusement of everyone, himself included, I suppose. There's nothing impetuous about it, because he calculates everything. Up to now, not getting married has been the path of least resistance. For years he's sat through his married friends' stories. He's heard about the boredom, the nagging, the money troubles, the pitiful little infidelities that have to pass for lust or grand passions. That's the worst part, I'll tell you. Listening to them talk about some poor sad cocktail waitress or secretary, and trying to convince themselves it was a hell of a good time. Anyway, he listens, he makes the right kind of sympathetic noise, and he thinks, Not me. He's too calculating, like I said, or maybe just too cautious. Plus he's got this idea, see, that his miseries are so much more exotic than theirs. When he's fogged in by depression or feels he could die in his sleep with perfect indifference, at least it's more interesting than crabbing at the wife about the electric bill. It proves he's a superior being, you know, all that grand gloomy solitary existential agony. He prides himself on it. Smug, melodramatic bastard, isn't he?"

He paused and finished off his drink. I said nothing, waiting for him to continue. I'd never before seen him in this peculiar, self-critical mood.

"So what happens. Well, he begins to think he's wrong. He gets bored, first with his posturing, then with the misery itself. He has a sneaking suspicion that he's just a self-pitying jerk like everybody else. He's ordinary. It comes as a relief. Then he meets a girl, nice girl, easy to get along with, soothing. Maybe she's not much different from other women he's known before, but this time he's ripe for it. And the hell of it is, he's still calculating. He can look at this girl and see just what he's letting himself in for. Nice, snuggly, claustrophobic domestic comfort. Squalid little spats over who's been messing up the towels. All the good old routines he used to hear about. He's ripe, all right. Maybe he just wants a nurse for his failing years. But he's really looking forward to married non-bliss, to the predictability of it. And you know what happens?"

He seemed to want me to answer this time. "He's wrong. It drives him crazy. I'm not surprised."

But Tim shook his head. He smiled down at his empty glass, almost furtively. He looks old I thought, then corrected myself. It was the draining away of confidence, of his old brashness, that aged him. "Oh, no. That would be too easy, if the sap got what he deserved. No, nothing mundane for our boy. There's no way I can put this without having to sound hysterical. It's Marianne. I think she's crazy, or going crazy."

"Oh, come on," I said. I meant to go on and tell him that women's quirks and scenes were not without their own element of calculation, that however oddly she behaved it was planned for maximum effect, as had happened at my party. But just then our food arrived. Someday I hope to be one of those people who can ignore the presence of waiters. When we were alone again I said, "You really mean it. What has she said to you?"

"It's not what she's said. It's the damnedest thing. She'll hardly talk to me at all now. And I have been trying to get through to her. I'm solicitous and attentive and—hell. I try to justify myself, that's mostly what I do."

"Tim, what in the world happened? This doesn't even sound like you."

"Yeah, I know. Usually I'm the world's greatest self-centered asshole." He gave a little sickly smirk and looked away.

We both stared down at the innocent table, with its freight of silverware and platters, as if it were the source of the curious embarrassment we felt. For it was surely embarrassment, though I didn't understand the reason for it. Tim said, "Friday, last Friday, I guess it was. I got home late—I'd told her I'd be late—and her car was in the drive but there weren't any lights on. I figured she'd dozed off watching television or something. I fixed myself a drink and a sandwich, read the mail in the kitchen—I didn't want to wake her—then I headed for the bathroom. I turned on the light and she was lying stark naked, face down on the rug."

He paused, then went on speaking in the same rapid voice. "You don't even know what you're afraid of when you see something like that, not until after it's over. She's fallen over dead, or somebody's broken in and raped and murdered her. I just stand there, I don't know for how long. I still had half a chicken sandwich in my hand. Here's the worst part. I'm so—I don't know. Stupefied, *I take another bite of the goddamned sandwich*. I didn't think people ever did things like that. Finally I come out of it, I bend down to touch her, and all of a sudden she rolls over and sits up. 'This is how you'll find me someday,' she says. 'You bastard.' Then she stands up, perfectly calm, and walks out. I wasn't even angry, not yet. More like having the wind knocked out of me. I sat down on the edge of the tub and didn't get up for a long time. All I remember thinking is, She's right, I am a bastard. When I did go to find her, she was in bed asleep."

I said, "Are you sure you want to tell me all this?" I felt cowardly, I even felt a little flicker of distaste. I kept picturing Marianne's white, sparse nakedness against the antiseptic tile.

He went on as if I hadn't spoken. "The next day, of course, I asked her what the hell it was all about. She pretended it had all been a joke, and she didn't seem to care if I believed that or not. So I made some sort of noise—bluster, really—because I *was* angry by then, as well as frightened. And she says, as if she's just thought of the funniest line in the world, 'You know, your face was absolutely pop-eyed. Like one of those fish they mount on plaques. I wish you could have seen it.'

"I was standing by the back door when she said that. We keep one of those little fire extinguishers on a hook, and I grabbed for it. And the second I'd done it, I felt stupid, and sick, because I knew it was exactly what she wanted me to do. You know, blow it, lose my cool. I wasn't even holding it like I was going to hit her, I didn't even get that far. I had the damned thing in the crook of my arm, like a baby. I felt ridiculous. She smiled at me and said, 'You'd like to beat me up, wouldn't you? Just once in your life, you'd like to do something you think you're too good for. That's why you married me. Because I'm the kind of woman you can imagine beating up. Somebody beneath you.'

"Then she picked up her car keys and went to work. I watched her walk down the drive. She was wearing a short skirt and a little rabbit fur jacket, and high-heeled boots. Maybe it was the skirt, nobody wears them that short now except hookers, or all that hair, almost like a wig, but she *did* look trashy. And I thought, As God is my witness, she's right. Maybe there's really something wrong with me. I don't beat her. But I'd find her reading one of her crazy magazine articles—I swear, all she reads are magazines—about increasing your charm IQ or turning the john into a greenhouse. Or she'd be putting some new silver glop on her eyes and staring into the mirror like she was performing surgery in there. Or she'd ask me why we couldn't go see the newest half-witted disaster flick. I mean, none of that stuff's really so terrible, is it? Why wouldn't I let her enjoy her silly magazines in peace? But I'd rave on at her for an hour about how disgusting or pathetic everything she did was. And I knew she was like that all along. Not stupid, because she's shrewd enough when it comes to putting the screws to you. But do we have any common interests? Forget it. So why did I marry her, if I was so hot for marriage? Why her and not somebody else? Why did I want a woman like that? What does it say about me?"

"Leave her. Break clean."

"It's not that simple."

"It's always that simple."

"No," he said, sounding almost angry. "You don't understand. It's gone too far. And there's something between us, I know that sounds crazy, after all I've said, but it's true. . . ."

He seemed to need to believe that. After a moment I said, "She isn't—unbalanced. Whatever else is wrong. I'm sure she knows exactly what she's doing."

Tim's eyes were heavy and unfocused, like a drunk's, though I knew he wasn't drunk. "It could have been us," he said. "Way back then. You and me."

"At least we both like the same movies."

"Don't laugh it off. Please, I'm trying to talk to you. I'm trying very hard to talk."

His eyes met mine and stayed there. Suddenly we became aware once more of the busy room, with its important-sounding clatter of dishes and voices. As if we felt too conspicuous, we hurried to eat a little food. I knew he was embarrassed by all he had allowed himself to say, and now he resented me for having heard it.

We ate in silence for a time, then he said, in his normal voice, "She mentioned you not too long ago. Apropos of nothing, as usual." I raised my eyebrows and waited. "She said she'd like to get to know you better. Figure that one out."

Marianne appeared at my doorstep the following Saturday after-noon. I had been dozing on the couch and I'd fallen into a brief, confused dream, in which someone unseen shouted at me in a language I couldn't understand, a dream-language composed only of furious sound. Then the voice became mixed with the buzzing at the door, and I awoke, feeling chilled and shaken. It was a mo-ment before I could collect myself to answer it.

The weather had turned as gray as concrete, and cold. Mar-ianne wore a little rainbow-striped tam perched on her blazing hair, matching mittens, and the rabbit jacket Tim had mentioned. She looked like the child of an overfond mother, trussed up and sent outside to play. She smiled, a little furtively, and from under the sparse cover of her fox-colored lashes, her eyes flickered across my face. "You'll have to tell me if you're busy. I was just in the neighborhood running errands."

I told her I wasn't at all busy. She'd caught me off my guard, yes, but it's also true that I was curious. I couldn't imagine why she was really here, unless she wanted to accuse me of sleeping with Tim. I thought I could handle that one. I suppose I was wait-ing for her to do something demented or startling. Instead she sat down on the sofa and arranged her skirt about her decorously. Without all those fuzzy garments she looked much smaller, and even less sure of herself. I wondered if she was already regretting that she'd come.

Had she said something? ". . . lovely flowers." I followed her glance to the pot of shaggy purple chrysanthemums near the hearth, and its little fringe of ragged shadow in the lamplight. "Thank you," I said. "It's an extravagance, I suppose, but one I allow myself."

"Extravagance," she repeated, nodding her head, as if she were committing the word to memory. Then she gave her little spurt of a laugh.

"Could I get you something to drink? Some sherry, maybe?"

She agreed, and I excused myself. On the way to the kitchen I peeked in the bathroom mirror. I looked rumpled and blotchy, and the dark shadows under my eyes were like a pair of small leathery wings. When I returned with the tray, Marianne had tucked her legs up underneath her. Somehow the posture irritated me, as if she were trying to demonstrate how agile and kittenish she could be.

"So this is sherry," she said after I'd managed the little ceremony of serving us. She tilted her glass so that the light was trapped in the rich brown pool, and frowned at it. "It's different. All this . . ."—she waved her hand at the decanter and tray— "it's like something people drink in books, isn't it? Very classy."

"I suppose so," I agreed, wondering just what sort of books she was talking about. Neither of us found anything to say for a time. Marianne contented herself with twitching the bare foot that peeked out from under her skirt. I was beginning to forget any apprehension I'd felt: it was diminishing into boredom.

"Someday I want to have a house like yours," she said finally, sounding triumphant at having thought of a remark. "One where everything looks like it belongs together."

"Thank you. It's comfortable, but too small, really."

"No, I mean it. Every time I try and decorate something, I just wind up with a lot of ugly vases and some fifty-dollar potted plant that dies in two weeks." She finished off the rest of her sherry and poured some more.

"I've lived here a long time, you know, I've had a chance to rearrange everything until it was the way I wanted it."

"I bet I could live in a place twenty years and not have it look right. You just have talent."

"Thank you," I said cautiously. There was an edge to her speech, some unconvincing mixture of brightness and complaint that I didn't trust.

"I'm just hopeless," she went on, in the same animated, brittle voice. "It makes me feel so stupid when I can't do something like . . . mix drinks the right way. You know, something people expect."

"Ice, water, and booze. That's all most of them are. Easy."

"No, it's not easy for me. None of the things I'm supposed to know are. None of the goddamned clever little things. Maybe other people just grow up knowing them, but I didn't. Not talking right, or acting right, or . . . anything," she finished lamely. Again she drained her sherry, and glared at the empty glass. I could see a crescent of tears glittering under her lashes. "Don't mind me," she said, "I'm just being stupid, as usual."

And what does one do with such a girl once she's installed on your sofa weeping? One sighs a little, then resolves to make the best of it, and one pitches in to console her. You tell her how mistaken she is, how attractive, how young, how much she has to offer. That other people aren't nearly as smart as they pretend to be. How when you feel blue about something, it's easy to think that everything's hopeless. I was well launched on this, I was feeling warm and generous and even almost liking her, such was the infectious power of my own words, when she squeezed a glance upward through her thin tear-matted lashes.

"You don't have to go on," she said, her voice now perfectly cool. "I know you don't mean any of it."

That stopped me all right. The little chit. "What would you like me to say, then?"

"Oh, it doesn't matter. It's all just talk to you, isn't it? How can you stand to go on and on, listening to yourself? Is there anything you won't pretend to know all about, anything you don't know how to explain? That's all you're good at, you know. Making the right kinds of noises. You and all your phony friends. You just impress each other to death, don't you?"

I had told Tim there was nothing really wrong with her. Now I wasn't entirely sure. She was already shrinking from her reckless speech, it seemed, as if she'd startled herself as well as me. Her body, without actually moving, gave the impression of edging sideways. And what is madness, what do we mean by it, after all, but this uncoupling of words and meaning, intention and action. I sighed. I said, "Marianne, believe it or not, I'm sorry if I upset you further. But why did you come here?"

"I don't know," she said, still without looking at me. Her mouth had gone sullen now; she shook out her hair, that floating, fine-spun cloud. "I guess I'd better go now." As she uncurled her legs, the heel of one bare foot struck the little table, hard. The crystal decanter rocked for a moment, each facet seen sharply, a field of opals in the light, then it toppled and smashed. Looking down, we saw the base of the decanter standing upright on the floor, like a crown or a jagged rose, still holding in its center a pool of brown nectar.

"Be careful of your feet," I said automatically.

"I am so sorry," she whispered, but by then I hardly cared if she meant it or not.

"It was an accident," I said. The sherry had splashed on my legs. It felt sticky and unclean, like blood. I felt I knew why Marianne had come to see me. She had come in order to break the decanter.

I didn't see either of them, Tim or Marianne, for quite some time. Winter settled in for good. Sidewalks were glazed with thin sugary ice, and trees raked back and forth across the low skies. The city took on its winter aspect of bareness and reclusiveness. All life retreated indoors, like a green plant set in a silent room. From the windows of my office, the windows of my rooms, I watched people hurry along the bitter wind-scoured streets, hurrying to return to their sheltered and secretly blooming lives. I thought about Tim and Marianne from time to time. I wondered if they continued to damage each other as recklessly as before, or if the marriage had reached some truce. I made no move to find out. I felt that the three of us had spoken too much and too unwisely among ourselves to ever undo. I had been drawn into a treacherous and queasy intimacy, and I would not make that mistake again.

The only news I heard of them was from a co-worker who, stopping by to strew my desk with papers, remarked, "You missed seeing Burten the other day. Came by to talk with Ed about some big-shot deal."

I asked how Tim was. My colleague regarded me earnestly for a moment. I'd known him almost as long as I'd known Tim. A wry, slow-talking man, whose luck had been sometimes merely bad, sometimes tragic. But all of his troubles—drinking, a child's death, heart attack—had left their mark on him. He sensed unhappiness or disaster the same way other people smell smoke. And he knew too well the limits of sympathy, how little it could extinguish. Because I had known him so long I knew all this, just as I knew, when he looked at me so earnestly, that he believed Tim and I had been lovers. "Looked like the devil," he said shortly. "You know how people look when they've given up on sleeping? Like they've been drying out in a slow oven. I didn't get to talk with him much, though."

I said I hoped it wasn't his health, and my friend agreed, and that was that. It was a few weeks later, during the holidays, that I encountered them at a party. One of those relentless Christmas gatherings where you're meant to drink eggnog and to be playful about mistletoe. I'd half expected to find them there. And it was Marianne herself who rushed up to me as I stood talking with friends. "I'm going to have a baby."

They were her first words, even before hello. She had always been one to blurt things. Always one to catch you off balance. I remember congratulating her, remember her telling me August, that was when, she'd just found out herself. I said that I hoped she was feeling well. That she was looking well. And she did; she looked rosier, less waiflike. Her hair was drawn up sleek on the top of her head, elegant and precarious. "I feel really healthy. Like I could jump hurdles and swim rivers." We couldn't have talked for more than a minute before the current of the party bore me away, someone else claiming my attention. And I didn't really have time to wonder why she was beaming at me so hugely, as if our last calamitous meeting had never happened, or why I got the impression that the others had drawn a little apart from us and were listening intently. . . .

I suppose she felt she'd finally triumphed over me. That was part of it. But I did not envy her pregnancy, only her faith in it. For I knew she was one of those women who believed that this would be the climactic achievement of their lives, the one true drama, and long after others have ceased to think of them as mothers, they keep insisting that drama be acknowledged and deferred to, insisting a little more querulously each time, oh, never directly, but through all manner of manipulations and petulance. . . . Well, there surely were such women, but why was I being so sour about it? Because I was envious after all? I didn't care to look too closely at my feelings. I went to find Tim and congratulate him.

I found him standing in front of the fireplace, alone. He had his nose in a drink as I approached, and not until I'd said, "Tim, what's this good news I hear?" did he put down his glass and turn to me. *Like he'd been drying out in a slow oven.* He looked bad and he knew it; his eyes reflected mine. "Thanks," he said. "Nice of you to drop by." And he turned back to his glass.

"What is it?" I said after a moment. Uncertainly, I touched his arm. "I haven't seen you in so long. . . ."

"Because you didn't want to, I'm sure. It got a little too messy, didn't it?"

"What are you talking about?" I said quietly, for now there were other people around, poking at the fire, arguing over whether or not a wad of cellophane from a candy box should be thrown in. "It'll just scorch and stink," someone was saying. "It'll smell like a plastics factory with gas."

"I'm sorry you're angry with me," I said a moment later, because Tim still hadn't answered. "I suppose it looks like I've been avoiding you. But what did you want me to do? I didn't want to make things worse by interfering." He made a curious gesture with his throat, like a man in a too-tight collar. "But if there's anything I can do now. . . . If you'd like to talk. . . ."

/29/

"All right. Sure, I'll talk. You want to know what's new? There isn't any goddamned baby, that's what. This is the third time we've been through it, everybody knows about it. I shouldn't pick on you. Nobody else wants to face me, either. She announces she's pregnant, she tells everybody, including people who don't know her and don't care, and she picks out names, and talks about going on an organic diet, and then, pop, suddenly she's not pregnant. She never was. And why isn't she? Because we don't fuck any more. There. Aren't you glad I told you? Now tell me what I should do about it all." He stared at me until I looked away."It's almost like—instead of a baby, she's having this—sickness. And it *is* my baby, in some weird way, it's a tradeoff. My responsibility."

"Tim, if she really needs help, there are people—"

"Should I have her locked up? Take her to a marriage counselor, or a shrink? Listen, I've tried those. She won't talk. All they can do finally is write her scrips for Valium. Listen, none of that shit helps, none of the easy stuff like the shrinks or the counselors or the clergymen or the hypnotists. Because people don't come apart easy. It takes time. See, they shed little gobs of hair and spit at first. Messy. Then hanks of skin and blood, then finally the springs loosen. So tell me what to do while I wait. Tell me what to do."

At that moment somebody ended the argument about the cellophane by tossing it in the fire. It crumpled at its edges with a thin green flame, and, propelled by its own burning, toppled out of the grate and onto the hearth. Then there was a charred, plastic stink, and the hostess hurried over to see who was vandalizing the yule log. I remember the crowd around us, excited by the little alarm, and Tim's dulled face, and Marianne across the room, smiling, her sleek and precariously arranged hair, and I remember thinking, It can't really be like that, not really. . . .

She wasn't pregnant, of course. I forget who told me. It doesn't really matter anyway. I still think of Marianne from time to time. Do we ever know what to do when we're confronted with madness, or grief, or disaster? Sometimes I think of it as some outlandish mushroom growth, sprouting out of a tree or damp ground, exotic, spiny, and colorful. And since we can't determine its exact species, since it's so singular and unexpected, we leave it strictly alone. Then one day it simply collapses in on itself, crumbling into powder and spores. Well, that's a prettier way to imagine such things. Marianne swallowed tranquilizers and liquor, so that when Tim found her she was unconscious, her hair matted with vomit. At the hospital they pumped her stomach and sent her home. The next time she was better at it. She checked into a motel and put up the Do Not Disturb sign.

The last time I saw Tim we managed to talk about it a little. It was winter again, with steel skies and a persistent, stinging wind laden with newspapers, gum wrappers, and grit. The seasons might never have changed, the last year never happened. We sat at a table in a bar, looking out over the streets and the traffic and the whirling garbage.

"She was better than we are," Tim said finally. "Or at least she was braver, more reckless. She wasn't afraid of going too far. I respect that."

I studied my hands folded on the tabletop, a bundle of coarse bones. I had no wish to contradict him. After another silence, he spoke again.

"Ah, Emily. My oldest friend. Sometimes I think we've lived too long, we've gotten too canny, too good at just surviving. Why are we still here? I'm not sure we deserve to be. What should we do with the rest of our lives, you and I? Tell me what we should do."

I looked up to find his dark, sad eyes on mine. And I wanted to tell him something true and hopeful, something that would redeem everything, but I couldn't think of the right way to begin. I couldn't think of one word.

REMEMBERING SONNY

Mothers hated him. He wasn't the hood type, with tattoos and a knife in his boot and a frozen sneer. If he had been, the mothers could have at least defined what they objected to, though it's still doubtful the daughters would have been convinced. Nor was he too good-looking, which would have been another cause for suspicion. No, as it was, they would encounter Sonny in their kitchens, scrambling eggs, or helping little brother put the batteries in his ray gun, the most innocent and pastoral of situations, and Sonny would grin and say, Good afternoon, Mrs. So and So, and the mothers would be struck cold. For they could tell he didn't ever mean a word he said, not to them, not to the daughters. And furthermore, he knew the mothers saw through him and he didn't care. His manners were a charade, one of their own weapons used against them.

(Fathers, of course, noticed nothing. They shook hands with him and remembered him as Johnny or Sammy or simply as one of those cars which was always blocking the drive.)

Well what's wrong with him? the daughters demanded, and the mothers were forced to use words like smart-aleck and dishonest. Which were entirely too vague. The daughters stamped their feet and said, You just don't want me to go out with anyone. You don't want me to have any fun at all. The daughters, of course, recognized Sonny's insincerity towards the mothers, even recognized that it was turned against themselves, but they weren't above using the mothers' confusion to best advantage. So Sonny would smile his too-tight smile, which made his face look narrow and foxy, and say, Good evening, Mrs. So and So, and usher the daughters out into the lurid unsafe night.

Alice's mother went so far as to come to her room once as she was dressing to go out with him and say in a rapid, rehearsed voice, Sonny is just not a nice boy, and maybe the others aren't nice boys either but at least they care about you and Sonny doesn't, so if he asks you say no. Her mother didn't look at her when she spoke; she seemed to address her recital to the poster above Alice's head. The poster showed Jimi Hendrix against a billowing formless background of purple, orange, and painful green, the one unequivocal adolescent note in Alice's Early American bedroom.

Alice, who was both embarrassed and resentful, nevertheless refrained from saying, What do you mean? Which would have been simply intolerable for her mother to answer. Instead she said OK, and waited, dryly, tapping a comb against the dresser so her mother could see she was intruding.

Alice thought that this episode was one reason her mother never said anything about Sonny's death, though she must have known about it. Her mother had wanted Sonny to be, if not quite dead, at least thoroughly absent. Perhaps she felt indirectly guilty. If she mentioned his death with regret Alice could accuse her of hypocrisy. If her words contained the faintest hint that his end was somewhat inevitable, or just-as-well, Alice would seize on it. Either way, the memory of that incident would shimmer between them, its embarrassment resurrected.

Therefore, nothing was ever said. By that time Alice no longer lived at home and the threat of Sonny was replaced by other threats and finally her mother was convinced that everything she had ever warned about had already happened anyway. So there was no real reason to mention him. Alice herself didn't think of him incessantly. Though since he had died at the rather ridiculous age of nineteen she felt, as she grew older, a sense of obligation. Not just to remember him as he was but to imagine him as he might have been with the silliness and mistakes outgrown.

Besides, there was a certain pleasure in having a dead lover. In songs and movies, after all, it was the very essence of romance. A part of her despised such morbid sentimentality and tried to keep her feelings genuine and uncomplicated. But sooner or later she would find herself thinking not of Sonny but of herself, how interesting her melancholy was, how poignant, how attractive. Sternly she'd force her attention back to Sonny. But she was like a Puritan trying to avoid the subtle sin of Pride and finding it instead at every turn. If she thought of his death, for example, she inevitably thought of how she had learned of it, what effect the news had on her, and so on.

What kind of person was she, she'd ask herself in a fit of disgust. Hadn't she cared about Sonny at all? Yet she knew her self-loathing was exaggerated too. Finally she was forced to accept her memories and the accompanying histrionics. After all, she had been very young when she'd known him. It was inevitable that some of those embarrassing younger attitudes should survive, twined around the memory of Sonny like vines around a stump.

So remembering Sonny was more complicated than it first appeared, because it meant remembering herself too.

The last time she saw him they'd spent all night skidding from one Chicago freeway to another in Sonny's brand-new van. It was a powder-blue Dodge with a windshield so large it was like flying an airplane, Sonny said, pounding on the dash, though of course he'd never flown an airplane. Alice thought it was more like driving a Greyhound bus, you were so high up and the seat pitched you forward into that slick bubble of glass. But she didn't say anything because Sonny was so perfectly happy and besides, she'd never driven a Greyhound either.

An April night, very black and frosty, wind shredding the new leaves. A shrill unsettled night, more like Hallowe'en than spring. In the back was a friend of Sonny's who was already out of the service. His name was Graham, she didn't know if that was his first or last name, and he kept getting tangled in the wires for the speakers. Or else he'd kneel between the two front seats to be part of the conversation, and every time Alice turned around his face would be about two inches from hers.

He had very round blue eyes and he kept grinning at her with this really *feverish* enthusiasm, Alice thought. The grin made his face look like a china plate that's been cracked and the pieces put back together wrong.

Once, when Sonny took a turn so fast it sent Graham somersaulting against the back door, Alice leaned over and asked, What did you do, sell me to this guy?

It's a trade. I'm getting two blankets and some venison.

Sonny, I'm serious, what the hell have you been telling him?

Aw, he's just so horny he's cross-eyed. Be nice to him.

I will not, said Alice, loud enough to be heard over the music. I won't be any nicer than I feel like being.

But Sonny was singing along with the tape, ignoring her. Graham was back in his place between the seats. She caught a whiff of body heat from him, a close, muddy kind of heat.

Old Sonny sure wishes this was an airplane, huh? The grin prodded her.

He sure does. Experimentally, she smiled. Graham's breath thickened. His eyes seemed to squirm. Good God, Alice thought, and pretended to rummage through the box of tapes so she wouldn't have to look at him.

The highway at night was a separate glamorous country of speed and loneliness, whispering of accidental death. The pavement hummed beneath the van's wheels. Shallow headlights swung past them on the opposite side of the road. They drove first west, then south out of the city, then doubled back into the intricate concrete ugliness of Chicago. Alice watched the landscape. A single farmhouse would materialize from the darkness, or a whole new outcropping of subdivision bathed in pink sodium vapor. They passed so quickly it was hard to imagine yourself actually there, standing in some spot you fixed your eyes on. For a moment she played that game with herself, trying to penetrate the frail lighted windows and their promise of mystery.

Of course, it was also true that there was not much else for them to do. Eventually what had been a whole range of possibilities went flat, so that by ten o'clock Alice said, trying not to sound querulous, Sonny, is there anyplace we can go?

Sonny shrugged and said I dunno, then, unexpectedly, We'll stop at my folks' crib. Again they reversed directions.

They were traveling a section of lighted road, the tall poles delicate and menacing, like giant insects in a science fiction movie. Stripes of numb light blinked over them in quick succession. Alice watched Sonny's face jump in and out of darkness. Every so often she could persuade herself he was good-looking.

Certainly if you were talking to a girlfriend, someone who didn't know him, you could make him sound OK, in fact she had often done so. He has green eyes, she'd say, emphasizing this as something especially intriguing and subtle, and the girlfriend would be impressed. His eyes were tilted at the corner and Sonny had a habit of narrowing them even further so they expressed nothing but irony. His hair, Alice might add, is reddish-brown, you know, waving her hand vaguely, chestnut-colored. Though just plain brown would have done, and Sonny wore it trimmed too short in back and too long in front, a peculiar compromise with his father and later with the Navy.

He had been too skinny, still a boy in spite of his booming voice and large-knuckled hands and black sprouting whiskers. She tried to be loyal, and she imagined him as he might have grown. After all, she herself had developed breasts and finally learned how to fix her hair. Yet she had to admit she felt something of the survivor's secret gloating, grateful she hadn't been stuck in adolescence like a gawky Peter Pan.

Sonny's parents' house was expensive and dull, like everything in the suburbs, she thought. His parents weren't home. It seemed they were never home, though maybe Sonny only brought people over in their absence. Alice had never once met them, and she formed her ideas of them from their empty house. The sign his mother clipped to the refrigerator: Think sex, not food! His father's fussy-looking humidor stand. Their bedroom, as neat and noncommittal as something in a Holiday Inn. It was the sort of house which at Christmas displays a white aluminum tree in the picture window, decked with blue lights and blue glass balls.

Graham was saying, Some spread, man, as they walked up the path between careful, vaguely Japanese arrangements of stones and dwarf evergreens creaking in the wind. Sonny just grunted. Any reference to his parents' money seemed to discomfit him, and it surfaced in cynicism. So that now, unlocking the front door, he said, Think of it as one of those period rooms in a museum. Middle-class interior, late twentieth-century American.

The living room carpet was white and frosty in the darkness, its clean expanse rather intimidating. Sonny flipped on a light and sauntered across to the kitchen. Graham was at her elbow saying, God *damn*, wish I had an apartment as big as this one room, huh? And while she felt sorry for him in an impersonal way, she wanted to watch Sonny. He was slapping cupboard doors, letting the water run full blast in the sink. Whenever he was in this house he seemed to be acting out an exaggerated contempt.

Now that they were out of the van Alice could see how short Graham was, no taller than herself, really, so she drew herself up, rocking a little on her heels. Yes, it is pretty big, she agreed, staring down at him. His grin flickered and he joined Sonny in the kitchen.

Sonny didn't get along with his own parents any more than he got along with the parents of his girlfriends. Nor had he lived long enough for rebellion against them to become less important, as it had for everyone else. In addition, the disagreements had been particularly violent. So that when Alice read the newspaper account of his father's remarks at the dedication of the flagpole (if that wasn't irony enough) with its standard words like sadness, duty, sacrifice, inspiration, she felt not just anger but distaste.

Granted, what could you expect him to say: My son often disappointed me. I would like to think that we loved each other in spite of our troubles, but I can't be sure? The ties among family members are often made legitimate simply by enduring over time, and we never had that time. Sonny would have laughed himself sick at the sight of this flagpole. I thank you.

No, you couldn't expect much honesty, let alone eloquence, from people at such times. But Alice remembered Sonny showing up at her house with a swollen jaw, the inside of his mouth still bleeding, saying, The old man did that, his voice a mixture of fury and queer pride at how bad things really were now. And Alice had fussed and exclaimed over it more than was necessary, until Sonny was a little embarrassed. The night before, he said, he'd ridden the train back and forth to the city until dawn because he had no place else to go. That night she snuck him in the back door after her parents were asleep.

She was thinking of that time as Sonny emerged from the kitchen with a bucket of ice, vodka, and a pitcher of orange juice. She wanted to mention it, in an offhand and conspiratorial fashion, something that would reestablish their shared past. But Sonny began singing in his exaggerated, operatic baritone, all tremolo and lushness:

> Do you remember Sweet Alice, Ben Bolt
> Sweet Alice, the girl from the town?
> Who laughed with delight when you gave her your smile
> and trembled with fear at your frown

It never failed to annoy her. Why do you always sing me that dopey song? she demanded.

Because you're sweet.

Bullshit. I bet it's not even a real song.

She watched him set the ice down carelessly on the top of the piano and mix the drinks. Here, he said, handing one to Graham. Take your medicine quietly and we won't have to give you the injection.

An injection could be interesting, said Graham, winking at Alice. Now that she was sitting down he seemed to have recovered some of his self-assurance.

Bend over and show us your best profile, then.

Aw Sonny. He was embarrassed again.

Madame. Sonny bowed and gave her a glass.

Thank you, Rufus.

Ole Rufus, he be happy to sarve you all, Miz Alice, don't ya'll pay me no nevah mind.

Please Sonny, spare us.

But he was off on one of his routines, on his knees in the white carpet, swaying back and forth with his hands clasped in front of him: Ah spect when ah stand befo dat hebbenly throne, de Lawd he 'member old Rufus, de Lawd he not fergit his chillun. Miz Alice, Ah be hearin dem bands o angels fore long, 'deed, Ah spect ole Rufus not see de sun rise tomorry. Effen only ah be 'lowed to spen this yere las Chrissmus Eve wif mah wife an lil chile . . . Aarrgh.

Alice had nudged him with her foot and he sprawled face down in the carpet. They were both laughing now, more than the joke deserved. Graham looked from one to the other, smiling expectantly, trying to edge in on things. After a minute he cleared his throat and said, Hey Sonny, what's downstairs?

Oh, the stereo, said Sonny, righting himself. The pool table, my dad's aquarium . . . the etchings. He said this last in a silky, theatrical tone. Graham gave him a look.

How bout it, he said, standing so close to Alice's chair that their knees almost touched. Want to listen to some records? He'd retrieved his grin, though one corner of it looked downright agonized. She had no doubt that this was all Sonny's doing.

I'll be there in a minute, she said, and smiled. Which left him no choice but to go downstairs by himself. They heard his feet echoing forlornly on the cold basement tiles.

She turned to Sonny. You ought to be ashamed of yourself.

Who, me?

Don't play dumb. Alice crossed the room to the piano and rubbed at the spilled water with her sleeve. She only managed to smudge the dark oiled surface.

Aw, I just thought maybe—

I know what you thought. She wasn't as mad as she was pretending to be, and in pretending she was threatening to overdo it a little.

Sonny got up and put his arms around her from behind. Don't be pissed off. He's not such a bad guy.

He runs with a bad crowd, she said, struggling against his hold, struggling to preserve her pose of anger. Having Sonny trying to appease her was an unaccustomed pleasure.

OK, so forget about Graham. I'm sorry. He turned her around, pressing against her.

You're really sorry?

Sorry I brought him along. He's in our way.

Mm, she said, not wanting to concede his meaning.

Sweet Alice, he crooned. She sagged against him, passive now. Downstairs they heard the stereo click on, and the sound of a Stones record came funneling up the stairs.

Poor guy, said Alice. Maybe we should go down.

Yeah.

But they stood, swaying together while the raucous music beat against them. Sonny was getting more and more insistent. His breath enveloped her. Finally Alice drew his hands away and said, When you going back, Sonny?

Tomorrow night I fly to San Francisco. Then I've got a few days before they ship me out.

Maybe it's just as well. She spoke with her face muffled in his flannel shirt. Her nostrils filled with the smells of wool, perfume, and cold air, a blend which reminded her treacherously of countless nights spent in cold parked cars.

Thanks a lot.

No, I mean your flying tomorrow, I mean . . . Why was she trying to talk about it? You could never talk Sonny out of anything, and once you were discussing it, both *yes* and *no* became possibilities. But it was too late.

There's always tonight.

You can't be serious.

Why not?

It's . . . She wasn't sure, in spite of everything, why she didn't want to sleep with him, or rather, she marveled at the fact that she still might want to. Finally she managed, It'd be too complicated.

What could be less complicated than a sailor's last night ashore?

Damn it, Sonny. I don't think you really want to either. Otherwise you might try to be a little more *winning*.

Sonny grinned. What if I wore my uniform?

You're impossible.

How long's it been?

Years.

Come on. Before I went in.

A year, then. All I have to do, she thought, is walk downstairs. All I have to do is stop talking. But she couldn't resist adding, I don't like the idea of you just gaily dropping in every shore leave and expecting all the goodies.

He raised his arms in astonishment. So what should I do, take you with me?

Oh come on, first you try to pawn me off on Popeye there, then you just casually take the notion to screw me. It doesn't mean anything to you, I don't know why you pursue it.

Because you want me to.

Sure, I'm really leading you on.

Sure. He caught her round the waist and set his full weight against her until she nearly toppled backwards. Sonny, stop! she demanded, but she only breathed it, and she knew by her lack of protest that she was assenting. He led her backwards into the bedroom and closed the door. It was always like this, she thought as she lay back on Sonny's unfresh sheets, they never made anything easy for each other. Warm air whispered continually from invisible vents. Once she thought she heard feet on the basement stairs, but if so they turned and retreated.

Sonny was motionless, his shoulder jutting against her chin. Sonny. She reached up and tugged his hair. We better get dressed.

He sat up, and in the blue-white dimness of the room his nakedness looked meager, his backbone too knobby and pronounced. She waited for him to look at her or say something.

Hey, she said finally. Is anything wrong?

He shrugged and reached for his shirt. Nothing. She followed him into the living room, where he snapped off the light and lay back on the couch. Downstairs another record was playing, though softer than before.

She stood, not knowing what to do. Should we go see what Graham's up to?

No. I don't really want to go look at my father's acquire-eum.

Alice sat on the opposite end of the couch. What had gone wrong? This was one reason she hadn't wanted it to happen, because of this inevitable separation afterwards, the feeling that she'd failed in some obscure but fundamental way, otherwise why would he go from wanting her to despising her? Why couldn't he be happy now? It would be years before she learned the aftermath of love could be anything but silence and cruelty. If she didn't say something, she thought, she'd start crying with the misery of it all.

So, she asked, What's it like over there, Sonny? hating the false bright sound of her voice.

What?

You know, the Navy, the war and all.

He looked impatient. It's not bad.

Well, tell me about it.

Not enough time for that.

She persisted. How about the war?

We don't see much of it. You know the Seabees? We work with them, mostly, construction and transport stuff.

The recital seemed to bore him. He scuffed at the couch with his heel. She knew if she kept asking him things he'd only get more and more abrupt. So she sat in silence. There seemed to be no way she could reach him.

Eight months later Sonny lay dying in a Japanese hospital from burns received in a boiler explosion. Even then there was no feeling that it was the war which killed him. The war was something people went to, like going to work or school. The war hadn't killed him, the boiler had, a sort of industrial accident that could happen anywhere, the sort of death that the war produced almost casually and which wasn't really supposed to count.

She knew none of the details. News reached her through letters from friends who knew as little as she did, through obscenely noncommittal paragraphs clipped from the suburban newspaper. Alice did not cry but that first night she lay on her bed and tried to evoke the delirium of pain, the raw, bacon-like scabs, the starched and acid air of the hospital, the gauze, the poisonous yellow ointment, as if by imagining it she could somehow lift the pain from Sonny, though by then he was beyond it all.

Sometime that night she woke, fighting sleep as if it were an unwholesome drug, something thick she had to swim through. In her dream they were making love, though the dream was not so much erotic a semaphoric, as series of brisk, disconnected pictures. Looking up at Sonny's face in the grainy and uncertain light she saw he was straining not to come, not to cry out. It was all right, she urged, go ahead, go ahead, and when he showed her his wounds she was overcome by tenderness, and finally they were able to weep together freely.

But in that glossy and astringent living room there had been no real premonition of these things, only her desperation at his silence. What else did he want from her? Why did they always end up so unhappy for no reason? She felt clumsy and ashamed. Were people meant to be like this? A part of her recoiled in weariness at the thought of love, the grasping and losing that might last a whole lifetime. Sonny, please, she said finally. Don't be like this. It drives me crazy.

What do you want me to do?

Just don't act like you hate me. She was starting to get teary now, and she struggled to keep it out of her voice. That would be the worst thing she could do.

He sat up a little straighter, though he still looked out the window, not at her. I don't hate you, Al.

Are you upset because of Graham?

Yeah, sort of. He hasn't had much of a night.

It'll be OK, she said, though she didn't entirely believe it. He'll understand.

He didn't acknowledge her, and said instead, Sometimes I think I'm the most fucked-up shit in the world, you know?

What do you mean?

But he shook his head, and she knew he wouldn't say any more. She reached over and squeezed his hand. Hey. Just tell him I seduced you.

She saw him smile faintly, and she could tell things were all right, or at least as all right as they could be. Still friends? she asked.

Sure.

They sat once more in silence and she was wary but content. In the oblique light from the kitchen Sonny's face was slack and rather tired. Somehow that moment seemed like the true end of the evening for her, though things had gone on. After a while Graham clumped back up the stairs, embarrassment making his feet sound thick and awkward. They'd sat in the van, still parked in Sonny's driveway, and smoked grass and listened to music for a time until Sonny drove her home.

She couldn't remember the last thing Sonny said to her, couldn't even remember if they'd kissed good-bye. Probably not, since Graham was there. No, she'd walked up to the door by herself in the black shrill unsettled night and waved to him and that was that.

Or was it? Again she willed herself to evoke that silent moment in the darkness, tried to make it like a clear piece of glass, a place from which you could view both past and future. The imbecile vision of a flagpole set in sparkling cement intruded on her for a moment but she brushed it aside. She would make her own monuments. And now her memory threw her a scrap, something Sonny said when he heard Graham (whose unhappiness, she saw now, was not just a comic grace note to the evening) clumping up the stairs. Ah now, said Sonny, and she could see him prodding himself back into his old antic irony, ah now, let's have some more fun.

SEX LIFE OF
THE SPONGE

Finally one night he called her frigid and she said That's because I can't come when you want me to, right? He said I've tried everything, I really have, but nothing works with you, it's like fucking a sponge.

A sponge, Evelyn replied, what a perfect indication of your attitude towards women, soft pliable creatures capable only of passive absorption. A cleaning utensil. The word has connotations of parasitism. Incidentally you have not tried everything.

Goddamn it I don't want you to be a sponge.

You want me to be a passionate sponge.

It's no fun getting off by myself.

So maybe you should find somebody who'll play along with your fantasies, she told him, somebody who'll fake an orgasm. I can do that if you really want. Here she gasped and rolled her head and twitched and shuddered. It was a very creditable imitation and when she was done she smiled and said See, it wouldn't be difficult at all to fool you and he hit her once in the mouth, with an open palm but moderately hard.

She began screaming, began it out of pain and rage, kept screaming because it was making him nervous. If you don't stop that I'm leaving, he said. Evelyn paused only long enough to hand him his tie when he couldn't find it. She followed him to the door, still naked, and when he was safely outside she laughed. With his shoes in his hand and his shirt unbuttoned, his hair lopsided and uncombed, he looked like a cartoon figure, a joke that needed a punch line. All she could think of to shout after him was You didn't even loosen any teeth.

She felt hungry so she sat down at the kitchen table with the leftover pork chops from dinner. The sponge turns carnivore, she said aloud. There was the beginning of a bruise on her lower lip; she could feel it every time she took a bite. But she ate two chops, including the stringy glazed fat on the edges, and washed them down with milk.

When she was sixteen she'd thought being frigid meant the boy couldn't get it in at all. Some kind of ice barrier he couldn't poke through. Of course, back then she also thought that orange juice and Coca-Cola would kill sperm. She remembered slipping into the bathroom with the pink rubber syringe and paper bag from the all-night grocery. It seemed pretty funny now, trying to open the bottles on the edge of the laundry hamper or straining the seeds out of the oranges. But of course it hadn't been funny at all. Thank God times had progressed.

But she supposed tonight hadn't been funny either, though if she told Freda later they would both roar about the inglorious exit. Freda would say You should have shouted Thanks, I had a very nice time.

And of course she would tell Freda; eventually she told Freda everything. The next day she called her and suggested they meet for drinks. You sound awfully sly, said Freda. What is it?

Just you wait.

So they were sitting in the ruby darkness, the soft leather of the booth tickling their legs and necks. Freda wore her black turtleneck, silver earrings and chains. She looked a bit like a gypsy today. She has that somber yet sensual look, Evelyn thought, shadowy and gaunt around the mouth and eyes, the nose properly hawklike through the bridge. Except her hair should not be red. These thoughts were interrupted when Freda leaned across the table and said Now tell me what the big secret is.

Evelyn let her fingernails chink against the glass and said carelessly Last night I was accused of being frigid.

You?

Yes, the woman you see before you.

Who said that?

Roger.

Roger . . . Roger. The one with the . . . ?

Afghan hound.

That one. Darling, why, if I may ask?

Evelyn shrugged and made her face very smooth. I'm afraid he's an unreconstructed type. Another champion of the vaginal orgasm.

Freda threw back her head and the red lamps made the inside of her mouth look inflamed. Then, said Evelyn, he hit me. The effect was all she could have asked for. Freda's mouth sank shut and she made a sound like a vacuum cleaner when the plug is suddenly pulled. The bruise was not really that bad, a blue smudge

smaller than her little finger. In the dark bar it was hardly notice-
able. But Freda was so upset by it she nearly cried and it took
them two more drinks before they could speak lightly about it.

Scratch a man and you'll find a man, said Evelyn.

Men are turds, said Freda.

Back home Evelyn felt the hilarity draining from her, overcome by the twilight that stained the corners of the rooms. No, it
really wasn't funny, you could joke all you want, but only afterwards. She had bad luck with men. Not usually as bad as with
Roger, thank God. She imagined herself trying to sum it all up for
Ann Landers. Dear Ann, I am a college graduate, a career woman
of twenty-six, a good conversationalist and dancer and my girl
friends tell me I am not unattractive. I have no problem meeting
men and in fact must exert considerable effort to keep things sim-
mering just below the boiling point of promiscuity. But all the ones
I can tolerate as human beings are either lousy lays or have three
kids back in White Plains or both; on the other hand the ones that
are good in bed talk about nothing but scuba diving or stereos.
What should I do, and how will I know if it's love?

Ann would write back: Remember, a lemon that's been
squeezed too often is garbage. When it's love, you'll know.

Oh Ann, said Evelyn, I believe it is the fault of my cultural
conditioning which emphasized romanticism to the exclusion of
everything else, which always showed one chiseled tear on the
chiseled cheek of the girl on the covers of *Teen Secrets*, thus inex-
tricably welding romance to suffering, which taught me to believe
in the Magic of a Kiss. Shall I tell you about Franklin, who said
we should live together for a three-month period and mingle our
souls?

Ann replied: Already I can tell he was a real shit.

You're right as usual Ann. We found a summer sublet and
moved in and he said it would be an interval of passion with all
the comforts of domesticity but none of the long-term tensions.
Then one night I mentioned extending the lease. We were in bed.
His organ, which had been tumescent, simply disappeared. I've
never seen anything like it. The same thing began to happen if I
said the word "September"; eventually he generalized to include
"autumn," "cold," and "radiator." He moved out two weeks early
and last I heard he was married to a woman who makes ceramic
jewelry and they were living in a commune.

Ann's voice was professionally stern. Wake up and smell the
coffee! You obviously want to get married.

At times, yes. At times I want nothing more than a tweedy
rumpled husband and kids with jam in their hair and fancy dish
towels that list uses for herbs. And these visions last about four
minutes and are sometimes referred to as temporary insanity.

Not every woman is equipped for the sacrifices and fulfillments of motherhood, said Ann.

A pox on your smug full-bosomed Jewish fertility, Ann. Choices aren't easy. I want everything.

I have heard all this many many times before, said Ann.

I know, cried Evelyn. I was simply reiterating my position.

But Ann had slipped away with the last blue daylight; she was beyond retort and somehow she had had the last word. Evelyn decided she would take a long hot bath with all her fancy soaps and oils and pretend she was Scheherazade lolling in the harem pool.

In the bath her knees and belly, the peaks of her breasts protruded from the suds, wet and sleek as seals. Tentatively she poked one nipple and it obliged by stiffening. Roger's accusation disturbed her, she admitted. She wasn't frigid, being able to achieve climax with oral or manual clitoral stimulation, but was she living up to her sexual potential? Was it something you could cultivate? All those books and techniques and questionnaires in *Cosmopolitan*. It was like studying to be an electrician or accountant from a matchbook correspondence course. And certainly the more you worried about it the more self-conscious it was. She wanted to be a natural, a ripe fruit bursting its skin with sensuality.

I want to be a ripe fruit bursting its skin with sensuality, she told Jacques at dinner the next night. He was one of her truly intimate friends, although she did not let him sleep with her for fear of jeopardizing their solid relationship.

A plum, Jacques suggested.

Yes, a plum, that's it exactly. Women today are expected to combine the sexual know-how of a high-priced trollop with the achievement drive of a Henry Ford.

Duality is a trap, said Jacques. We should aim for being unified human entities.

In spite of his Gallic name Jacques was a tall fair boy with a long face the color of pale cheese. Evelyn always found him delightfully sympathetic. Perhaps, she told others, it is because he is almost androgynous in nature (though a definite heterosexual), possessing as he does the so-called feminine qualities of intuition and dependency.

God, said Evelyn. When I think of my childhood, the expectations and assumptions I was raised with. Do you know the kind of things little girls say when they skip rope? Jacques shook his head. She described in detail the sound of the rope, the dry light scrape as it drags for a moment on the asphalt, the whipping noise when the rope cuts the air. The line of little girls waiting their turn. Then the chant:

Down in the valley where the green grass grows
There sat Mary, pretty as a rose

She sang, she sang, she sang so sweet
Along came Bobby and kissed her on the cheek

How many kisses did she get?

The number of kisses, of course, determined by the number of unobstructed turns of the rope. A really accomplished jumper could hit the boys for dozens of kisses, 1 . . 2 . . 3 . . 4 . . 5 . . 6 . . .

Jacques thought this was terribly amusing and he nearly choked on his zabaglione. Evelyn thought how much more attractive Jacques would be if his parents had been able to afford orthodonture.

She thought she might write a poem to capture the bitterness and confusion of the contemporary female sexual trauma. The poem would not use the word thigh. It might not even use the words cock or cunt, but it would still be shocking in its images and honesty. It was a slow morning at work; she could safely hide in her frosted glass cubicle. Evelyn took out a clean piece of stationery. Under the letterhead, Bronson and Van Slyck, Fraternal Regalia and Supplies, she wrote

> The stems of flowers do not
> tremble at the
> bee's raw thrust

She paused, frowned, crumpled the paper and got out a plain second sheet. At the end of an hour she had written

> The stems of flowers do not
> tremble at the
> bee's raw thrust
> the suck of his
> urgent lips, no,
> the pollen clings without
> dissent to the tiger-striped
> fur, the petals spread, the
> moist center throbs

She had meant to go on and say that it was more complicated with men and women, but several things bothered her. She was comparing flowers to women but someone had told her flowers have male organs too. Did bees have lips as such? Wasn't the whole bee and flower thing awfully worn? There were problems, problems. Evelyn sighed and looked out her office window, down thirty-five stories through fluffy gray layers of the city's air. Obviously her poem was a nineteenth-century conceit and how could such pastoral imagery be relevant to her essentially urban concerns.

She thought again of last night and Jacques's appreciation of her humor. She wondered if little girls still said such things on playgrounds. She wondered . . . Was not the contrast of childhood naiveté and adult reality bittersweet and ironic? Could not such juxtaposition encompass both sentiment and anguish? The idea charmed her. She would begin it that evening.

But Evelyn had forgotten her date with Gregory and it was simply too late to break it. A man would never understand if you said you would rather stay home and write a poem than go to a movie. Though men certainly did that to women. Besides, she wanted to see Gregory. He had a coarseness and sheer physical presence that she found extremely compelling, despite the undertones of submission implied in such a relationship. As she dressed in her unbleached muslin caftan Evelyn bemoaned woman's eternal conflict between self-actualization and the demands of biology.

Gregory looked impressive in his khaki safari suit, like the young Hemingway only much more elegant. His hair was black and his teeth were as white as piano keys and his gluteal muscles bulged winsomely. Evelyn did not even object when he suggested going to see *Supervixens*. Sometimes it was fun to pretend to be dominated.

What did you think of the movie, she asked him later. Weren't you slightly embarrassed at the transparency of the wish fulfillment, the coupling of sex and aggression?

I liked the part where he put the dynamite between her legs, said Gregory. He was not a man with whom she had an intellectual relationship.

But physically she couldn't ask for more. He leaves me feeling drained, she thought, freed from myself. When she asked him Gregory, do you think I'm frigid? he pointed to his still-swollen member and said Kid, you do wonders for the big guy. Oh, thought Evelyn, with him I am truly a ripe plum.

How many kisses did she get, 1 . . 2 . . 3 . . .

Yes, he was undeniably sturdy, but she wished he were more of a conversationalist. Was not the mind the most sensitive erogenous zone?

4 . . 5 . . 6 . . .

Evelyn confided to Freda that the term "unprotected intercourse," as it was used in the literature of contraception, had always been charged with ironies for her. In view of woman's essential receptivity and vulnerability, what intercourse was not unprotected?

Freda was enthusiastic. I should think you could work that up into quite a nice little essay, she said.

It would remain a personal and anecdotal essay, said Evelyn. I do not have the temperament of an activist.

Political awareness is only as valid as the personal experience it springs from, said Freda.

True, said Evelyn, ordering another daiquiri. That cheers me a bit.

Freda placed her fingertips to her temples and leaned forward on her elbows. Evelyn thought, With her hair falling loose to her shoulder and in that square-cut neckline she has the mysterious heavy-lidded sadness of a Pre-Raphaelite painting. Freda looked up. Something's been bothering me, she said.

My dear, can I be of any help?

I hope so. It's Carlo. He's dissatisfied with my tits.

Carlo was Freda's second husband and while they had both agreed that marriage was a social contract to be entered into without illusions, apparently there were still difficulties.

Evelyn said I'm not sure there's much I can do.

You can advise me. It seems that Carlo has always connected large bosoms with sexual appeal. He knows, of course, that it's an irrational association, and up until now he's persuaded himself it was superficial.

And now?

Now he says he dreams frequently of balloons and grapefruits and he leaves all my magazines open to the ads for Mark Eden Bust Developers.

Evelyn frowned. It doesn't sound good. But perhaps he's only trying to keep you on your erotic toes, so to speak, wanting you to compensate for your alleged deficiency by more imaginative sexual performance.

Oh, said Freda, sounding relieved. I do hope you're right.

Let me know, said Evelyn.

> Policeman, policeman, do your duty
> Here comes Sue, American Beauty
> She can wiggle she can wobble
> She can do the splits
> But I bet a million dollars that she can't do this

Hey, said Gregory. You're really good at that.

You mean it? asked Evelyn.

Of course I mean it. You're great.

You liked it then.

Boy, it made me want to stand up and sing the Star-Spangled Banner. Where did you learn stuff like that?

Actually it's one of my mother's recipes.

Ha ha. Mom must be quite a cook. Hey are you hungry? Thinking about recipes made me hungry.

No, not now.

I could really go for some potato chips. Do you have any potato chips?

No I don't.

How about ice cream? You got ice cream or maybe some fried chicken?

I'm afraid I didn't get to the store today.

We could go out and get a pizza, come on.

Right now?

Yeah, I'm starved.

Wouldn't you rather stay here for awhile?

Maybe one of those rib houses is still open. Are you sure you're not hungry?

Mmn.

Well maybe I'll let you get some sleep then. Hey that tickles. Ha ha. Have you seen my shoes?

> Cinderella dressed in yella
> went downtown to see her fella
> On the way her bloomers busted
> How many people were disgusted?

Freda and Carlo had come over for lamb pilaf and now the three of them were sitting on the bean bag chairs drinking chartreuse. Carlo had begun a discussion of deficit spending, and he did most of the talking with an occasional assist from Evelyn. Carlo gave the impression of being a large man although he was only five foot eight. His hands were enormous and thickly furred. Tendrils of black hair escaped from even his tightest shirt-collars and his nostrils were tarry cavities. Secretly Evelyn was appalled at the thought of what he must look like with his clothes off. Though Freda claimed hirsuteness had a charm of its own.

The evening had not quite congealed. At dinner Freda had been animated, almost feverish, speaking of acquaintances and current events. With that high flush in her cheeks, thought Evelyn, she resembles Heathcliff's Catherine just back from a romp on the moors. But as the meal progressed she had fallen silent, and Evelyn noticed the putty-colored bags under her eyes. Freda's last remark had been twenty minutes ago when apropos of nothing, she had lifted her chin and said Jesus, if there's one thing I hate it's synthetic whipped cream.

Carlo was saying An unbalanced budget can be a stimulus for a time but sooner or later the pressure must be counteracted. Otherwise we have economic rupture.

I quite agree, said Evelyn. She noticed Freda was plucking bits of lint from the carpet, rolling them into pills and lining them up in squadrons before her. Rupture, said Freda. No one ever speaks about the positive, liberating aspects of rupture.

Carlo's eyebrows were formidable at the best of times. Now they closed ranks. An economic rupture is not a pretty thing, my pet.

I was speaking generally.

I was speaking metaphorically.

I was speaking ironically, said Freda, shooting a lint pill at Carlo's nostril.

Evelyn admired the calm distate with which he removed the lint. It reminded her of an eighteenth-century nobleman accepting a challenge to a duel. I don't suppose you'd care to explain that, he asked.

I tire of verbal sallies, said Freda. Ka-pow, ka-pow, ka-pow. All three pills hit their target.

Well my squirrel, said Carlo, fortunately your physical assaults are no more deadly than your arguments.

Let's not bring up physical assaults. Some problems which seem to have physical solutions are hopelessly complicated by unhealthy mental attitudes.

Would anyone like another drink? asked Evelyn.

Why don't you stop mincing around the issue, said Carlo. You feel sexually inadequate.

Not until I met you.

So you're a late bloomer, said Carlo.

The ashtray was a very old one and had no sentimental value whatsoever, Evelyn assured them. Carlo apologized for the mess the bean bag chair made but Evelyn said it would be no problem. She loaned Freda a wide-brimmed straw hat to cover the gash above her eye. In it she looked very young, the daughter of a respectable French provincial family on her way to Mass. Before she closed the hall door Evelyn heard Carlo say Secretly you love to be degraded.

Not by you, Freda replied.

> Little Miss Pinkie, dressed in blue
> died last night at half past two
> Before she died she told me this:
> You better get out before you miss

Evelyn and Jacques had drunk a great deal of wine and now at dusk they were pretending they could see the city's skyline from Evelyn's windows.

I feel triste tonight, said Evelyn. She rememberd her unfinished poem. Triste, triste, triste.

Doubtless it is the violet afterglow of the vanished sun which lingers so poignantly and makes the city's lights seem to promise something that can never be attained, said Jacques.

Maybe, said Evelyn. Jacques was nuzzling her ear and while she was grateful for the animal comfort it afforded, she sensed an undercurrent of tension. Evelyn, he said, I think we should become lovers.

Why, said Evelyn.

Must it be analyzed and argued? We love each other. We've shared so many secrets. Why not share our bodies.

It would be incestuous, said Evelyn. You know me too well. I would feel psychically naked.

Sometimes you have to take chances, said Jacques.

We've drunk too much. It would be less than the best.

I don't care.

I have grave reservations.

Perhaps we could reach a compromise, said Jacques. Ease into things gradually. Why don't you take off your clothes and I will leave mine on and we'll see what happens.

Would we touch each other?

Perhaps you could touch me but if you have reservations I won't touch you.

Perhaps we could both undress but stop short of actual penetration.

Or we could achieve mutual climax by auto-stimulation. What the hell. He shrugged. We'll make up the rules as we go along.

The shadows in the room were ripening to purple. Yes, agreed Evelyn, stepping out of her shoes. We will. It sounded like something she had heard many many times before but she couldn't think exactly where.

LITTLE FACE

"You're hurting me," she told him. But he wouldn't stop now. She squeezed her eyes almost shut and waited. The sheets were a soft intricate landscape of furrows and ridges. Through the shadow of her lashes she watched it melting and reforming again and again. It was like those animated films about the solar system, with the strange boiling planets. Venus? Mercury. It was hard to get air into her lungs. Although she was not crying, tears were jolting to the rims of her eyes and the sheet-world blurred and swam and finally disappeared.

After a while he said "I'm sorry. I didn't mean it to hurt."

"It's OK. It's just from behind like that, when you pull me up on my knees, then it can sort of hurt."

"It wasn't on purpose. I wouldn't ever do anything like that on purpose."

"I know," she said, because he seemed anxious that she believe it. Although she felt it was not entirely true. Not that he wanted to hurt her, but that tenderness was only one part of what happened between them. Apologizing was like saying the rest of it was a mistake. She didn't want him to apologize for any of it.

He raised himself up on one elbow and stroked the wing of her shoulder blade, polishing it. "Sometimes I forget how easy it is to hurt you. You aren't used to it."

She was embarrassed and resentful at any reference to her age, which after all was something she could not help. She didn't answer him and the hand on her shoulder grew lighter, patting her. He was thinking, she knew, that it was almost time for her to leave.

He wasn't good-looking. She didn't try and pretend he was. Sometimes girls did that. She'd done it before, convincing herself that some boy she liked was everything she wanted him to be. It was a little like throwing your eyes out of focus. You saw them that way for as long as you could keep the effort up. She didn't do that with Willie, maybe because everything about him, even his homeliness, seemed extraordinary, as if no one had discovered him before she had. He had a heavy face with deep hinged lines around the mouth and nose. The skin itself looked heavy, like you could push the lines into it with your hands. It was grayish and you could see the pores in it. It was the only thing about him that really looked old. When he was asleep or resting she watched him greedily. Now she rolled over so they lay together from shoulder to toe. "I don't want to leave."

"You never want to leave. But you know you have to."

"I know." She ducked her head and looked into the sheets again for the miniature world she had discovered. But the angle of light had changed and it was gone.

"It'll be dark soon and I don't want you out by yourself. They'll be worrying about you too. Come on, Little Face."

That was Willie's name for her, he said because her hair was so shaggy and drooped so low into her eyes. He said she looked like she was peering out from behind shrubbery. She liked him calling her that, not so much because of the name itself, but because no one else in the world would ever use it.

He'd already gotten out of bed and put on his robe. His bare legs looked cold in the sunless afternoon light. She heard him running water in the bathroom. She wished she could dress by just draping something loose around her. Her neat stack of discarded clothes always seemed forlorn, even ludicrous, not what she should be wearing at all. Cotton underwear, plaid skirt, sweater, socks gone all stretched and shapeless around the cuffs. By the time she finished dressing she always felt self-conscious, even if he hadn't watched her tugging everything on.

She waited for him in the living room. The books on his shelves were familiar to her by now. She remembered how guilty and excited she'd felt at first, trying to learn about him from them, like a spy. The German she couldn't read. The oversized art books, Klee and Picasso and the rest, and their stiff glossy expensive paper. Too expensive, Willie said. Every time he bought one he was taking food out of his mouth. He always talked like that, as if he were poor. And maybe he was, but to her, having your own apartment and shopping for groceries and paying bills and all the things he complained about were signs of the most desirable wealth. There wasn't much else of interest in the room beside the books. Willie never made any effort at arranging things, except in piles, and the place managed to look both bare and cluttered at the same time. The floor was uncarpeted and wads of gray dust tumbled across it in the arid breath from the heating vents. It disappointed her that Willie wasn't more interested in appearances. Lately the apartment made her feel as if nothing really belonged there, including her.

Now he padded into the room. "All set? Ready to march?"

Leaving was always like this. He would be brisk and nervous about it, and she would implore him with her silence and her misery not to let her go. She knew it only made him impatient when she got teary, but she couldn't help it. She sank her face into his chest. His bathrobe smelled of closet. "You know what I keep thinking," he said. "This isn't good for you. That's what I keep coming back to."

"Don't say that, that's silly. Why do you want to talk like that?"

"Because I have to think about these things. I have to worry about you."

"No you don't. I don't want you to. It's all right, really. I'm just being sad because I don't want to leave. You don't make me sad, not one bit."

She was talking too fast again. He smiled down at her, his narrow, quizzical smile. It meant he was thinking that she was too young even to know how she felt. How unfair it was, and always would be, for him to be able to use that against her. And then he could resent her for making him feel responsible for her, making him worry. It was unfair both ways. She supposed he did worry about her, but it was so wrapped up in his worry for himself that she was most afraid when he talked like this, about what was good or bad for her.

"It's OK," she said. "Remember? We talked it all out. Nobody's going to know, not ever. It's OK."

"A lot of people wouldn't think so."

"Well, we aren't a lot of people. We're just us, and that's all that matters. You shouldn't let yourself get upset about things that won't ever happen."

When he laughed the lines around his mouth and eyes folded in on themselves. "What an amazing girl. Now she's giving me advice. What a wise little person. All I do is snivel. How do you ever put up with me. Oh I like you too much, Little Face, I do, that's what I worry about."

And she wanted to tell him that this was why it was good for her, the only good thing she had, and that no one else would ever call her amazing or worry about liking her too much. But it was late now, and once she'd gathered up her books and kissed him again there was nothing to do but leave. He closed the door softly and she was on the other side. She stared at it but it didn't budge or change, nor did the airless hallway and its single cloudy light bulb. It was always the same and she would never get used to it.

And then the street and the lights coming on and turning the air blind, and the growl of the bus as it stopped in front of her. Inside it smelled metallic and overheated. She found a seat and closed her eyes, but it did no good. She was still there. She was still traveling away from Willie and into the ordinary world that existed everywhere else. Nothing had changed except herself and now she had to change herself back again to fit. She was swaddled in ordinariness, like her ill-fitting clothes. Already she was thinking of things they would ask her at home, how was your day and your math test and your cold, and what she would answer back. And they would notice nothing. She supposed she ought to be glad. At times it was thrilling to have secrets, to be able to reach down inside yourself and touch them. But at other times she wondered how she could live and talk and move among them without their knowing a single thing about her, not a thing, and it might go on forever, this life that meant nothing.

She looked around her at the people on the bus jolting heavily in their seats, their stiff going-home faces, the way they clutched their packages to them like parts of their bodies that might stray if not tended. They were ordinary. But then she knew she looked nothing if not ordinary herself. A girl with lumpy bare knees, huddled so far over her armload of books that her shoulders rounded. Her dopey, rabbity expression. She knew very well how she looked. And that meant (no matter how many times she rediscovered it, it amazed her all over again) that the heavy shapes around her were every bit as alive as she. How terrible to think that they too were unknowable, burdened with secrets, each one separate and confined to separateness, like the mad little planets she had imagined earlier. And that was the worst thought of all, because if no one understood anyone it meant that she did not really know Willie, nor he her.

The one good thing about the bus ride was that it always made her so tired from thinking, nothing could touch her for a while. The lights of her house were tiny and harmless. She could cover them with her outstretched hand. It was beginning to mist; her hair felt damp, as if covered by a net. She exhaled and left all her breath outside. Her mother was scraping carrots for dinner. The steam from the cooking made the kitchen seem smaller, and everything within it bright and loud. Her mother's face was sharp with worry and relief. "It's about time," she said when Paula opened the back door, and "You know what I've told you. Dinner in this house is at six, and I will not have you sauntering in at the last minute." And Paula said that she was sorry, it was just that she had so much to read and the buses were late, and she'd set the table if her mother wanted.

Her mother held up her cheek to be kissed. It tasted dry and powdery, in spite of the room's heat. "Angela did it already. Never mind, just go wash up. I don't mean to be cross, sweetie, it's just that I worry about you after dark."

"It gets dark early now," said Paula, and she waited a moment to see if there was anything else. There wasn't, so she picked up her books and headed for the stairs. Everyone worried about her, it seemed, but none of it did her that much good.

She was glad she was hungry. She felt safer among them when she could feel what she was supposed to feel. Her mother had cooked the chops too long again; they were thin and dry, and the little curls of fat edging them had hardened. Mashed potatoes. The carrots smelled of steam and nothing else. She made herself busy with her plate until she could manage to look up at them. Her mother's face was tired, as always. Her father chewing impassively, as if he'd forgotten what eating was for, that it had something to do with hunger. Her sister saw Paula staring, and shifted her mouthful of potatoes so that one cheek bulged.

"Mom, Angela's being gross."

"Paula Maria, you are not to use that word."

"She's playing with her food, look at her. Well she was, just a second ago."

"I don't care who was doing what. Do you know how tired I get of hearing about it? I will not have the dinner table spoiled with another one of your squabbles."

"How am I supposed to eat anything? She's making me sick. *Look* at her."

"You heard your mother," Paula's father said.

Angela rolled her eyes and when no one else was looking, shot her tongue out at Paula. A circle of carrot balanced on its tip. Gross. She was gross. Her mother always talked as if dinnertime were some festivity, something to be treated with reverence, when it was only burned chops and Angela making faces and everyone too hungry to care what they ate anyway. She supposed that her mother aspired to some vision of Dinnertime as it was on television commercials, where everyone looked so hugely delighted to be together in such gleaming, well-appointed kitchens, it hardly mattered if food was in front of them or not. And then it occurred to her that maybe her mother *did* see them that way, in spite of everything, the irritation and indifference, that this was her mother's family, her home, the food she had prepared for them. That it actually gave her mother pleasure to sit back in her chair, exhausted, already worrying about the next chore, or that worry and exhaustion were what she made herself feel after allowing herself pleasure.

She lowered her head. She was going to cry, really cry in a minute, and it was because of the smallness of what gave her mother enjoyment, and because every time she moved her legs she felt where Willie had been, and how could she ever tell them, her own people, of her love and sadness or anything else she knew, when she had set herself forever so far apart?

"Paula, honey?"

Her mother who loved her too much to know anything about her.

"You look flushed. Let me feel your cheek. After you finish eating I want you to go straight up and take a hot bath. Angela can clear the table."

"Oh great. I'm sick too then, I'm sick and I don't have to do anything."

"Finish your milk."

And her father, who would never know what to say to any of them.

"It's not fair. First her and her big deal homework so she doesn't have to help and now she's sick. She isn't sick one bit. She's faking everything."

Upstairs in her room, which was at least all hers and she could be alone. She drew the sheets up over her shoulders. They were soft and thin from all the washing, and if you left them on too long they only got softer and began to smell perfumey. Willie's sheets were stiff and creased. You were always afraid of rubbing against grit, even if he'd just put them on. She supposed this was why when she lay in her own bed and tried to remember what it had felt like with Willie, she couldn't. Her legs shifted underneath the load of blankets, warm and secret. It wasn't the same at all. She couldn't even imagine him here. She would be a little ashamed to have him see her room anyway. There wasn't a single thing special about it. The posters and the little scraps of paper and yarn that were supposed to give it personality. They only looked messy and pathetic, as if they were trying too hard. Maybe that was her personality. No, she wouldn't want Willie here.

She slid deeper into the covers. She felt sore from him. Maybe they were doing it wrong somehow. (She had no word that meant sex, even when she was only thinking to herself.) It wasn't at all the way she had imagined it. Not at all. She watched Willie's eyes, and his mouth twisting like a wound. *Do you feel what I feel? Tell me what I feel.* Bewilderment, and the violence of her body. Songs and books and the way people talked about it were all wrong. Everything she'd heard before must have been a sort of code, as if people had agreed to make it a matter for rhymes and jokes and slyness, disguising what it was really like, a secret. If so, she was in on it now, but in some ways she understood less than ever.

She'd met Willie in the library. "Of all places," her mother would have said. Her parents' familiar and persistent voices. She turned on her pillow, but they followed her. "You must have read every book in there twice by now." What her father would say, and say again and again, with such heavy playfulness she wanted to scream. He made it out to be a joke, but she knew it meant he (her mother too) was disappointed in her. Why wasn't she happier? "Such a nice afternoon and you sat inside the whole time?" Exasperated, still pretending to tease her. She wished they'd just come out and say it.

She liked the library's high windows and the sunlight drifting down from them, brown and dusty gold. And on cloudy days the big globe lamps on the ceiling, making everything warm. And the little ordered noise of people scraping chairs or asking the librarian questions in murmuring, respectful voices. She liked all of it. She didn't really read. She looked at magazines or daydreamed, and no one bothered her. She liked having people all around her as long as they would not pay her any attention or wonder why she was there. Anyone could sit in the library forever, and no one would care.

And Willie, with his pale stiff hair and his knobby face and old green sweater, and piles of important-looking books all around him. It was funny to think back on him then, when he meant nothing to her. He was frowning and peering at the book, then at his paper, writing a word or two each time. It was hard work, whatever it was. He looked up and shook his head. "Scribble scribble. And no end in sight."

He sounded angry. No, he was smiling. He was making a joke. Caught staring, she was so mortified she had trouble telling. He was still smiling, as if expecting her to say something. "What are you writing?" And then felt stupid all over again, for being so nosy.

"My dissertation. What a mess."

"Dissertation?"

They were seated on opposite sides of the long blond wood table, a little distance apart. Now he scooted his chair closer, so they wouldn't have to talk so loudly. "Yeah. I've only been working on it since the year one." She must have still looked puzzled. "I'm at the university," he explained.

He looked too old to be in college. He looked almost as old as her parents, thirty at least, but he dressed younger, more carelessly. He kept leaning towards her, grinning hugely, as if delighted by something. She wondered if he'd confused her with someone he already knew. For politeness' sake she asked, "What is it about?"

"What?"

"You know, your paper."

"You'll be sorry you asked. It's about the connection between economic climate and the German expressionists. There. Isn't that sexy?"

She smiled to hide her alarm. Sexy? "I'm great at parties," he went on. "I start talking about it and crowds gather. To throw things. Strong men weep and women faint. Ha ha."

Paula smiled again. Whatever he meant, it had not been . . . She felt stupid, sitting there nodding and agreeing when she had no idea what he was talking about, German whoevers or anything else. He seemed embarrassed too. He sat up straighter in his chair and fussed with the notebooks in front of him. Maybe he was only bored with her. It was hard to tell. He seemed to keep changing his mind in the middle of saying things. "Sorry," he said. "I forget. I start going on and on. I get tired of it myself."

"Why are you writing it then? I mean, is it something you have to do?"

"If I want to be officially overeducated, I have to finish it. I mean if I want my degree. But nobody's making me do it. Nobody ever really makes you do anything, do they."

She couldn't have disagreed more with him, but it seemed rude to say so. She wondered what sort of life he led, that no one made him do anything, and stranger still, why he should seem unhappy about it. She was starting to feel shy about talking to him for so long, or at least, about listening to him. She tidied her stack of books and cleared her throat. "I have to go now. It's been nice talking to you. I hope you can finish your, ah, work soon."

He laughed. He had a wide, haw-hawing laugh that embarrassed her a little, at least in the library, where it was conspicuous. "You and everybody else. Sorry I bent your ear."

"No, really, I enjoyed it." It made her feel good to be using her manners so well, and to have sustained a whole conversation, no matter how peculiar, with a stranger.

The next time he showed her pictures by the expressionists. She wondered why anyone would draw such ugly misshapen people, and why Willie would want to spend all his time looking at them. They were like cartoons that weren't funny. Bloated, green-faced little men, mincing scarecrow women. She listened and frowned intently, as if that would help her understand everything. He explained that to do the right sort of research he would have to go to Germany. He couldn't afford to on his own, he was waiting to hear about some grant that he probably wouldn't get because it was all political. You had to brown-nose the chairman, he said. Begging your pardon. They, by which he seemed to mean the whole university, would just as soon he'd quit. They didn't know quite what to do with him anyway, because although he was in the art history department, his topic involved so much of economics and German. It was all very complicated and difficult. She imagined him struggling to fit his little piece of knowledge in its proper place, like a chip in some enormous mosaic, while the university poked and prodded at him. His long knobby hand brushed against hers as he turned a page. "I talk too much," he said, and laughed, haw-haw, as if that were funny. She told him no, it was just that she talked too little.

"So tell me something about yourself."

They were in his apartment, drinking tea he'd brewed in a green china teapot. "Oh," she said, "there's nothing to tell. Nothing special." She could have told him that she'd never even drunk tea out of a real pot before, much less been up in a man's room. Her heart was growing larger and larger, gathering strength to leap out of her. She hurried to say something, so he wouldn't get bored. "I go to school, I go home. That's about it." She shrugged. She was miserable, hearing herself say how dull she was.

"I'm trying to remember what I was doing when I was your age. Probably playing cowboys and Indians."

He grinned at her. He was making one of his jokes. They were so corny, she never knew what to say back to him. "Well, I don't do that."

"So tell me about something you like to do. Anything."

"Like? Oh. I like being by myself."

"That's a sad thing to like."

It had been all she could think of. She hurried to explain. "It's not sad. I don't always feel that way. But other people pull and push you so much. You have to keep doing what they want, being what they expect you to be, different things all the time. Like those mirrors that make you fat and thin . . ."

"No, don't stop. That's interesting."

"It's dumb. It's just something—I don't know what I meant."

"You're so modest. Yes you are. I like trying to figure you out. You know more than you ever let on."

"Me? I don't know anything about anything. Really." She was trying to imagine herself with some store of secret knowledge, smiling enigmatically at the rest of the world.

"Sometimes I wonder what you must think of me."

"Think of you?"

"This peculiar character you've taken up with."

"Come on."

"The world's oldest grad student. How pathetic. I should have learned a trade. TV repair, maybe."

"That's silly. You're a, you know, a scholar. You know all about things I'll never know. I feel so stupid next to you. If I don't say much, it's just because I don't want to sound stupid. But I'm always interested. I'm interested in everything you talk about." Not what she wanted to say at all.

He laughed his too-loud laugh. "Good Lord, girl. Such flattery. I'd better enjoy it while it lasts, before you wise up to me."

"That's silly," she said again. He confused her. Why wouldn't he just let her like him? Maybe both of them had the same sadness, something that made them keep apologizing for themselves. She knew more than she let on. She knew absolutely nothing. Her heart was still too large, clenching like a fist. "Maybe I should go now," she said.

"Why? We just got here. Are you afraid to be here? Are you afraid of me?"

"Afraid?"

She didn't want to be. She wanted whatever was going to happen to happen. She wanted something to happen to her for once in her life. He had green eyes. No, gray. He was waiting for her to say something else, bending towards her over the little table with the tea things on it. She was going to cry. That was all that ever happened to her. She said stupid things and cried.

"Hey now."

He was bending closer, pushing her heavy hair aside with one hand. Carefully, so as not to alarm her. "Hey, are you in there?"

She shook her head. She'd ruined everything now.

His face was still close to hers. She could see smaller lines around his eyes, like pale scratches. She lowered her head. Her hair lit up with sunlight, and she saw him through a blurred tangle of brown and gold. He was leaning over so far she was afraid the chairs would topple. Then his hands were all mixed up in her sweater, rubbing her hard. His mouth on her jaw. It was wet and soft, and his breath whistled in her ear. She was embarrassed. She wondered if there was something she should be doing. The next minute, without warning, it had all stopped, and she opened her eyes, feeling dazed. He was across the room with his back to her, looking out the window.

"What's the matter?" she said finally. He shook his head. "Please."

He reached for his coat on the chair next to him. "Come on, let's go."

Their cups were on the little table where they'd left them. The same streaky sunlight and the dust turning slowly in it. Nothing changed. She kept waiting for him to say something.

"Please, Willie." He had to tell her what she'd done wrong.

"You're fifteen years old."

He turned around but still he didn't look at her. "Let's get out of here. I'm really sorry."

"No," she said.

He didn't understand. "I don't want you to be sorry," she said. "I'm not sorry."

"Oh hell."

"Look at me, please Willie?"

"I'll walk you back to the library. Come on."

The sun dropped like a bullet. Long slats of glare fell between buildings. They were walking so fast the spokes of light seemed to revolve around them. He was walking so fast, with his hands jammed into his pockets. Why was he angry, what did he want her to say? She opened her mouth to speak but the light cut across her face. Willie halted on the sidewalk in front of the library. "Isn't this where you get your bus?"

"Willie, what did I do wrong?"

"Nothing."

"Tell me."

"Jesus."

"You have to tell me."

The sidewalk was in shadow now. The wind made his hair stand up in spikes. His nose all pink and rubbed-looking. Sometimes he didn't look very old at all. He kept wheeling away from her as if he wanted to leave, then swinging back impatiently. "It's nothing you did."

"You're angry at me, I can't stand it."

"I told you already. It's not you at all."

"It's because you're embarrassed now. I'm a dopey stupid boring *kid*, and you're embarrassed that you had anything to do with me, it makes you ashamed of yourself, like you ought to be able to do better. Never mind. Never mind any of it."

"What are you talking about? Don't you know how I feel?" He clutched at his hair, rumpling it even more. "Like a child molester. I keep waiting for a cop to come up and grab me. Look, it was all a mistake. It was all my fault, OK?"

"You don't even want to look at me now."

"It's not what I *want*, for Christ's sake . . ."

There were other people coming out now, and he had to stop talking. She was waiting for it to be over. She only wanted it to be over. The bus was at the end of the street, small, like a toy. He touched her elbow.

"Look, don't feel that way. Would you feel better if we talked? Tomorrow, OK? I'll be here tomorrow and we'll talk."

Talk? I don't know how to talk. But she nodded and turned back to the curb. He was still there on the sidewalk when she got on. He looked thin and lost, as if he had no reason for standing there, but nowhere else in the world to go. He gave her an odd little wave, like a shrug, and she knew right then everything that would happen. She knew she could make it happen. Looking back, she thought that might have been the best it ever was, riding home in the last tarnished daylight and knowing he was thinking about her.

When it did happen she didn't cry at all. She cried at all the wrong times. She kept her eyes open all the while, as though she'd been told to. What strange creatures they had become. Pale and unnatural, like shorn animals. His breath was everywhere, roaring at her. She felt like a kite, stretched between her light bones. She wanted to say something, to be reassured. That she was still herself. Maybe she wasn't. This made her someone different, it was all a mistake and it was too late now. Outside the windows traffic rolled and rolled. From somewhere very close, the other side of the wall perhaps, a dog barked. Left inside all day while people worked, she supposed. She tried to shut out hearing it, it seemed wrong to be hearing or thinking of anything else. Lord, he was heavy. Willie? She wanted him to talk to her. It hurt, it kept hurting. She tasted his hair in her mouth. *Willie?*

He told her it would get better, she'd relax and it wouldn't hurt so much. Like learning to play tennis or something, he'd said, and laughed. Why was he always making jokes? It wasn't like that at all. The dog barked every time. It startled her, she always thought at first it was in the room with them. She'd jerk her head on the pillow, looking for it. She'd known some people who had a dog with two different-colored eyes. A normal sad brown dog's eye, and a blue staring one. A glass eye, the people called it, though it wasn't at all. The dog's name was Milo. Silly thing to remember. How did it see? Blue and brown. Silly. She shouldn't be thinking of that at all.

You look so sad, Little Face, he'd say. Why are you always sad. She tried to explain. She wasn't really sad. She just thought about things a lot. When you thought about things it couldn't help but make you a little sad. How being with him made her think of all the secrets there must be in the world, all the things people said that meant nothing, all the things they meant but never said. She felt as if she had achieved some new and perilous vision, but it was not allowed her, there was no use for it beyond the four corners of Willie's bed. She knew more than she let on. She knew absolutely nothing.

It was a rain-day. A school day. The sky at midmorning was as low and sad as four o'clock. Cold rain puddled on the ground. The air was full of mists and stinging water. Paula sat next to the radiator in American History. The radiator thrummed and clanked. She felt shivery, lightheaded from all that stuffy warmth. The teacher was talking about railroads and the development of the West. It was always something like that. Outside the window bare trees dripped like candles melting. Waves of heat pushed at her. She tried to follow the teacher's voice but it floated out of reach. She supposed she would never be a good student. A, you know. A scholar.

In the row ahead of her a blonde girl in a red sweater bent her head, laughing silently but shaking her shoulders, so you could tell she was doing it. Her blonde hair swung over her back like ribbons. She mouthed something to one of her friends across the room and the friend rolled her eyes. Paula wondered what it was they said. Girls like that were always saying something to make each other laugh. *Oh riot. Tough titty. Better believe it. Hey, no lie.* It was the way they said things, not the words themselves. There was a way you were supposed to say things and a way you were supposed to look. She wasn't like that, well, so what. The few times she'd tried, laughing along with them or saying something tough and smart, they'd just ignored her. That was something else you were supposed to do, ignore people. Everyone had to watch you having secrets.

The bonde girl was folding up a note for her friend. *Isn't she out of it? I mean. Isn't he fine?* So much time spent deciding on who was what. She supposed she ought to be glad she was too dull for them to pay any attention to. Secrets no one knew she had. She wondered what they'd think about Willie and her. But she knew exactly what they'd think, or at least, how they'd act. They'd make it out to be something to laugh at, something queer and dirty. They'd twist it around and brand her with it, even though they giggled and swaggered about the things they themselves did with boys. They'd make it out to be queer and ugly because it would shock them, really shock them, and because she wasn't one of them. She wasn't one of them and Willie wasn't one of them, neither she nor he was right, somehow, and never would be. The two of them were freaks. Like the people in the German drawings, pursy or gaunt, staring out of the pictures with goggling, frightened eyes. She hated thinking it. She hated them for making her think it. *Isn't he too much? Tammy. Steve. Cathy. I swear. Believe it.*

The rest of the day her head hurt. Sleep buzzed in her ears. It was the first time she'd admitted to herself that there were things about Willie that disappointed her. He was what he joked about being. He was ashamed of himself for not working harder, not being something else, but he only made jokes about it. He wrote about ugly drawings because they were something he would not have to like too much. Something beautiful he'd have to take seriously. She didn't want to think that way about him. She tried to force herself back to the way she'd seen him before, when she had only admired him. It was like seeing two of him. A blue eye and a brown one. She dug her fists into her eyes, rubbing. She thought too much and there was no way to stop it.

It was still raining at three o'clock, a dull rain, like a tap left running. Water splashed up her legs each time she took a step. Her head was heavy and thick. She could feel blood squeezing through it painfully. She was going straight over to Willie's. She would almost rather have gone home to sleep. But that made her feel guilty, disloyal even. Funny how thinking critically of him also made her feel more tender. She had something to forgive him for.

When she knocked, he came to the door with a book in his hand. "Is it still raining? What a rotten day. Filthy stuff, rain."

The desk in the corner was heaped with papers. They were piled every which way, the corners splayed outwards like the petals of an enormous untidy rose. She watched him shuffle through them. "You look busy."

"It seemed like a good time to hit the books. What else could you do on a day like this. I really hate this weather. I feel like I'm growing moss."

"It's not so bad." He only shrugged and pursed his lips at the book he held. "So what are you reading?"

"I'm through reading. I'm starting to write the thing, finally. I figured it was about time. Enough of the bloody research."

"I thought you had to go to Germany before you had all the research done." There was never enough heat in the apartment. Her shoes were wet clear through.

"Oh, I would, to do it the way it ought to be done. But I've decided to limit the topic. It'll be more emphasis on the aesthetics, less on social conditions. A shift in focus. Something I can handle."

"That's terrific. That you're starting to write, I mean."

"It'll be especially terrific if I actually get it done."

She put her wet things in the kitchen and started the kettle going for tea. It made her feel good to be able to rummage through the cupboards, knowing where everything was. It was her kitchen more than her mother's ever would be. She warmed her hands on the stove and felt a little of the chill leave her. When she came out with the tray, Willie was back at his desk, writing. "Hey, thanks." He sat the cup next to the page. She watched the pen scratch up and down. He had cramped little handwriting, black and furious-looking. She sat in the one good chair, next to the window. The rain looked steely now, solid unbroken lines, like in a Japanese print. She wondered why they were still sitting here, in the living room. She wondered why the dog wasn't barking.

After a while she said, "Are you very busy? Is it a bad time for me to be here?"

"Well, sort of. What with trying to get the writing started."

"Oh. Sure."

"I'm going to have to make a real push. Really concentrate on it. It's going to take up a lot of time."

She watched the pen scratch and scratch. The desk lamp made an oval of light around his hands. It quivered on the edges like an egg in a dish, a little wavering brightness.

"Oh hell." Something he was mad about.

"I'm no good at this sort of thing. I'm no good at anything like this. Listen, I just think it would be better if we didn't see each other for a while. I've been thinking about it and it just seems like the best idea. For both of us. For all sorts of reasons."

He frowned at the desk, then turned back to her. "Say something, OK?"

"I can't."

"I'm sorry. God, if I was any good at any of this. I know how it must look. Like some high school jerk who gets what he wants off you and then backs out. Christ. It probably just makes it worse to say things like that. I really am a jerk. I'm no good for you."

She was thinking of the little secret planet-worlds in the sheets. How they shivered and boiled and it was hard to breathe. On Venus? Mercury?

"It's not that I don't want to see you," he was saying now. "To talk and things. I'll for sure see you at the library. But anything else is asking for trouble. I knew that all along, I was just selfish. I didn't think. I take full responsibility. I wish you'd say something."

She cleared her throat. "I used to think of things to say to you ahead of time. I used to rehearse them, so I'd have something to say."

"You deserve better than me, you know? Somebody your own age. Somebody you can go on double dates with, and eat pizzas with. Somebody *normal*, for Christ's sake."

"I'd make up little stories about us, where I wouldn't have to talk. Things like I'd faint in the library, and you'd have to bring me glasses of water and take care of me."

"I really wish I could make you feel better about this. I wish I could make you see it's the only right thing."

"Oh, never mind," she said vaguely. She was looking around for her things. She couldn't remember what she'd brought. What of it belonged to her.

"Look, I'll call you a cab. You can't go out in this rain. It's too awful, you leaving this way."

But she was already buttoning her coat. She was looking not so much at him as at the walls and furniture, as if they were what she ought to remember. None of it belonged to her, although she seemed to belong to it. "Good-bye," she said, and let him hug her. A hair-tussling, embarrassed sort of hug. He was saying something else, but she wasn't listening. It was like leaving all the other times, except that she wasn't listening to him.

She cried at all the wrong times. She wasn't crying now. She had a picture in her mind of how she looked, walking through the rain, and how sad it was, and that kept it from really being sad. She was just walking. There was nowhere to go except the bus and home, and while she would do that sooner or later, she wouldn't just yet. She walked in L-shaped patterns, C-patterns, cement alphabets. The street was one she'd seen a thousand times, with buildings of soaked red brick jammed together. She knew she'd seen it, although never before had it been so tricky to walk on, expanding and contracting, like a skin. But it hadn't changed, not really. She was simply nowhere at all. Little Face. No one in the world would ever call her that again. No one in the world would ever know what she knew. There was no place for her to be what she was, now that everything was a secret. Rain like glass hair. Cloth nipples folding up tight. *Willie? I don't know how to talk. Little Face, growing smaller and smaller.*

NAOMI
COUNTING TIME

She was a big girl, and in fact there always seemed to be rather too much of her. She wore the universal schoolgirl's clothes of the times, lint-covered sweaters and drooping socks and kilts, with the belts pulled so tight she overflowed them above and below. Her voice honked and stammered. There was too much inside her that wasn't words, too many itches and confusions and untidy longings. She startled herself when she laughed, the enormous sound of it exploding so close, like a flock of hidden birds boiling up out of a field. Her name was Naomi Hess but at least there was a girl in her class named Velma, and that was even worse. Her head was filled with too many trashy daydreams, the sort that combined songs from the radio and various square-jawed movie stars, though never very satisfactorily. It was even less satisfactory to put herself into them, because as she was she didn't fit, and if you imagined yourself as someone beautiful, that stretched things to the point where you lost interest. She was almost always in love, though sometimes she forgot just who it was she was supposed to be in love with. Most of them were boys at school she never spoke to, and it was hard to keep things in focus when nothing ever happened. Love was the important part of it anyway, just as hunger was more important, finally, than the food you ate. She was resigned to the idea that her love didn't fit anything properly, but she couldn't help it, love kept bursting out of her. She yawned through geometry class and summer vacations and Sunday dinners. She was fifteen when her mother decided she should take violin lessons.

Mrs. Hess was a practical woman, but when she looked at her daughter she saw the need for ornament. What mother wouldn't feel concern? Live off her wits the girl couldn't be expected to do.

A good disposition she had, for whatever that was worth, and all the sturdy housekeeping skills Mrs. Hess could impart. Naomi knew how to chop stew vegetables and she knew that for a broken glass first you picked up the big pieces, then swept, then used a wet paper towel. Now she was to have an accomplishment, something to act as leavening, to give her an outside interest. And since lying about on sofas and skewering her head with bobby pins were hardly accomplishments, one had to be procured. It couldn't hurt, was one way the mother put it to herself. Don't expect miracles, was another. For a while Mrs. Hess thought of ballet, which might at least improve her posture. But she must have foreseen Naomi mutely suffering in tights. Naomi with a violin wedged under her chin, swaying gravely over a music stand, was more plausible. The violin was a serious instrument, Mrs. Hess felt, unlike some others.

So here's Naomi on the downtown bus one sullen November day after school, on her way to becoming accomplished. The cold air made her nose itch. Her books kept sliding off her knees. Mashed bits of paper protruded from all of them, and these she absently frayed and crumpled as she looked out the window. A docile girl, she had not really argued much about violin lessons. She never won arguments with anyone. The bus jolted and wheezed and stank. She liked the bus. She liked going downtown, liked especially the grimy, forbidden neighborhoods that swam alongside the windows. The pocked brick walls and yawning doors, the murky little taverns at the corners and unkempt children crouching on porches, all this suggested some fiercer, more important world than her own. For different reasons she liked the small tidy shops farther down the line, their lights blooming warmly in the gray air. She liked the enormous stone blocks of the downtown offices, and the smartly dressed, knowing secretaries clipping along the sidewalks in their high, needle-toed shoes. She would have liked to live everywhere at once, she decided. She would have liked to be everyone else too, while she was at it, at one time or another. It hardly seemed fair that you had to be yourself for the whole of your life. As it was, she almost missed her stop.

Once she was off the bus she began to feel a quite predictable dread. To walk into a place where she was unknown, to announce herself and speak reasonably to strangers, as if she expected them to answer reasonably (but what if they *didn't*?), all this seemed an impossible trial. She dawdled in front of store windows. It was all stupid anyway, she thought, feeling mutinous. The violin was stupid, and playing it, she saw clearly, would just make her into a different category of freak. It would be as bad as wearing your hair in braids. Besides, none of the songs on the radio had violins in them, none of the good ones. They all had words, not violins. Stupid. She had reached the music store before she realized it, and after frowning at the sheet music in the window in case anyone was watching her, there was nothing to do but go in.

It was a small store, one she'd seen before but had immediately forgotten, since there was no reason to remember it. A bell crashed against the door when she opened it, pushing too hard. The inside was dim, and while she could see nothing clearly at first, she was very much aware of the smell tickling her nose. Oil and polish and the dusty bouquet of plush. Leather, metal, maybe a whiff of smoke. It was much later that she learned to sort it out and give it names. Right now she stood, breathing it in, blinking, vaguely aware of the shining glass countertops and other breakable-looking surfaces that surrounded her.

At the far end of the shop, which was long, almost like a corridor, two people were standing. There was a look about them that she knew at once, though like the smell it couldn't be immediately described. It was the look of belonging exactly where they were, of comfortable proprietorship. One was a man who perched on a high stool at the end of the counter, a coffee mug cradled in his hands. The other was a woman, leaning one elbow on the countertop, her chin in her palm. They might as well turn it into a regular swimsuit contest, the man was saying. There's no point in pretending there's anything else competitive about it. Or anything professional, or anything that has to do with standards of excellence, heaven forbid.

The woman said she thought he was exaggerating. Oh am I? the man went on. It's supposed to be a *scholarship*, correct me if I'm wrong, and everybody knows she went out of her way to display her shapely ankles for old Hogan, at least, that's one way of putting it—

Naomi had been afraid that they were going to sit there forever, ignoring her until she'd be forced to intrude on them. But at some almost imperceptible sign from the woman, the man slid off his stool and came reluctantly forward. Help you? he said. He was very thin and hollow-chested, and wore a black turtleneck with some large faint stain, resembling the map of Asia, across its front.

I'm here for a lesson, Naomi managed, easier than she would have thought. She was relieved when the man turned away, calling, Diana?

The woman was already walking towards her. You must be Naomi. I'm Miss Greer. Would you like to come back with me?

Naomi nodded, and said something stupid that roared in her ears, like Yeah, or Oh yeah sure uh-huh, and clutched her toppling armload of books. Maybe it wouldn't be so hard. They'd just keep telling her what to do. The back of the store was even darker, stacked high with cardboard boxes. The corridor between them turned a corner and Naomi realized Miss Greer had vanished. She halted, afraid of knocking things over. No, Miss Greer was just ahead, her heels tapping sharply on the tile floor. Weeks later, when that few feet of corridor would become as familiar to her as her own upstairs hallway at home, she would wonder how she'd ever gotten lost, even for an instant, would wonder how she failed to appreciate Miss Greer the second she laid eyes on her.

It wasn't until they had taken their places in the small practice room that she really looked at her. Even then she was distracted by the effort of bundling her knees and books into the proper places, and trying not to make the folding chair squeak. Miss Greer wore gray, a sweater and flannel skirt. Naomi saw in an instant what gray could be; not just a safe no-color you had to choose for your winter coat, but something pale and fine and irreproachable. Miss Greer was unbuckling a leather case lined with rose plush. This instrument is old, she was saying. But its condition is good. Its tone is good. And she swept it under her chin, plucked at it for a moment, frowning, then raised the bow and out came the music as easy as turning on a faucet.

You see, said Miss Greer, stopping in mid-note and smiling slightly. She went on to explain: The care of the instrument. The principle of bow against string, the different thicknesses and tensions. The neck. The frog. The bridge. Naomi wasn't listening, though her eyes were wide and attentive. She was still trying to sort it all out. The music, the violin, with its beautiful deep caramel finish and the two black S-shapes that curved so exactly, most of all Miss Greer herself. How old was she? As much as thirty? Her hands were very long and white and she wore no rings. Her dark hair was pulled straight back from her forehead. It was unfashionable but it looked exactly *right*, somehow, so that once you saw it you couldn't imagine it any other way. Her eyebrows too were very dark and straight, with just a hint of arch to them, like the violin carvings. Naomi, who read all the makeup articles in the magazines, decided they were neither plucked nor penciled. (Back home Mrs. Hess had a set of little clear plastic strips with different shapes of eyebrows cut in them, thick or spidery or surprised. You were meant to tie them around your forehead and color the eyebrows in; they had puzzled Naomi greatly when she'd found them in a dresser drawer at the age of seven.)

Naomi divided all women's figures into *little* or *big*, meaning good or bad; she didn't know what to make of Miss Greer's. Miss Greer was round. No, that wasn't right. It made her sound fat and she wasn't. There was so little about her that was ornamental, her beauty, once you saw it, was startling. Naomi was suddenly reminded of a waitress she'd seen once leaning against a drugstore counter, not a pretty woman or a young one, just a tired waitress in a pink uniform, standing with her hands on her hips. But there was something about the curve of those hips and breasts, something about the soft, far from trim slope of her waist that had stirred Naomi oddly, had made her think, this is a woman's body, this is what a woman should look like . . .

Naomi?

Her eyes focused again, and she gulped air. Do you, Miss Greer was repeating, bearing down on her with her eyebrows, do you have any knowledge of the scales or the values of musical notes? No? I will give you some simple exercise books to complete for next week. We will begin with that, and with position. The left hand and arm are like so. The elbow held well under the instrument, thus freeing the arm and back of the hand to form a single straight line. Turn the nails of your hand towards your nose. (Naomi, mortified, faced her horrible ragged gray-rimmed fingernails.) We bow from the forearm, not the elbow, with the wrist supple but not limp. Like this. No, the forearm. The fingers of the left hand in this position. Stroke. Stroke. With the forearm. You hear the difference now? Above all, the violin requires a good ear. Naomi, are you listening?

She was trying to listen now, but she'd gotten all tangled up in what she was supposed to do and not do, and in trying to pretend she had been listening all along. She clamped her knees together and looked down at her fuzzy plaid lap.

After a moment, Miss Greer said Naomi, was it your idea to study the violin?

Ah—my mother. My mother wanted me to.

And you don't?

Oh—She was afraid of insulting Miss Greer. Or worse, being yelled at. Miss Greer looked as if she could yell. Naomi moved her shoulders, one at a time, in apology.

You must do as your mother wishes, at least for long enough to give the instrument a chance, said Miss Greer, sounding, if not insulted, at least not overly pleased. You must give yourself a chance. If it was easy to play, no one would need lessons. We'll begin again.

It was nearly dark when Naomi emerged from the store, balancing her stack of books in one hand, the violin case in the other. At the last minute she had remembered to fish out the thin dollar bills wadded up in her wallet, three for the lessons, seven for the violin rental. Miss Greer had accepted them gravely, without counting through them, as if the money wasn't important, or perhaps it simply looked soiled and she didn't want to touch it more than was necessary. The last glimpse Naomi had of her was when she looked back through the shop door. Streaks of gold light, lozenges and bubbles of reflected gold shone on the curved surfaces of the instruments on display, the trumpets and the great bells of the French horns. She saw Miss Greer suddenly swing her arms high overhead, stretching, then let them fall to her side. It was startling, somehow, to see her move like that. She said something to the man in the black turtleneck, lifting her chin sharply and smiling. What a dunce, what a clumsy stupid girl, Naomi could imagine her saying, but she thought it more probable they had returned to their earlier, more absorbing conversation, to something which was at any rate more interesting than herself. Out on the street the air had turned damp, and the lights as they streamed past her were wreathed in mist, like comets. Although she did not know it yet, she was in love again.

Of course she drove them crazy at home. She sawed and squealed and twanged. She chased the notes all over the scale, and when she finally pinned one down, she showed no mercy. The family waited for something that was recognizably music to emerge, and when it did, in timid, wavering phrases, they would cock their heads, frowning. Twinkle Twinkle Little Star? Begin the Beguine? It might have been either, or something else entirely. Mrs. Hess pursed her lips. She wouldn't have gone so far as to say you weren't supposed to enjoy music lessons, but this was hardly expected. She couldn't help feeling she'd been gotten round somehow.

Naomi played scales and counted beats with her foot, one-de-and-uh, two-de-and-uh. The music store was a place of such importance, with so much of beauty and delight, she felt like a spy, an impostor who would be banished once her true nature became known. Everything amazed her. A customer might lounge against the counter, examining a piece of music swarming with impossible notes, and shake his head disdainfully. Mozart, Naomi learned, was an interesting technical challenge, but for interpretation you needed the Bach. The ranks of instruments on display cost thousands and thousands of dollars. Trumpet players were a bunch of hammer-handed jerks. It was incredible, Naomi thought, that this entire world of knowledge had existed in the very same air she breathed, and that she had never suspected it until now. Best of all was when Miss Greer would play a passage to demonstrate how it ought to be done, and the music would leap into the air like a rocket.

Oh Miss Greer. What is it like being you, how did you get to be you, where is the world you live in? All this Naomi wanted to ask, but of course she would have died before she said any such thing. Miss Greer was a student at the conservatory and lived in an apartment not far from the school. She let this information out carelessly one day and Naomi, hardly believing her good fortune, had gobbled it down. She had a vague, satisfactory notion of rehearsals and meetings and coffee drinking and serious conversation and late nights practicing, the sort of glamour that came from being always busy and always absorbed. This excused much that was odd, or old-fashioned, or even cold about her. She had other things to think about. Miss Greer seldom said anything about herself; Naomi had to rely on what she saw and heard, things like her covert examinations of Miss Greer's shoes (black pumps, stretching out at the instep), or the overheard conversations with the man at the counter.

His name was Jones. Just Jones, no other name, or at least that was all Miss Greer ever called him, while he called her Diana. He seemed to be some sort of student also. He was thin and rumpled and unsmiling and always wore black. Naomi wondered if he was a beatnik. If Miss Greer excited her because of her severity and dedication, someone who lived in the pure world of art, Jones appealed to her because he suggested corruption and decadence. She pictured him sleeping late in the mornings and smoking in bed.

At times Naomi thought the two of them, Jones and Miss Greer, were friends. Other times she was sure they weren't. You know what your problem is, Jones? Miss Greer said. You think nobody does anything for simple reasons. If they order good wine in a restaurant, they're just trying to impress the waiter. If they loan you money, they're trying to obligate you. Everyone is devious, everything is sinister. It can't be healthy, thinking like that.

Jones' narrow chest seemed to ripple, as if he were trying to get a full breath into it. Oh, I'm brimming with health, he said. You couldn't be more wrong. Health and right-thinking and good cheer and clear-eyed optimism. After all, why wouldn't I be?

It's an abnormal life, said Miss Greer. It can't help but be. I'm not making judgments, just stating a fact. It makes you bitter.

And how about you, sweetie? Don't tell me about abnormal. In another few years you'll be raising African violets and talking to a cat, like a regular little old lady.

All this going on while Naomi struggled into her coat at the end of a lesson, trying to look as if she hadn't heard. They paid no more attention to her than if she'd been a heap of bricks. Though once or twice she got the odd impression they spoke that way only *because* of her, not for her benefit, perhaps, but . . . She couldn't understand it at all.

Naomi advanced to minuets, playing them carefully, much as she'd been taught to cut up her meat at the table. Miss Greer stayed stern and graceful and preoccupied, occasionally dispensing encouragement. Much better this week, she might say. Much better attack. You must count out your measures, though. And it is andante, remember, not a jig.

Only once did Naomi succeed in asking her anything personal, and that, oddly enough, came after a lesson in which she had not done at all well. She sat with the violin dangling over her knees, waiting to hear what she already knew, how bad it had been. But Miss Greer said nothing, just flipped through the pages of the music book. It was almost worse, having her say nothing. Miss Greer, Naomi heard herself asking, did it take you a long time to get good? Playing, I mean.

Miss Greer closed the book absently on her hand, as if it were a leaf she meant to press, and looked at Naomi with mild interest. Today she was wearing a brown plaid jumper over a brown jersey. All her clothes were like that, plain colors, the colors of the city birds. I suppose it did, she said. To gain any skill at all. It's hard to remember back that far. I suppose I still don't think of myself as good.

Oh, but you're—of course you're good, said Naomi. You're wonderful. When you play, I hear what I'll never be. I mean, you have talent.

You need more than talent, after a time, said Miss Greer, sounding pensive. Talent, aptitude, all one's little skills can only get you so far. You need more than hard work, even. You realize that sooner or later. We all have limits. What you start out with can only be improved on so far.

Did you start playing when you were very young? asked Naomi, just for the sake of saying something. She wanted them to keep talking like this, but she didn't know how to go about it. And sure enough, Miss Greer seemed to shake off her mood, and opened the music book again.

Very young, she said briskly. To learn the discipline, you're never too young. Now, Naomi, these arpeggios were sloppy. You rush them like you were galloping down a flight of stairs.

Whatever did one do with such a love, if love it was? Naomi wasn't even sure of what to call it. It didn't seem to keep her from the usual mooning after movie stars and such. If Miss Greer had been a man, everything would have been easier. Everything would have been the way it always was, in fact, the daydreams and the gradual, inevitable dwindling of it all. But as it was, there was no place to put what she felt, no place for it to go. She wasn't even sure of what she wanted. She wanted to be like Miss Greer. No, she wanted to *be* Miss Greer, that was it. At times she felt simply frustrated and embarrassed at her own feelings. At other times, she felt this love, or whatever else you might call it, was the best thing about herself, the thing that made her most alive, most important, and whatever sadness came of it was good also. It was a kind of knowledge, this sadness, that otherwise she might have had to accumulate piece by piece. It was better this way, having the sadness come all at once. She treasured it like a chocolate Valentine's heart too perfect to eat.

The winter deepened. Ice piled up on the sidewalks like heaps of slag, and the low clouds might have been made of soiled smoke. At school Naomi struggled with congruent triangles and French verbs. Her friend Joyce Stanzik smuggled copies of her mother's romantic and vaguely forbidden novels from home. They took turns reading them and crying over the parts where people died or lovers parted. The tears came easily, but Naomi knew they weren't for anyone in the books, weren't even for herself, perhaps. She cried because it was so satisfying to read about love, to see it given its proper scope and importance. When people said they admired such a book or such a movie, she felt a thrill of secret pride, as if they had actually complimented her. After all, wasn't she in love, wasn't she a part of the mystery and grandeur of it all? One afternoon, doing the marketing for her mother, an old man came up to her and touched her arm. Excuse me, he said. I just had to tell you. You look so much like my own little girl, we lost her years ago to the polio. Just such hair she had, the color of wheat, with a curl to it. Excuse me. I didn't mean to frighten you. And Naomi, mute, transfixed, watched him shuffle way. This too, she felt, was happening because she was in love, there were wonderful, terrible things all around her, just waiting to be discovered.

It was March before the weather broke at all, and then raw cold rain fell for days. Naomi wore a hideous old brown slicker that smelled like the inside of a shoe and crackled when she moved. It was a Saturday and she had gone to the library to work on a history report, economic factors in the Civil War. All afternoon she had lugged encyclopedias down from the shelves, copying out the parts about cotton and manufacturing and export and import, until she was paralyzed with boredom, until she was certain that no war was ever fought for such dull reasons and why was everyone so determined to convince you that it was? She stood on the street corner waiting for her bus and yawning generously. Miss Greer walked past her in a black raincoat, carrying a red umbrella.

She was already at the far end of the block before Naomi started after her. It wasn't that she hesitated; in fact, the impulse to follow her had come at the same moment she'd finally recognized Miss Greer. She saw her and she followed her, as simple as that, without any plan or purpose, like you blinked at a bright light. The slicker that enveloped her so completely made her feel secret, invisible. Drops of rain thumped against the hood and she heard the traffic noises only dimly. Miss Greer was walking very fast; the red umbrella bobbed and dipped. Naomi increased her pace, but she wasn't afraid of losing sight of her, not really. The strength in her legs elated her. She knew she could walk for miles if she had to.

Where was Miss Greer going in such a hurry? They were nowhere near the music store. The streets were clogged with late-afternoon shoppers carrying damp bundles and elbowing their way around puddles. They passed the Rialto and its Now Playing ads, which at any other time would have halted her in her tracks for a good twenty minutes. Past the Pig 'n' Whistle and the big Kresge's with the posters for fried chicken lunches and pink milkshakes. The red umbrella entered the door of a newsstand and Naomi, her heart booming in her chest, followed.

Fortunately it was a large shop, and rather crowded. Miss Greer was making her way down the center aisle, to the books-and-stationery part; Naomi ducked behind the magazines. She could always say she'd been—to the movies? The dentist? Something. Already she was rehearsing the pleased, surprised expression she would adopt when Miss Greer recognized her, the courteous, adult tone that was proper for two acquaintances. Dreadful weather to be out in, isn't it, Miss Greer? Absolutely dreadful, Naomi, that's the exact word for it. Miss Greer was standing in front of the bookshelves marked Fiction, staring straight ahead of her, the red umbrella furled over her arm. Naomi could see the smooth knot of hair and the shadowy nape of her neck just above her collar. Miss Greer plucked a book from the shelves and wheeled around. No inefficient browsing for her. She turned and marched towards the cashier and Naomi, in a passion of cowardice, turned her back. When she dared look again, she saw that the book tucked under her elbow was . . . *Forever Amber*? Who would have thought it? Oh, lovely Miss Greer, to have such secrets, such surprises! She felt a kind of gratitude. She waited until Miss Greer left the store and passed by the front windows, then she hurried after her.

The sensible thing, of course, would be to go on home. Once she'd told herself that, she felt free to remain. Miss Greer seemed to be heading into a neighborhood that was little known to her. The people on the sidewalks looked warier, more inclined to stare. The stores were smaller and had a frowsy, unprosperous look to them. Naomi's mother would have sniffed and said you wouldn't dare drink a glass of water from places like that, not if you were carried in dying off the street. The rain had slackened to a drizzle, the air seemed bluer and colder. Miss Greer entered a Walgreen's and bought a box of Kleenex and a sack of jelly beans. Jelly beans! Naomi could have wept with delight. Everything she did was a revelation, everything was perfect.

They continued their halting progress up the street. Miss Greer went into a shoe repair and came out again almost immediately.

She walked into a small, odoriferous grocery that Naomi dared not enter; instead she stood on the sidewalk, pretending to be absorbed in the pyramids of hair tonic in a barber's window. She would have just as readily stared at empty glass. She felt as if her entire being had exploded outward into her skin, where it fluttered and shivered violently. She was an enormous spiderweb of nerves, all crisscrossing and short-circuiting. When Miss Greer emerged ten minutes later with a brown paper sack, Naomi wasn't even sure she was glad she hadn't lost track of her. It would have been simpler if she had, for as long as it was possible to follow her, Naomi knew she would. There was no longer any question of pretending to encounter her by accident, no longer any fantasies in which Miss Greer invited her for cups of coffee. She no longer knew what she wanted, except to follow Miss Greer as long as she could, watching her select emery boards or vegetables forever, anything normal and ordinary and therefore amazing, following her inside her front door, inside her very skin. She felt weak with terror, and at the same time, extraordinarily reckless. The wet sidewalks glistened as though they'd been oiled. She could no more have left of her own free will than she could have flown. The blue air and shining streets had become like the landscape of a dream in the moment before you wake, something already slipping away even as you pursue it.

More than an hour had passed since she'd first spotted Miss Greer. Lights were beginning to come on, deepening the shadows. Miss Greer walked more slowly now, perhaps because of her packages. Naomi drew the folds of the slicker closely about her. The crowds were thinning out. Once or twice Naomi thought Miss Greer turned her head sharply, and then she hung back. But nothing came of it and, encouraged, Naomi crept forward again. Soon she'd have to leave; already she was perilously late getting home. But not quite yet. Not yet. There were fewer shops now, and more of the massive, liver-colored apartment buildings that turned the streets into canyons. Hurrying round the corner of one of these, Naomi saw Miss Greer standing squarely in the middle of the sidewalk, waiting for her.

She felt hot, and then light, and then there was nothing left to feel. There was no hope for it but to go forward.

Naomi, said Miss Greer. Naomi had halted a little distance away. She was trying to make herself faint. Naomi, have you been following me?

I just wanted to say hello, Naomi mumbled. I didn't want to bother you.

There wasn't really anything she could have said that made sense. Miss Greer shifted her packages. It was too dark to see her face clearly, even if she'd dared to look at it, but she knew the awful fixity of those eyes. I just don't know what to make of you, Naomi, said Miss Greer, sighing. I truly don't.

And she stood as if waiting for Naomi to explain herself. Trees dripped sadly about them. Naomi felt impossible weight bearing down on her, she was dying. At the same time she felt, against all hope, that Miss Greer could have helped her if she'd chosen to, or had known how, that it wasn't impossible even now to be rescued from her shame. The rain had started again; veils of it blew across them as they stood and stood. Finally Miss Greer said It's late, you need to go home. I'll walk you to a bus stop. You shouldn't be out by yourself.

No, said Naomi, because that would be the worst of all, to be marched back like a misbehaving child. But Miss Greer was already steering her back towards the corner. And that wasn't even the worst, because in those few dreadful, silent minutes of walking, she began to cry. Quietly at first, then with unmistakable snuffling noises. Miss Greer brought out her box of Kleenex and passed her some. At least she said nothing. Naomi was grateful for that now. She felt weak and fouled with crying, and she was beginning to shiver. When the bus came Miss Greer said, without any inflection at all, Please go straight home, Naomi. I'm sure they're worried about you. The streets were black glass. She didn't even dare look out the window to see if Miss Greer still stood there or was walking away.

She didn't die of it. She found that out soon enough, that you didn't die of shame or misery any more than you did of a head cold. All week long she tried to bring it to some bursting point, to heap on enough misery to crowd herself right out of her body. It couldn't be done, and it frightened her to think of that endless capacity for pain, of the enormous amounts of it she still might be able to hold. All week she waited for Miss Greer to call and say her lessons were terminated. All week she thought of excuses to try on her mother, none of which, she knew, would hold up for a minute. She thought of simply not going. But on Thursday, her lesson day, she walked into the shop as usual. Perhaps she was looking for the final perfecting quantity of pain.

As usual, Jones nodded indifferently to her from his high stool behind the counter. Since he never even pretended to take any interest in her, this meant nothing. She took her seat, alone, in the usual practice room, and tuned up. Normal. You couldn't tell a thing by looking at her. And when Miss Greer walked in and shut the door behind her and said, as she always did, Good afternoon, Naomi, you may begin with the chromatic scale, for a moment she might have believed she'd imagined the whole hideous thing. But the next instant the shame crashed down on her with new force, as if to punish her for forgetting it.

Nevertheless, she did as she was told. C-sharp again, said Miss Greer. Was she going to act as if it had never happened? Forefinger more relaxed, said Miss Greer. She was wearing blue today. The color tugged at Naomi's eyes even as she bent her head over the violin. Pale blue with a white collar. It couldn't go on like this; she would begin to weep again if something wasn't said.

But Miss Greer was talking now, rummaging through the music. Something new to try, she was saying. For the first time, Naomi saw that Miss Greer had brought her own violin with her. She was unpacking it now from its smooth black case, tuning it, testing the bow. Naomi, daring to raise her eyes at last, saw that the music was called Polonaise for Two Violins. Go ahead, urged Miss Greer. She gave the page a little nervous pat with her hand, smoothing it. Try your part first.

She played, stumbling a few times, but she got all the way through without getting lost or tripping up the measures as she sometimes did. Miss Greer nodded gravely. Not bad. Watch tempo, she said. Watch this diminuendo. Now, again, from the beginning. It was not until Miss Greer raised her own violin to her chin that Naomi was able to believe it. Miss Greer was forgiving her, in perhaps the only way that was possible for her. Miss Greer cleared her throat, waiting, and Naomi hastened to begin. Her part began first, and she concentrated on the rests and attacks, the thicket of close black notes. One-de-and-uh, two-de-and-uh. She played industriously, without ease, it was true, for she had no native skill of ear or hands. What we start out with can only be improved on so far, and we must labor for the rest, to play with grace or to allow love in our lives. All Naomi heard was the second violin gliding and twining around her own, building the music into a reaching spire of sound, clear as glass, simple as air, and every note fit exactly.

A COURTSHIP

It's awful music, really. Shrieking, repetitive, insipid, and about as durable as popcorn. There's something more manufactured than musical about it, something that makes me think in terms of product distribution and shelf life. But Terry turns the radio up and sings along with it. He's slouched back in the passenger seat, his long legs crossed at the knee. One foot swings, keeping time and menacing the windshield. "Waitin for my baby," he sings, his voice both light and husky. "Waitin for my baby," watching me, or rather, looking so elaborately elsewhere that I know he's watching. It's taken me some time to learn to recognize this. Most of Terry's behavior is so inexplicable to me as to seem downright exotic, like observing some fabulous species of tree-dwelling snail, or the Lesser Hoopoe.

I'd like to be able to join in, but I'm too self-conscious. It's easy music to sing along to, it's pumped so full of noise and echo. I know this for a fact because when I'm alone, and only when, I too sing along with it, I too turn the volume all the way up to its full epileptic force, and in spite of my established and articulate distaste for such music I love it, each song threatens to pull my heart out through my throat. It is the sort of contradiction I live closely with these days. Each song can be classified as either love-is-happy or love-is-sad, and they succeed each other randomly. Love is happy sad happy sad, or happy happy sad sad, or sad sad sad, and who could possibly argue with that? I only have two moods I'm comfortable with lately, the ironic and the sensual, and neither mood is particularly comfortable with the other.

"So you're still mad," says Terry after five minutes of what would have been silence, without the music. "So what am I supposed to do about it."

"Nothing. I don't want you to do anything."

"Now that's a laugh. There's always something you expect me to be doing. A whole program. And I'm supposed to know what it is without being told."

"Oh, get off it," I say. We've been having this argument, in bits and pieces, all afternoon, or, in another sense, ever since we met. He pokes at the radio and we switch songs in midstride. Happy to happy.

Meanwhile, I'm trying to drive without hitting something. "You make me nervous," I've told Terry on other occasions, with what is meant to be coquetry, but like most of my attempts it didn't quite connect. He frowned and said, "Well, I shouldn't, you shouldn't say things like that. Why do you want to say things like that anyway?" And I think he was annoyed because he'd been trying so hard not to be nervous himself. He's just about convinced himself of it now, in fact, with his lounging and his negligently swinging foot and the hand perched like a butterfly on his knee, lightly tapping. One more missed signal. Sometimes I think we don't speak the same language at all, and we need the music as a kind of Esperanto, emotion reduced to its lowest common denominator.

Meanwhile, the driving. I'm trying to be careful. But I'm deathly afraid of each cartwheeling speck I see out of the corner of my eye, each blown leaf or newspaper that will turn out to be something else entirely. I won't see it, I know. The first thing I'll feel is the bump and shimmy of the tires. Even then, it's not a big jolt, because the car is new, well engineered, chosen for all the right reasons, for its fuel-efficiency, its safety features rather than luxuries and so on, an altogether sober and admirable car. It's hard to imagine it hitting anything, stepping out of character like that, but it has. I know it the instant I feel the tires shudder. Not a pothole, no, it's an entirely different sensation, like a mouth biting down on something soft. The blood is oddly violet, iridescent on the new green paint, laid on in elegant, spear-shaped lines. And I'm looking at whatever it is under the tires. Cat, child, an old woman in a lumpy wool coat on this too-warm day. I can still determine all too well exactly what it is, or was. I'm staring at it as if it could tell me something, as if it is a sort of ritual sacrifice, something to divine from.

But I haven't really hit anything. Nor have I yet slept with Terry. When I do, I expect some instant catastrophe, like the old ballads of the demon lover. The fatal move made, the castle disappearing in a clap of thunder, Hell swallowing us whole, the works. It's a nice conceit, I think, but hardly one I can share with Terry. He doesn't understand literary allusions, among othe things. Sometimes I think I ought to keep a record of all my witticisms and insights and present them to him when he's old enough to enjoy them, like a baby album. For Terry is younger than I am, by how many years I don't like to think, though I could tell you down to the month if I had to. And while I am aiming for an attitude of worldly tolerance and indulgence, something like Colette's *Chérie* (now there's a book I'd like him to read), it doesn't usually work that way.

Waitin for my baby. Waitin for my baby. Today we had lunch together, and he was forty minutes late. I was the one who suggested lunch; it seemed like a good forum for elegant flirtation. At least that's the way it is in Colette. Instead I get there five minutes early and arrange myself at a table with a clear view of the door and try to look like a woman who is confident of being met on time. The restaurant is a good one, with linen on the tables and dusky, venerable paneling and waiters crisscrossing the room like little wheeled toys. I order a drink, knock back half of it right away for courage and leave the other half there for a prop. A lady dawdling over a drink, trying to work up an appetite for lunch. I tell myself that I won't begin to get upset until he's ten minutes late. Ten minutes, I think, is a reasonable time to be late if one insists on lateness. Ten minutes requires little of apology or indignation on either side. Meet me halfway, Terry. Pretend your watch stopped. Bring a note from your mother. One of the baffling things for me about Terry is his utter lack of such tactful stratagems. Once when I phoned him he said he couldn't talk, he was busy, but he didn't say why. In the background I heard the TV, and the beginning of "Gilligan's Island." Maybe I imagine too much.

Ten minutes comes and goes, as does fifteen and twenty, and I pretend to study the menu and wonder why the hell I asked for a table for two. The other menu, folded neatly on the place across from me, is a giveaway, an admission of failure, and at any moment now the elegant, well-trained waiter, too well trained even to show sympathy, is going to ask me if I want to go ahead and order. "Not yet," I say when he does. "But another drink, please." Maybe, I consider, people will think I am merely waiting for another woman. I don't allow myself to feel ashamed of even that thought for long. I know in any case that I exude the specific haggard glamour which marks a woman waiting anxiously for a man.

Funny, how with Terry I never think of car accidents or earthquakes or illness, all the catastrophes I imagine for other lovers when they fail to appear as expected. With Terry, I think in terms of broken elevators, somebody dropping by to see him, or else he had to do his laundry. The life he lives when he's away from me is a complicated network of obligations, encounters and pleasures, all of it of great interest and none of it seemingly planned out in advance. Of course I plan everything. The world for me these days is divided very simply into Terry and not-Terry. At any point in my not-Terry existence I can pause and calculate just how long until we're meeting next, like one of those inner biological signals that tells bees when to swarm. When I am not-Terry, things that I used to find unremarkable and harmless now madden me. Old couples shopping together in the grocery store, getting querulous about lunchmeat and instant coffee. Schoolgirls lurching along the sidewalk and giggling at their reflections in shop windows. Men yawning on buses. Magazine ads for porcelain birds. Everything is unenchanted and intolerable. When I am with Terry I am a menace to pedestrians, a connoisseur of adolescent melodies and clocks in restaurants and this of course is a much preferable existence. It is all just too ludicrous, I'm thinking, too absurd, and even irony won't save me forever.

The dusky walls of the restaurant seem to be elongating, growing steeper. I have the sensation of huddling in the bottom of a long dark tube. And while it is only anxiety, and the alcohol ripping through an empty stomach, for a moment I think, this is it. Pretty soon I'll start throwing up or setting the table on fire, something even the gliding waiters and the other discreetly lunching patrons can't ignore. I will have attained complete loss of control. Just then the glass doorway of the restaurant, an oblong of white smeared glare, darkens. The body within it is reduced to silhouette, a purple-black cutout rimmed with light, its edges dissolving. It has the same apocalyptic quality of a figure seen in a cathedral window, or of hallucination. Yes, it is exactly like a hallucination. I am just congratulating myself on my perceptiveness when the figure moves and solidifies and it really is Terry, tall and lounging and not overly apologetic.

"Hey," he says, dropping into the chair. "Been waiting long?"

"Yes," I say, because I have decided to allow myself at least this much irritation.

"Wicked night last night. Tell you about it. I overslept. Hey, I couldn't help it."

He is wearing an overwashed knit shirt, baggy at the neck and sleeves. It always surprises me when he manages to look ordinary. Some trick of perception makes me see a dozen memories of him at once. So that even now, if he smiles, or raises his chin in a way that shows the architecture of the throat and the jutting bone beneath, I see him again and again, like a pack of cards fanning.

"You're mad at me, I can tell. So shoot me."

"You're beautiful," I say. But no, I haven't really said it, any more than I've driven my car over a sidewalk. Maybe I should say it. It would be sincere, if nothing else. Instead I tell him "Somebody's probably going to shoot you sooner or later. Not me, but somebody."

"Is that nice? Give me a break."

He starts in on the rolls, looking aggrieved. It is not a promising beginning. Conversations between us are always this muddled and edgy lately. For instance. He peers into his wineglass, tastes and frowns. "This isn't bad. Have you ever had Chablis wine?"

I wince. I say, "So tell me about your party." He looks blank. "What party?" I say, "You know. The one that made you oversleep." "It wasn't a party. I didn't say that. Just got high." "Oh. Well, how was it?"

"Fine."

And we're really hitting our stride now. The perpetual mad monologue going on within me only surfaces in such squeaks and chirps. With other people I am thought to be a dandy conversationalist, a good listener and so on. With Terry, words scatter and escape me like a bag of spilled candy. I say too much, or too little. With other people I am not like this at all.

When the waiter comes I order whatever Terry is having. I know I won't eat and I might as well get something he can finish. I'm rather proud of this lack of appetite. I've also begun to get nosebleeds. I am looking at Terry and thinking how little I really know of him. Circumstances, I mean. He works occasionally for a veterinarian, exercising dogs and feeding and such. An animal lover? He complains about hair on his clothes, and the way the place smells when it rains. He's from Pennsylvania and has three sisters. He talks about going back to school someday. He lives in a cheesy modern appartment building with another fellow his age. I've been there once. The walls are covered with posters of rock groups, the same ones no doubt that festoon the airwaves, and laundry grows in all the corners. None of these things are really important.

"You're not hungry?" Terry says, glancing at my plate, and I shake my head. "So why do you want to have lunch at all? Waste of money."

"I thought I'd be hungry," I say, because at this moment I can't bring myself to say, You're right, I don't want lunch at all, I want to be in bed with you, I want to murder the sheets, I want to see your long body unrolling over mine and my heels rising above your shoulders. I don't say any of that, though I occasionally say other things that alarm him. I am looking for some password or spell, an alphabet for the deaf, semaphores, anything to get through to him. So after he eats all of his roast beef sandwich and half of mine, I say, "You know, sometimes I think you're afraid of me."

He is tilting back in his seat, looking at the ceiling, being Cool. (I have forgotten the importance of Cool to someone of Terry's age, and I doubt if I will ever entirely relearn it.) His chair doesn't skid but his eyes fight for balance. "Afraid. There's nobody on earth I'm afraid of," and this is so exactly what I expect him to say, I have elicited it so effortlessly that I feel tender and even protective of him. "Man," he continues, shaking his head, recovering now. "You come up with some wild shit sometimes. Why am I supposed to be scared of you?"

"Because I don't bother hiding how I feel about you. I don't even bother hiding that I want you more than you want me. You're not used to that."

Shaking his head. "Wild shit. Wild."

"This really isn't working out the way I planned," I say, even more recklessly. "Though God knows what that was."

"Give me a break, OK?"

"We have absolutely nothing in common. That was even fun for a while. Like trying to learn Icelandic. Now I don't know."

"Well what the hell are we supposed to be to each other? We're not in love. Sometimes I think we don't even like each other. So give me a clue."

"You know, I hate conversations like this. I hate the word relationship."

"Nobody said it except you, did they?"

So now I'm driving him home, and the radio is dripping tears, and he is being Cool again. I am being Depressed. I am in motion, yet getting nowhere, no longer even sure of where I want to go. This has been a Bad Idea all along, which I very well knew, which has no doubt been a large part of its attraction. My intrigue with Terry has gone on for weeks now, far longer than I ever thought it would without coming to some climactic point. Things have gotten complicated, in ways I should have expected but didn't. We are too chronically irritated at each other even to get to bed. We are suffering from failure-to-thrive syndrome. This afternoon has been just one more episode in our curious history of advance and retreat, desire and hostilities. I am beginning to think maybe it is all Just As Well.

I glance over at him for just long enough to smash into a parked car, if one were in my path, and I see him finally looking at me. "You make it all so hard," he says unexpectedly. "Talk and talk, and I never know what you want me to say back. Make it sound like I don't think about you, and I do."

He sounds both sullen and coaxing, and I'm trying to sort

through this one. Yes, but, I want to say. Why weren't you thinking of me at noon today, why are these things so difficult. Look, I want to say, we don't speak the same language, or at least, we don't keep the same time, Terry, here's a bus stop, here's change for the bus even, here's a handshake, have a nice life, we can't do anything right, why should we imagine sex would be any different? "Pull over," Terry says. "Right here."

I find a spot on the curb and manage to park without killing more than an already flattened can. There is a thin spring tree overhead, a locust, I think, and it covers the hood of the car with airy shadows. "Come here," says Terry. "Come here to me." We've kissed before, but tentatively, as if through a screen, and the shock of his tongue in my mouth is something new. It is a root seeking its own darkness again in me: enormous, blind, alive. How it blocks out everything else. It could break through my skin like a tree in cement, but strange to say it is not my wanting I'm most aware of at this moment but his, his weakness too, what he won't allow to be said, this red root which will only speak in darkness. "I want to see you again," he says, getting out of the car. "I'll call you. We'll talk." There's really nothing more to be said for now, and I watch him saunter across the street in the mild sunlight as if none of it has happened.

It is still spring. Spring has lasted forever this year. It was wet and warm and tentative when I first saw Terry in the park, walking dogs for the vet. I went up and started talking to him. It was that easy. The grass was gauzy pale green and the bare trees dripped with buds and I was elated by my own daring. I am not a woman who does such things. I am a woman who drives sensible cars and gives money to Save The Whales. My hobbies are films and Oriental cooking. I am not a woman who does such things, which is no doubt why I'm doing it so badly.

Terry and I met often in the park after that. I still believe it's a voluntary process, this giving oneself over to infatuation. You can do it consciously. It's the getting back that's hard, the retreat from sexual drunkenness. The trees fanned into leaf. The grass turned long and sweet. What could be less complicated, I thought, than such an affair? The scratching of a small, specific itch of vanity. Of course, that is not the way it's turned out.

I drive to the park and walk along the lagoon. It would be a sentimental consolation to me if now, when things have gotten sour and difficult between us, the weather had turned bad. But the air is drenched with blossom. Each small life in the grass sends up its own thread of sound, like the workings of an enormous engine, so the earth itself seems to hum, to be on the edge of some violent explosion of sweetness. Warmth drizzles down on my skin.

If I close my eyes I see the dull red bloom of my lids. Strange to say, youth in itself does not automatically appeal to me. Where I work there is a young man of about Terry's age who is in love with me. I know it from the way he approaches me with his eyes averted, and the shy shape of his mouth. He carries his love carefully, like a candle. He is happy to be in love with me. We talk pleasantly about car trouble, vacations, our jobs. Nothing more is ever said between us, nor will be. We gratify each other in this way. It is a little ceremony of admiration given and accepted. It is not really what I want.

There's no rational explanation for sex, I think, as if this were a new and commendable piece of wisdom. I watch white flowers shredding from a branch, dropping into the lagoon. They float and spin in the dark green water. The warmth and scented air are beginning to daze me. There is a bed of tulips to one side of the path, yellow, pink and red. They are just beginning to bloom and the thick petal tips are folded into tight cones. One of the flowers. Is black. No, purple, so purple-and-steel as to be nearly black. It seems to me a bad omen. Such glossy, bruise-colored flesh. It's too alive, too lush, a throat about to speak something cruel. Silly, I think a moment later, continuing my walk. To be afraid of a flower. There's no explanation for any of it.

Terry and I arrange to meet at his apartment. It is raining and the green world has turned emerald in the odd, chalky light. Terry's building has a frill of dusty grass around it, and a vast, lunar-landscape parking lot. Today the grass is aflame and I dodge gray asphalt lakes on my way to the door. Terry's curtains are closed, carelessly bunched and wadded in the window frame. Up until now I haven't considered the possibility that he won't be home.

He won't be home. It would be just like him. I'll have every right, even an obligation, to go and never come back. It will be almost a relief. I can see myself doing it, retracing my path through those sad puddles, driving home in the rain with the radio on, softly this time. Going home and sorting through the dry-cleaning and arranging to take the car to the garage for a long-overdue oil change. Maybe I'll have a drink. Maybe I'll call my friend Jim and we'll go out for a drink and I'll tell him all about it. The prospect of indulging myself in confession appeals to me. I've known Jim for years. There was a time when we even imagined ourselves in love, but we probably made one too many jokes about it. In any case we're old friends, we can talk. He'll say all the right things, sympathetic and humorous, and flirt with me and buy me more drinks. Maybe we'll even go to bed, though we've never done that before. I enumerate his many good qualities. He's attractive, intelligent, witty, and so on. ABCDE. It seems like an appealing program. Clean the house and sleep with Jim. Reasonable alternatives. So clearly have I imagined all this that even as I'm knocking on Terry's door I'm already pondering my first drink.

The door swings open under my hand. Terry peers out. "Hey," he says, retreating into the dim, disordered interior. There is nothing very enthusiastic in his face or in his voice. I close the door behind me. He's already left the room. Through a gap in the curtains I watch the rain sliding against the glass and the undisturbed dust-freckles and dead moths on the sill. I wait for Terry to return, a minute, more than a minute. *Screw him,* I think dangerously, him and his deliberate, boring rudeness, but I go look for him anyway.

He's in the bedroom. As I walk in, he seems to be tending to several appliances at once, barricading himself behind cords and switches. The iron is out and a pair of jeans is laid neatly in front of it. He turns the television on, off. Fits a cassette into the tape player, fiddles with the volume. Picks up the iron and glides it over the cloth. I almost expect him to start making toast. He still hasn't looked at me.

"What's the matter with you?" I say after a minute.

"Nothing."

He realigns the seams and bears down again. I sit on the edge of the bed to watch. He's doing an admirable job with the ironing, really. This is one of the things I'm thinking. Another is that sometimes it's easier to understand Terry if you realize he means exactly the opposite of what he says. And another is that when you've been anticipating lovemaking, when your nerves are tied in small, intricate knots, like embroidery stitching, then watching someone iron is a poor second best.

"You want to talk about it?"

"About what."

"What's not the matter with you."

"Shit." He yanks too hard and the cord of the iron comes loose from the wall, dangles in stiff, dead-snake coils. Muttering, he retrieves it, plugs it in again.

I clear my throat. "Would you like any help with that?"

"With what."

"The ironing. I mean, if you've got a lot to do."

"Nope. Just this."

I watch him iron and iron. Those jeans are immaculate now, flatter than Kansas, the stitching all white and puckered from the heat. They are a triumph of artisanship. I wonder what he's angry about. There's really no telling. Observing the Lesser Hoopoe. It's sad. I don't know a thing about him, this gloomy, iron-wielding creature. Sometimes I imagine that, like me, he is a different, better person when we are apart. More loveable, upright, kindly. He is a skin filled with secrets. An outside, an inside. Everything divides itself too easily. Happy-sad. Love-sex. Body-mind. Yin-yang. Terrific. Once you get going, it's easy to comprehend the tragic symmetry of the universe. Meanwhile, there's Terry.

"Do you want me to leave?"

"I didn't say that."

"I know. You haven't said much of anything."

"So stay or go, whatever you like."

Outside it's still raining. A green branch, its leaves new and crumpled-looking sways in the wet wind. Stay-go. Life an endless series of fascinating options. The person I am with Terry. The person I am with everyone else. Duality is a trap, I've always believed. We should strive to be unified human entities, who wouldn't agree with that. But a chunk of me is intent on breaking loose, tumbling free, like an asteroid. "Do asteroids have orbits?" I ask Terry.

"What?"

"Asteroids. Those big pieces of rock out in space. Do they have orbits, like comets, or do they just kind of bounce around from one thing to another?"

"How in the world should I know?"

"Did you ever try and learn the constellations when you were a kid? All those critters and heroes they said were up there. I could never see them. How about you?"

"Just why do you need to know?"

"I'm gathering data on you. Range, habitat, diet. Distinctive markings. Humor me."

"Look, you feeling OK?"

"Tell me if you ever learned the constellations."

"This is really a stupid conversation, you know?"

"Tell me."

"I forget. The Big Dipper, maybe. Are you happy now?"

"Next question. Why you're acting like such a jerk. Why you ask me over and then act jerkish. Jerkishly."

"Because I never know what to say to you. I never know what you want to hear. I don't know what you want from me in the first place. You want to mouth off about stars? Swell. I can do that."

"Next question."

"Shit."

"An easy one. Do you want to go to bed?"

Which at least gets him to put the iron down. He stares at me over his shoulder. "Jesus Christ."

"That either means you do or you don't."

"One screwy woman. That's what you are."

"I'm not, really, except with you. Funny how that works."

"Hilarious," he agrees.

He will either reach for the iron, or for me. I will either stay or go. Things diverge this neatly. Either: I stand up from this bed, I shake hands with Terry, give him a few words of advice about fabric softeners or life in general, and leave. I go home and clean the oven. I call Jim, or maybe even the young man who is in love with me. I remain the persona I have always been. Or: I become the person who sleeps with Terry. I am being humorous about this. I am being serious. Maybe this is exactly what I want, these separate visions. Maybe that's why I'm here, to peel away words from meaning, logic from loving, myself from myself.

"None of this makes any sense," says Terry. He sounds cautious. He is unbuttoning his shirt and his chest is bare underneath it. He is either undressing or simply changing his shirt. His shoulders slip loose from the cloth. His hand on his belt. "No sense at all, you and me. You want to try it anyway? How come?"

Because with no one else can I be this person. Because I am spilling out of myself like a seed from a husk. But no, I say something else entirely, something soft and easy like the songs so we both understand it, and I lean back against the sheets for him. Am I really this person now? Is this the person I will remain? It occurs to me that there was another alternative. I could be the person who drives endlessly through the streets with love beating against the sparkling windshield. I could do that forever. It occurs to me that this was the only time I was truly happy, on the edge of all possibilities, fainting at flowers, sick with hope. Strange as it sounds, I was happy. Happy-sad. It's one and the same thing after all, I'm thinking.

LENNY DYING, PACIFIC STANDARD TIME

The things that go through your head at times like that. It's never the way it's supposed to be, but then neither is death. When Ruthann, Lenny's wife, called to tell me about the accident, the first thing I thought was, it's like it already happened a long time ago. It was so easy to see it coming if he didn't stop the drinking. And I was angry at Lenny because he hadn't stopped, angry that he let it happen. Ruthann was crying. It was the first time I'd ever known her to cry. I thought of that too. "He's gone, Jack," she kept saying, and I kept saying I was sorry, like it was really my fault. All the while I was thinking how everyone always said how strong Ruthann was. How she'd had to be, getting through the thin times with Lenny. And how that would be something we could use to console ourselves with now, to keep from worrying too much about her: Ruthann's strong. She'll make it. I say we, but I mean myself. I'm telling Ruthann to try and stay calm, I'm asking about the kids and the funeral, if there's anything I can do, and I have a vision of how easy it will be for me to keep saying the right things, to make phone calls and write letters and do everything that ought to be done and all the while none of it has touched me, not yet.

"Do you feel like talking?" I asked her. "I don't want to keep you on the phone if it only makes things worse."

"I'll talk for a little while. It helps to talk. But I'm so tired, Jack, all day long it's been so crazy. All the things you have to think about when somebody dies, I always thought dying was simple."

"Can you tell me how it happened?" I wanted to know, but I didn't want to press her too much.

"He'd been at a roadhouse." Matter-of-fact. "It was late, I mean, early morning, about two, and it was foggy and he missed a curve and hit a tree, and his chest was crushed. It was instant."

I really didn't want her to go on now. Her voice had a dullness in it that meant she'd said the same thing too many times already. Nobody should have to hear themselves say things like that.

But she said, "At least there weren't any other cars. At least he didn't take anybody else with him."

And then a minute later: "Somebody I know saw him that night, at the tavern. They said he was having a really good time. I'm glad for that."

You console yourself any way you can. But later, when I thought about it, those things did make a difference. We only talked a moment longer. The funeral was in three days. Lenny wanted to be cremated and have his ashes scattered over duck-hunting country. And Ruthann was going to do it, by God. If he'd said he wanted to be put out to sea in a Viking ship she would have done that too. She was that kind of a wife to him.

I hung up the phone and looked at the clock again. 1:30. The digital numbers squirmed in the dark room, an unnatural cold orange, a color you'll never see anywhere else in the world. It had been nearly twenty-four hours since Lenny died. But no, I was getting the time zones mixed up. That was one of the things that made it all seem so far away. Barbara had slept through the phone and everything else. I could hear her shallow breathing from somewhere in the mounds of blankets. I thought about waking her up to tell her, but there wasn't much point in it. "Lenny's dead," I'd say, and she'd gasp, *whassat*, the way she always did when startled out of sleep, and then I'd probably have to remind her who Lenny was. He was my friend, after all, not hers. She'd be innocently relieved it wasn't something worse or more immediate, burglars, alarms at night, who could blame her, but it would only make me angry. If I persisted, she'd say something like well, it's awful, but what can you expect? And her reaction would be too much like my own, I who ought to be feeling so much more.

I found my clothes, dressed, and padded out to the living room. I wanted to sit, just sit in the dark for a while, and give the grief a chance to catch up with me. I knew it was out there, like putting your ear to railroad tracks and knowing a train's coming. But it wasn't there yet, wasn't real. I thought about flying out for the funeral. But I hadn't seen Lenny for three years, and it seemed backwards, hypocritical somehow, to go now that he was dead, when I hadn't taken the trouble for him alive.

It had snowed a couple of days earlier, a heavy, icing-like snow that weighed down the evergreens and scalloped the roofs. The street outside my windows looked like a child's drawing of winter, with the stick trees and line of snug houses and the puffy snow. Sometimes New England seems like that to me, a simplified landscape, hard to take seriously. Everything's too symmetrical, composes itself too easily into charming vistas. I'm from the Midwest originally. I'm used to flatness and angularity and downright ugliness. It makes you mistrustful of anything more prepossessing. The West, Lenny's country, was even stranger to me. I'd only visited a couple of times. I remember being overwhelmed by sheer geography, the immensity of everything. It seemed like dinosaurs should still be roaming around through it, uprooting trees and starting avalanches with their footsteps. Now I found it difficult not only to imagine Lenny was dead, but to visualize that far, improbable edge of the continent, to believe it existed at all.

It was a failure of imagination, emotion, and memory. I'd known Lenny for fifteen years, ever since college. Maybe I was just unable to squeeze everything I knew and felt about him into one tidy epitaph. That wasn't all of it, though. The friendship hadn't aged well. Doesn't everyone have a friend who must, on some occasions, merely be tolerated? Through all of Lenny's escapades and misbehaviors, the drinking, the debts, the pointless feuds, I tried to keep from judging him. I can't say I was successful. I measured his faults against my loyalty, and I disliked myself for doing so. Any love I had for him came to seem doled out and grudging, exasperated and ungenerous. And all the while I knew that whatever his other faults, Lenny never doubted me the way I doubted him. Sitting in the dark house, with the furnace muttering at intervals like a beast in uneasy sleep, I tried to decide what I felt. I wanted to think better of him. I wanted to think better of myself.

Dutifully, I set about remembering. Lenny and I, impossibly young, at college in the baleful midsection of the country. Lenny at parties, trying to start earnest, deadly conversations with anyone who'd listen. "How do you ever know, I mean, *really* know, if you're acting out of free will? You could think you were making a decision, but all the while you could just be responding to some stimulus. You know what I mean?" Sure Lenny. I'll get back to you, OK? People thought he was odd, and he was, I guess. Everybody else would be nursing their plastic cups of thin beer, trying to convince themselves they were having a hell of a good time, and here's Lenny cornering people about Life and Truth. You'd see him coming at you like the very apparition of boredom, his gingery eyebrows puckered, genuinely perplexed about the nature of man or whatever, and determined to get some answers. He didn't drink back then. He didn't know how. He never grew an inch past five foot six. He had chronic insomnia, migraines, colitis, all the ailments of the nerve-tormented. He wore clothes that even among college students seemed haphazard: stretched-out T-shirts, khaki pants, clodhopper boots. He looked like what he was, a lower-middle-class kid from a town nobody ever heard of, shipped off a thousand miles to dwell among alien cornfields. Back home in Washington his old man ran a gas station and complained about the government and lost a little more money each year. The family wanted Lenny, the bright one, to get an education, even though it would make him an incomprehensible being to them, and maybe to himself also.

I suppose we got to be friends because I was just as odd as Lenny was, just as socially maladroit, though in a milder, more furtive way. At the same parties, I'd be the one sitting by the record player or on the stairs all night, glum, relentlessly observing. I was overwhelmed by my own sensitivity. Of course Lenny seized on me, a stationary object, and I'd have to say I enjoyed his company. I wasn't above talking about Life and Truth myself. I admired his nearly unbearable intensity. At least he wasn't superficial, and being superficial, I thought at the time, was what was wrong with nearly everyone else in the world. I took long walks alone at night, I wrote bad poetry. I remember a girl I had one of my hapless romances with, stalking out of my room. "I give up. There's always something wrong with you, but it's never anything *real*."

For Lenny, I guess things were always too real. He was one of those people who take the world very personally. By which I mean, he felt betrayed by all misfortune. He had bad luck and a worse temper. While I think I know why we became friends, I'm not at all sure why we stayed that way. Over the years he must have quarreled with everyone he knew, and alienated most of them. They were snobs, tight-asses, jerks, bullshitters. Fuck em. You couldn't let them get to you, man. I've known other people who've had what you could call adversary relationships with life. They keep looking for an explanation for pain. And when they don't find any, no rules or logic, no way to organize the universe that makes sense, they figure the fix is in. The deck's stacked, nobody plays fair.

"Jack, you fucker, you worthless piece a shit." It would be the middle of the night, bleary predawn, actually, and Lenny's voice would be kindly and slurred. The bars would have just closed out there, and who knows what else he'd been taking. This last year he'd gotten his hands on a prescription for speed, which was the last thing somebody like him needed. He drove around for hours in the country with a mayonnaise jar full of black beauties in the back seat and a six-pack in the front. Stopping at all the pokey little bars and roadhouses, the places with the deer heads wearing sunglasses, the restrooms marked Pointers and Setters, the shimmering electric landscapes of beer signs. Swapping stories, making bets on the game, dancing with somebody's wife, I think he was happiest then. Looking for life's sweet aching mysteries, man, and this one's on me, and what's the lady drinking? So Jack, whatha fuck. What're you good for, huh?"

If Barbara was awake I'd cover the receiver and say, "Lenny," and she'd sigh and say Honestly, and I'd settle in to nurse the phone. "So how's it going, Lenny?"

"Terrific. Just terrific. Go get on a plane."

"You know I'd like to, Len."

"So do it. The red-eye special. Be here by morning."

It was nearly morning anyway, but I didn't tell him that. The windows were the color of pale stone, and in a minute the bird-racket would begin, and in little more than an hour it would be time to worry about whether the car would start, and meeting my classes. There was no way. But for a moment I imagined myself doing it. Flying west through the shimmering, tender sky, watching the light flood all around me. Lenny and Ruthann meeting me at the airport, Lenny whooping at me, his eyes cracked and small from being up all night. Ruthann smiling and smiling, their youngest child wrapped up in a blanket in her arms, pink and smudged with sleep. We'd go back to the house and Ruthann would fry potatoes and eggs and sausage and the kids would bounce around in their pajamas, not sure exactly why they were excited, but making the most of it. And Lenny would bellow at them and keep hauling things out of the refrigerator for me to try, homemade plum jam and kippered salmon and cheeses, more than I could ever eat, and we'd sit at the table for hours while the house filled up with plastic toys and coffee cups and our talking. For a moment I saw it all.

"I wish I could, Len. I really do."

"So what's stopping you? I'm buyin the ticket. Come on."

"I've got to go to work, Len. I've got all these fuzzy little undergraduates who ask intelligent questions about Robert Frost."

"Screw em." But he could tell I wasn't coming. I heard him breathing, long, snore-like gusts, as if he were falling asleep or had forgotten what he was doing. Then he came back. "So how's life. How's it treating you."

"Fine. Everything's fine." As always I spoke a little too quickly and heartily. I'd gotten into that habit with him, as if I were ashamed to say anything about my own successes, too delicate and tactful to imply comparisons between us. "They overwork me, that's all. How about you? How's the shop?" He'd started a used furniture store a couple years back. I already knew how it was.

"Killing me. I got loans to renegotiate at mile-high rates. I got a lease they want to pull out from under my feet. You read about your basic small businessman eating it? Tha's me. Mr. Statistic."

"Hey, I'm sorry. I hope it changes for you."

"Screw it."

Again the sound of his breathing, and the black crackling static of the line. "So Lenny," I said, wanting to nudge him either into speech or hanging up, "it's really good to hear from you."

"Yeah? Yeah, good talkin. You gotta come out here, I mean it."

"If I could get away I would. Maybe you should come visit me." I knew he wouldn't. And if he ever did, I didn't want to think about how we'd cope with him if he went on a genuine spree, how Barbara would keep getting more and more polite and ironic, how after a while I wouldn't enjoy it either. "How's Ruthann and the kids?"

"Fine. They're fine." The phone must have slipped; he sounded small and faint.

"Lenny?" I didn't want him passing out with the phone in his lap. "Lenny, I have to get off now."

"Yeah, OK. Come see me. I love ya."

"I love you too, Len. Thanks for calling."

"Sure."

"Take care of yourself."

"Sure."

I don't remember the last time we talked, although I'm certain it was like all the other times. He only called when he was drinking, and whenever I didn't hear from him I figured maybe he was having a good spell. The drinking was just one reason the calls depressed me. It was depressing that I'd fallen into the pattern of merely indulging him, and that we no longer had any way of imagining each other's lives, and depressing that he had not been happier and that now he was dead and everything was too late. I touched the cold glass of the window. It looked like it would be night forever. I would sit up a while longer, though I was beginning to feel melodramatic and worse, a little sorry for myself, a little too conscious of my own very interesting melancholy funk. Being superficial is what's wrong with nearly everyone in the world. I made myself think of Ruthann and the kids.

Then I started thinking about yesterday, the day it happened. No premonitions; it had been a perfectly normal day. Although as soon as I labeled it, I began to wonder if there ever was any such thing. It might be like putting a drop of pond water under a microscope and watching things churn and breed and get swallowed whole. Perfectly normal, but like all life, a little alarming when examined closely. All that day Lenny was dying, hour by hour, and nothing was left for me now but to think about how far our lives had diverged.

My day began at seven a.m., like any day school is in session, with the clock radio chuckling to itself about full-service banking. It's like waking up with a madman in the room. I'm a quick starter, a morning person, and once my eyes are open I'm ready to march, ready to do battle with plumbing and razor blades. (Four a.m. out West, and Lenny surely asleep by now, even if he'd made a night of it.) I like to get to the bathroom before Barbara does, though more often than not she wanders in looking for her eyelash curler or pumice stone or some even more exotic appliance. She works too, and in her case it's eight to five, buddy, is what she reminds me if I complain.

Breakfast wasn't much, it never is with us. Barbara had half a grapefruit dosed with Sweet 'n' Low, and V-8 juice. Dieting again. I had cereal and toast and refrained from pointing out that all the acid would make her stomach start digesting itself in the space of an hour. There are certain conversations in every marriage, I suppose, that are repeated so often they become instant provocations. If I said something critical about her diet, Barbara would counter that it was hard enough to lose weight without my negative attitude. Then I'd say she really wasn't overweight, it was all in her mind, like those teenage anorexics. For some reason that always made her angry. "Do you think I don't know how I look? Am I allowed to have an opinion you won't contradict?"

So I just watched her pry up the little grapefruit triangles, and wished she wasn't so defensive. The truth is she's not a bit fat. But she's so firmly committed to the vision of her own inadequacies, to console her is to deprive her of her one area of expertise. Or so it can seem. Like most couples we have only one real argument, but there are many weary permutations. Her mingy breakfast, and the air of righteous grievance with which she consumed it, was enough to summon up all my irritation. I swallowed it like she did her bitter grapefruit, as a conscious act of virtue. You learn to do that in marriage, to detour around trouble, wait for the next good stretch. Barbara smiled at me over the breakfast debris. "Don't say it. You hate even looking at grapefruit. It makes you think of brain surgery or something."

It must have been about the time I got to school that Lenny and his household began waking up. The two youngest kids padding out to the TV, making chocolate milk messes, eating cereal out of the box. Ruthann would wake and gauge with radar-like accuracy if they needed immediate refereeing, or if she could afford another five minutes in bed. Later, after she'd showered and dressed and herded the kids, she'd wake the others. The oldest girl, the beauty like her mother, thirteen years old and dreaming all the time, awake or asleep. The smiler at mirrors, the singer of small beauty songs, the heroine of a thousand invisible dramas. Who would not be in love with the pillow at that age?

And Lenny, deep in his last sweet mortal sleep. Dreaming? A treeful of birds all taking flight at once, and the dull sound of wings like water ruffling in a pond. Somebody said There, that one, and one lone bird broke off from the others, rising in the pure sky. There was a perfect shot if you ever saw it, but before he could aim here was Ruthann shaking him, and it was morning all over again, and the sky not blue but gray. (A front moving into the Northwest. I saw it that morning on the news.) "All right," he told Ruthann. "All right, I gotcha." She left early for work, and it was his job to finish packing the kids off to school and make sure the house didn't catch on fire. It took one good heave to get out of bed, and a minute to let his head slide around and steady. Drinking last night? Probably, but nothing a shower and coffee wouldn't cure. He opened the store at ten. Should leave it closed all bloody day, hell with it, not now. Behind the bathroom door his oldest daughter was perfecting her hair. "Let's look sharp in there, you hear me?" and God his mouth tasted like sin and he hoped he lived long enough to take a piss.

Finally the house was empty, and he stood in the shower letting the steam heal him. He should start working out again. Running. Weights too. Christ, there wasn't one dry towel in the whole place. He wiped the mirror with his hand and scowled into the smeared glass. His face was boiled and puffy, and his hair looked like somebody'd wiped their feet on it. Not getting any younger. Sometimes he couldn't get air all the way into his chest. His kidneys leaked. Teeth probably rotting away at the roots, little secret festering stumps. All sorts of pestilence building up in you. You'd never know until it was too late. Cancers the size of walnuts. Heart going flabby, arteries backing up like drains, doctors looking professionally sad while they gave you the bad news, needles, pain, blood, bloody vomit, more pain. Now he was just being silly. The only thing wrong with him was a bad night's sleep.

But fat? Look at that gut. He kneaded it with his fist and peered critically into the mirror to see if it looked as bad in profile. He never used to be fat. He never used to be thirty-five either. Let's get with the plan, fella. He found a pillow and hunkered down on the living room floor and did sixty sit-ups, the hard kind, elbow to opposite knee. It got him sweaty again, and the blood beat hard through his head. But it felt good to know you could still crank it up if you had to. Tomorrow he'd do a hundred.

He made the bed and took out the garbage and set the dishes to soak in plenty of suds. He was feeling better all the time. The next thing was breakfast. He wanted something healthy, something so chock full of vitamins and energy your whole system would stand up and cheer. He poured orange juice, sliced a tomato and broiled it, soft-boiled an egg and had it on a piece of wheat toast. After he ate he finished the dishes, scalding them, the way it ought to be done. He sat back down at the kitchen table, lit a cigarette and watched the smoke curl in the air. The cigarettes would have to go for sure. He knew that, but he was in too good a mood to worry about it now. You could lick anything after a good breakfast, take on the whole mothering world. If it could always be just like this. Morning is like gold in the mouth. Something he'd heard, he couldn't remember where, but he liked the sound of it. Gold in the mouth. You could sneak up on trouble and wrestle it to the ground, and nothing that had gone before mattered, and weren't you a lucky bastard to have this fine new day and a full belly and a head start on everything. It was all so good that he went to the cupboard and poured himself a single shot of brown-gold Bourbon to make the feeling last.

I like to get to school with plenty of time before my first class, which meets at eleven. It gives me a chance to look over my notes and do whatever busywork's accumulated. A request to appear on a panel at the next articulation conference. A questionnaire on teaching effectiveness, put out by some statistics-crazed fellow in the Education Department. An announcement of the next visiting distinguished/extinguished scholar, lecturing on the Form and Theory of the Critical Imagination. On: Ripples in the Mainstream, a Rationalist Perspective. On: Robert Lowell's influence on Walt Whitman. It's almost too easy to make fun of things like that. I never fail to note the stuffiness and the little pretensions, the rich unintentional comedies of committee meetings. You see, my irony says, what a regular all-right guy I am, what a down-to-earth fellow, seeing through all this. My refreshing irreverence. My homespun qualities. The professor with the heart of gold. The muscular scholar.

But in fact my job is a good one. I was hired four years ago. I was very young to get such a position, and I've maintained a certain precocious notoriety. My scholarship attracts regular and respectful attention. (I still write bad poetry, but I show it to no one.) I teach dutifully. I'm an up-and-comer. I have my place among the cherubim and seraphim who sitteth on the right hand of the Chairman of the Department. I walk through the halls with a pleased unfocused smile that indicates I am delighted to encounter my colleagues on the stairs or in the toilet.

My first class was English 241. (Major American Authors II. Survey of prose, poetry and drama after World War I, with concentration on the themes of alienation, social realism, romance and anti-romance.) I marched in, straightened my little stack of notes and looked out at the rows of upturned faces. It was not one of my better classes. There was a collective timid quality to them, a mute sullen plea for anonymity. Their eyes were furtive, their faces unformed and lumpy. Not exactly petals on a wet black bough. "Today," I began, "we're talking about Sherwood Anderson, one of the most idiosyncratic and even peculiar of American writers. His style is unadorned, awkward at times. His subject matter can seem mundane. His characters are rarely articulate. Yet he is ranked among the geniuses . . ."

Long bars of light came in through the high windows. Somebody coughed. There are those moments in a classroom when you know you've lost them. It's nothing you can put your finger on. A drifting quality to the air. You tell a joke and no one laughs. Your voice goes on and on, receding through a long tunnel. "He is above all a regional writer, and his regionalism must be understood in terms of . . ." You pause at certain points to foment discussion and nothing comes. No matter how often it happens, you never get used to it. You hate them all by now. A girl in the front row is scraping lint from the sleeve of her sweater, rolling it into little pills. You want to stop and ask her a question about the lecture she's not listening to, the book she hasn't read, just to embarrass her. (Lenny would have roared at her, reduced her to pink-nosed blubbering. Then he would have quit the job.) Finally it's five minutes before the bell, and you can give up. "Any questions?" You know there won't be. Any complaints? Anybody home?

They shuffled out, making ugly scraping noises with the chairs. Nobody met my eye. Like family pets, they know when they've misbehaved; they knew I was exasperated with them. One of them paused by the desk, a tall, insubstantial shape. Even before I turned I knew who it was. "Yes, Mr. Holpuch?"

It was that kind of a morning. I might as well have Mr. Holpuch too. Mr. Holpuch is writing a paper on Faulkner. His favorite authors are Faulkner and Isaac Asimov. He is tall, as I say, or rather, overgrown, with a mealy complexion and worse teeth. A loner, a boy of average intelligence but limited wisdom. He asks lots of questions because so many things puzzle him. It depresses me to think of Mr. Holpuch graduating, for there is nothing to keep him from doing so, and wandering at large through the world with his puzzlement and his bad breath, trying to find someone to listen to him.

"Yes, Mr. Holpuch?" And I waited, as I knew I had to, the extra thirty seconds it would take him to formulate his question.

"It's about my paper. I've been thinking about changing it so the emphasis is on Faulkner's mythic qualities. I made a list of all the myths I found in his work and I wanted to know if you thought I should put them all in, or just some of them."

He held out a piece of unclean-looking yellow paper. I took it reluctantly. In his loopy wavering script he had written:

Oedipus **
the underworld
Medea   (?)
Prometheus
rape of Europa

I tried to imagine the paper that might result, how his scanty and cryptic list would sprout roots and branches, sentences and paragraphs. I thought of the strange illogical growths he would twine around Faulkner. I felt more sadness than exasperation. He was unequipped not only for literature, but for living. What should I say to him? Tell him to fall in love? Join the Army? Take vitamins? How many times in a day, or a life, do we encounter a Mr. Holpuch, and the limits of our own response. I told him to write an outline. I doubted if he had ever written an outline for anything. I went back to my office, locked the door behind me, and sat there with the lights off.

Lenny was just at that moment opening the store. Like me, he enjoyed having time to himself before the business of the day geared up. He came in through the back door. The rear of the place was a succession of narrow cement-floored rooms used for storage and repair. The low ceilings bulged with piping. Partitions of ancient gouged wallboard made the space seem even more cramped. Bolts of upholstery fabric, staple guns, tacks, hammers, glue, tags, invoices, hanks of uncoiling wire, a dismembered vacuum cleaner, various three-legged tables, easy chairs with the stuffing exploding through the fabric like fuzzy cauliflower. He tried to keep the place looking trim, but it was a losing battle. The front of the store kept up a braver appearance, but the farther back you went, the more everything succumbed to secondhandness, to carelessness and age.

He pushed aside the curtain that led to the front showroom. Unlocked the door and brought in the paper. Opened the cash register. Gave a few swipes with the furniture polish and rag. He sat down in a leather armchair, the best piece in the shop, though he could feel the springs shifting treacherously underneath him. A familiar, dangerous mood rose to greet him, as if it came from the chair itself. There was nothing else to do all the effing day but sit here. Sit and calculate just how much money he was losing per hour. He wondered if losing money would be more tolerable if you did it in a nice clean office. There was nothing more depressing, he had long since decided, than other people's furniture, the smells and stains and scars, the messy residues of their lives. Nothing, unless it was the people themselves. The way they'd drift among the furniture, trying to decide which cheesy piece would look the best in their cheesy living rooms, frowning, trying to imagine it, failing entirely, 'he was sure. I dunno. I didn't want to pay more than forty. I need something in blue, you know? He knew. Knew their soiled wads of money, knew how little enjoyment they got from their dubious purchases, or anything else for that matter. Poor, sorry bastards. Everything was pathetic and small, picked over and tainted. Life was a bitch.

"Life is a bitch," he said to Mitchell, several hours later. They were smoking weed in the back room. Mitchell was nineteen and dreamy and he did deliveries and pickups. Lenny had long since given up trying to make him do jobs the way they ought to be done, as he had given up on most exercises of authority. Mitchell just slit his eyes and turned politely silent. Sometimes Lenny wondered if he had the energy for an existence of his own outside the shop, or if Mitchell materialized only when Lenny needed him, like the genie of the lamp.

Now Mitchell pinched the end of the joint open and inhaled. "Life is a bitch," he agreed, holding the smoke. He was slouched so far on the chair that he rested on his meager hips. His feet balanced on an upended mattress. He looked rather like a human hammock.

"Shoot, Mitchell, what do you know. What've you got to complain about? I'm paying you good money to sit on your ass and get wasted. So what's your problem?"

"I got to listen to you carry on all the time, that's my problem. Give me a break, Holmes."

"A break. Yeah, I apologize, Mitchell. It's been quite a while since I bought you a car or a new suit. You mind unhooking your lip from that number long enough to pass it?"

A minute or two of silence while the smoke drifted. Then Lenny began again: "What you are, Mitchell, is one of the lilies of the field. You toil not and neither do you spin. You hear me? One of the goddamned lilies. Nineteen years old. Nobody nineteen has any problems."

"Except unless they boss is crazy. Lilies? Shit man."

"Funny thing is, I wouldn't be nineteen again for love or money. Don't look at me that way. I mean it. What does anybody know when they're young? Nada. Goose egg. Your brain's still teething. Listen up here, Mitchell. I'm giving you advice. I'm laying wisdom on you. You don't know just how much you're up against in the bastard world. You don't appreciate nothing. Dig me please, Mitchell. Happy's when you can steal a little time off from being alive. There now. You're a wiser man, Mitchell. You just don't know it yet."

"That's cool," said Mitchell, with his eyes closed.

Six p.m. out East. Barbara and I met for dinner after work. Dieting doesn't keep her from enjoying the little formalities of dressing up and being waited on, even if all she orders is soup and salad. And sometimes it's a good idea to meet on neutral ground at the end of the day. It keeps whatever grievances you might have accumulated against the world from spilling over into the familiar patterns of irritation. There is a certain pleasure in being a handsome couple out to spend money. I watched Barbara walking towards me in her elegant, impractical shoes, watched the way she used her head and eyes, watched other people watching her. I had an odd thought then. I thought that my marriage had turned out no worse than I had believed it would. No worse, maybe even better. As if right from the start I had mapped the terrain of domestic anger and boredom, as if I had made certain there was nothing in me to be disillusioned. I watched her hips moving secretly within their circles of silk. She was a very attractive woman.

Three o'clock Pacific time. Lenny had sent Mitchell home early and locked the store. Let the fat ladies and derelicts find their broken-backed sofas and ugly lamps someplace else. What good was being your own boss if you couldn't give yourself a break now and then. He stood for a moment outside the back door, contemplating the broken pavement and stray trash of the alley. He felt pretty fair, pretty fair. Even the air seemed clearer, less damp in it, the sky lifting. It would've been a good day to be out hunting. A good day for whatever you wanted it to be. He felt expansive, light, paddling gently in the mild air. And wasted? His car keys had fallen in the gravel at his feet. Grunting a little, he stooped for them, but it was like reaching through water. They kept jumping away from his hand. He had to laugh. Christ on a bicycle, he wasn't good for much, well, why fight it. Why the hell fight it.

Barbara ordered fish, I ordered steak. No potatoes for her, and the salad dressing on the side, please. "Mr. and Mrs. Jack Sprat dine out," I said.

"You've got it backwards. He's the one who wouldn't eat fat. You thrive on it."

"Unkind."

"Accurate."

She smiled. There was one of those thick red glass candleholders on the table between us, a little domesticated campfire. Its wavering glow picked out the gold at my wife's ears and throat. But we were not gypsies squatting over a roasting haunch of venison. It was only a trick of light, a crude and sentimental approximation. We were Mr. and Mrs. Jack Sprat.

"So what kind of a day did you have?" I asked, and she told me. So-so. Fairish. I said that mine had been the same. I provided anecdotes. I made exasperated noises about my students and about the weather. I took a pull at my drink and declared how much I needed it. Life as a series of small grievances. Neither fat nor lean. The emotional median, the average daily balance.

Six p.m. Pacific. Lenny in the bosom of his family. If one were watching from outside their warm windows, the scene would have the blurred, imprecise quality of those miniatures inside glass domes, awash with artificial snow. They were seated at the dinner table, eating chicken and rice. Eating tacos. Pork chops. There were mild arguments about the kids' table manners. About who didn't walk the dog. Lenny was drinking beer. He told a joke, one he'd told before, the youngest child laughed. Jokes, his father's jokes, are to him like reading Shakespeare or *Wuthering Heights* is to some adults. Pleasure is in no way diminished by knowing how things turn out at the end. The other children's faces were more remote, their attention focussed on their dinners. They had learned to be cautious at mealtimes, to read the shifting weather of their father's face. Lenny was not really that drunk. He was riding a wave of feeling that had not yet crested, something building all day or maybe all his life. He had the bastard licked. Had it all knocked. They could only get you down so far and after that they couldn't lay a glove on you. Tell another joke, his son demanded. Tell another.   Another? You sure? Well now. What time is it when the clock strikes thirteen?   I know, I KNOW!!   And the kid was practically bounding out of his chair, well, why not, how often did you ever know anything for absolute sure. All right, don't keep us in suspense, buddy, what the hell time is it?   It's . . . . The ecstasy of knowing almost kept him from getting it out. TIME TO GET THE CLOCK FIXED!!   Right on. Terrific. He had all the answers. He had it knocked. Before he left the house, Ruthann kissed him and told him to be careful.

That night before I went to bed, around midnight I guess it was, I made the rounds of the house. Turning off lights, rechecking doors. Oven off, smoking materials extinguished, nothing likely to explode overnight. In the darkness the solid bulky shadows of the furniture looked peaceful, like sleeping animals. Everything would still be there in the morning. One accumulates a life just as one acquires these household artifacts, chairs, lamps, books, clocks, marriage beds. It had all turned out no worse than I expected it to. Perhaps I had never allowed myself to expect too much. There is no room, in an ordered life, for large discontents or fantastic hopes. There is room for only so much. I checked the front door one more time and went to bed.

Sometime later that night, two headlights, very small, made snakelike patterns on a country road. The sky had grown low again, a filmy, shifting darkness. The twin beams of light were narrow and indistinct, their edges dissolving into mist. The car did not seem to be moving, for all its impressive noise and solid metal bulk; it was the lights pulling it along effortlessly.

And then the headlights' sudden corkscrew, and a tree grown too large, and the sound of the crash that he was no longer alive to hear, and myself too far away. Grief is an echo that can take a long time to travel, or a light hurtling towards us. A life is composed of a thousand frail strands, like the rainbow tangle of telephone cables. Somehow, we make connections.

ACCIDENTS

He thought of himself as a man of little imagination, and that judgment sometimes found its way into his conversation. "I'm afraid I've never been anything but a plodder. Down-to-earth. Dull of me, isn't it?" Those he said it to, friends, or more often people he didn't know well, would wonder just why he had. It would be the sort of conversation, the sort of gathering where many such things might be said. People offered themselves up like hors d'oeuvres, their opinions, histories, and so on, tricked out, garnished, witty and insubstantial. But Marshall gave the impression of admitting, humorously, to a virtue. Smiling a little over his drink, dropping his eyes in modesty. Or was he only being ironic? Whatever he lacked, you felt, he had done very well without it; it would only have been excess baggage. One could just as easily picture him saying, I'm afraid I'm not an intellectual. I'm afraid I don't know much about music. He was a solid-looking young man, dark-eyed, affable, self-possessed. He had a good job which absorbed him, but not to an unhealthy degree, and the pleasant expectation of better jobs to come in the future. People liked him. There was little not to like. He made few demands on anyone. He had no need to. Whatever he wanted he was usually capable of getting on his own. If he was not particularly interested in things that lay outside his nature, all which was not industrious, substantial, easily social, he at least recognized that fact. Marshall deceived no one about himself, nor did he wish to. His occasional proclamations were perhaps only a kind of preventive routine, like making dental appointments.

Then he became involved with a woman, and it ended badly. It had not begun any too well, in fact, but it had seemed volatile and arousing then, instead of merely tedious, as it became. With most women, you could reach some understanding. It was over, for one reason or another, and perhaps you even agreed on the reasons. With Trish—that was her name—they had not even agreed it was over. There had been scenes and messiness. That was her style, though certainly not his. On their last encounter she provoked him into striking her. That was how he thought of it, for he had never done such a thing before in his life, and even now he had difficulty believing it had happened.

He remembered little of what led up to it. Their argument had gone on for hours, it was late, he was exhausted by it all—there were reasons, he supposed. "You and your stupid stupid bloody fake cool," she said. "Don't you get tired of pretending everything bores you?" He smoked a cigarette and waited for it to be over. Her apartment was small and hot. The air conditioning had broken some time ago and she hadn't managed to get it fixed. A small rotating fan stirred the air uselessly. It gave a thin stream of freshness, then the heat rushed back in, like water parted with a stick. Each turn of the fan only increased his irritation. She couldn't be bothered to do anything right.

"You know," he said wearily, when she began to cry, "making yourself this miserable is really pointless, Trish. You don't have to put so much effort into it. Try getting some perspective. A little balance."

"You make it all sound like a goddamned vitamin deficiency. Nice of you to be concerned, though." And on it went.

The place stank of cats and defeated carpeting. The posters she'd put up with gobs of tape—art prints, mostly—were buckling and sagging from the walls. In the bedroom her clothes lay in soft, bright-colored heaps. It used to drive him crazy to watch her dress, rummaging through the bottom of the closet, scattering makeup. Staring into the mirror as if nothing mattered but the perfectability of her eyelashes, as if she couldn't even see the rubbish-pile she lived in. Leaving the place a mess, he thought, was probably gratifying for her. It was meant to demonstrate that she had other things to concern· her, that she was a woman of grand, brooding passions who couldn't be much occupied with cleaning sinks. Everything about her he imagined as calculated for tragic effect. Lady Macbeth in a cocktail lounge. Jane Eyre goes to the dry cleaners. She was really only theatrical and loud. He couldn't for the life of him remember why he'd ever found her appealing. She was launched on one of her endless complaints now. He watched her without really listening. He'd heard it all before anyway. She was calling him shallow, insensitive, cruel, a shrill and boring litany. Her mouth worked rapidly, like it was spitting seeds. What was he doing here anyway, in this airless disordered room, listening to a woman he cared nothing for berate him? Her eyes were veined with red, and her makeup had smeared from the heat and the crying. No one should have to listen to such things; no one should say them. He was not here, not really, there was no part of him that belonged here. "You think of having sex the same way you think of having lunch," she was saying. "I had shrimp for lunch. I had sex with what's-her-name. You push away your plate, you zip up your pants, God, if you only knew how pathetic you are."

And then he had hit her in the mouth with the back of his hand, hard enough to send her stumbling against the wall. One leg bent underneath her and she fell. She said nothing, only looked up at him with her long hair wrapped around her throat, tasting the line of blood on her lip, smiling crookedly. Although she was a pretty woman, at that moment she looked fouled, distorted, like a face seen through unclean water. Even then a part of him stood ready to apologize, a familiar reflex, as he might have to a stranger he'd bumped into. But that smile, the lip peeled back grotesquely from the wound, the tongue flicking out so slyly, tasting— The more he looked at her the more unreal it all became. Himself, her coarsened unrecognizable face, the notion that they had ever touched each other in love. Then she was getting to her feet, almost briskly, as if she had only tripped. "Terrific. Deadly. Such a hook. The kid's a natural." She spoke with some difficulty. There was by now a fair amount of bleeding. She turned to peer into a mirror, touched her mouth. Then she turned again and her hand snaked out at him, smearing bright blood across his shirt.

He got himself home somehow. The next morning he awoke feeling shamed in some far more complicated way than his single action could explain. As if he'd been soiled, or caught in a lie, and every morning from now on he would wake to it. He had not been himself. The whole thing was ugly and unwholesome, not just last night, but all of it. A mistake from the start. She was neurotic and unbalanced. She had probably wanted him to strike her. It dragged him down to her level, the better to make more unreasonable demands on him. She brought out the worst in him. He could not be responsible for someone who refused to be responsible for themselves. So he talked to himself, like a reassuring friend, and gradually he felt better about it. He made a conscious effort not to think about her, and like most of his efforts, it was largely successful.

He had not seen her for weeks now. He was not thinking of her on this brilliant late-summer day as he lay beside his club's well-groomed swimming pool, trying to read. The sun's glare made the print swarm and gave the page itself a porous, grainy appearance. Bad for the eyes, he supposed, but he only had one more chapter. He bore down on the page once more, trying to will the black swarm into words, the words into sense. The sun was tricky, histrionic. It made things look two-dimensional, like the false blue of the swimming pool, enamel laid on with a single brush stroke. Or else objects revealed impossible complications of texture, like the pebbled concrete deck he lay on. Close up, it was a landscape of lunar boulders, receding gradually into white sugar smoothness. Everything seemed intent on slipping loose from its normal shape, distracting him with unnecessary visions. Marshall lowered his eyes again and made a new attempt at concentration. It always irritated him when he found himself repeating sentences.

Three drops of water fell heavily on the page. The black letters within them swam like one-celled animals under a microscope. "Hello Marshall. I've been trying to get a tan."

His first instinct was to stay completely still, as if that would render him invisible. Camouflage. Too late. He wished mightily that she would go away, or better yet, that she had never existed. Instead he glanced up without moving his head. "Good for you," he said.

"Do you like me better tan, or pale?"

"What?"

"It's not a trick question. Either you like me tan, or pale, or both ways, or neither."

"I haven't thought about it," he muttered.

"Ah. A man who knows his own mind."

She sat down next to him then. She smelled hot and baked, even through the chlorine scent of the water.

Against his better judgement he said "I'm curious. What would you do if I said I liked you with a tan?"

"I'd get more tan."

"And if I liked you pale?"

"I'd stay indoors until I faded. I'd wear a veil and long sleeves. I'd be positively nun-like. Can you imagine that?"

Marshall didn't reply. He was wondering why he hadn't realized she could be here. He should have kept a lookout, or not come at all. Now that he thought about it, he couldn't even remember her casting a warning shadow.

"Actually," she said after a moment, "I'm still pale here, underneath."

She lifted the edge of the red nylon at her hip to display the whiteness of the skin. Marshall found himself feeling a nearly adolescent awkwardness, an embarrassment at their lack of clothing.

"What are you reading?"

He lifted the cover for inspection, holding his place with his thumb as if to demonstrate how momentary her interruption was, how imminently he was going to resume his reading.

/111/

"A serious book. In fact, literature. Let me commend you."
She seemed not at all dismayed by his silence, as he'd hoped. "Are
you reading it because you have to for some reason, or just for
amusement?"

"Amusement. Pure amusement. Grins." He hoped he sounded
sarcastic and unfriendly enough to dislodge her.

"But then, amusement is never pure with you, is it? There's
always some purpose to it. Hygiene, say—"

"Look Trish. All this is done. Remember? All that's finished."

"Getting to you, huh Marshall?"

"Don't you wish."

"Oh, I know. Nobody can lay a glove on you."

She stretched out full length on her back, as if bored. Marshall, who lay on his stomach, buried his head in his arms. Much
as he wanted to leave, it would have smacked of retreat. He felt
childish, both guilty and irritated. He would have liked to find
the right thing to say to her, the right combination of apology and
firmness to dismiss her forever, but that seemed even harder to
do. Yes, he would have apologized, if that were possible; again
he felt the unreasonable shame, crowding his throat like vomit.

A long minute passed. The sun was brutal. The other bathers
lining the deck seemed dazed by it also. They hardly moved; they
looked like rows of fish laid out to dry. Marshall thought about
the water, of submerging himself in its coldness, layers and layers
of it. He realized how rigid he was, waiting for her to do or say
something. That was stupid. After all, what was the worst that
could happen? It was all finished, as he'd said. You had to expect
hysteria and accusations from her. That had been true all along.
That was precisely why it hadn't lasted, and maybe also, he could
admit now, part of why it had started.

"None of this is what I want to say to you."

She had spoken almost in his ear. The nearness of it made
him set his teeth. He turned his head towards the mirrored discs
of her sunglasses, which were staring straight up, silver exploding stars. The eyes themselves were invisible.

Again he waited, saying nothing. "It's just what comes out
first." She shrugged, or seemed to. It was an awkward move-
ment, her shoulders scraping along the cement.

"Don't worry about it, OK?" What he meant was, please stop
talking. If he were quick enough he might have been able to end
it there, on that note, but he wasn't.

"What I want to say is this. The last time we were together.
In bed, I mean. Remember?"

"What about it."

"I remember it very well indeed. Believe it or not, Marshall,
among my attributes I have a good memory. I remember it was

raining. One of those steamy rains, when the sky just goes on forever being hot and gray, and the leaves drip. That's how it was. Funny. That's what sexual frustration feels like too after a while, I've decided. Something flat and gray you can't budge. Anyway. I remember you were so hard I hurt myself on you—"

"For Christ's sake."

"—remember how you tasted and the way you closed your eyes. You want to hear more?"

"No."

"I remember how your legs felt between mine. Listen to me, please. You need someone to say things like this to you, that's why you liked me, because I'd say them. Here. Do you feel my hand? Do you hear me talking? It was good, Marshall, really, if I ever said any different it was just to hurt you. Please—"

He was on his feet now, striding away. *Bitch. Bitch.* When he came out from changing clothes he looked around cautiously to see if she were waiting for him. She wasn't anywhere in sight.

Marshall did not return to the club for some time, though he hated the idea of letting her alter any part of his habits. Yet once or twice he saw her, or imagined he did. Walking on a busy street, he'd glimpse her car, or one like it, the brake lights winking on just after it passed him. Then the traffic would carry it out of sight. That small electric flaring filled him with dismay. She might even be following him. He wouldn't put it past her. She probably got no end of a charge out of it all. It was grand opera to her, with plenty of daggers and revenge and breast-beating. *Carmen? Rigoletto?* He couldn't remember which ones ended unhappily. He supposed they all did. He supposed he should feel sorry for her, but it made more sense to simply forget her.

Then one night he saw her in a bar with another man. They were seated at a table by themselves and Trish was talking earnestly, her arm fluttering on his sleeve. Poor bastard, thought Marshall. She was probably telling him about her dreams, or her unhappy childhood. The man surprised him; he didn't seem her type. Young, with a little fair moustache and a slice of fair well-tended hair. He looked stiff, even a bit prim. He was managing to seem polite and aggrieved at the same time. He nodded at whatever she was saying and stirred his drink violently. Even from across the room Marshall could see his straw galloping through the dissolving ice. Poor bastard. He probably turned up at her door selling encyclopedias, and she'd carried him off. Shoes, thought Marshall, observing more closely. He sold her a pair of shoes.

They stood up to go and Marshall realized they'd have to pass near him on the way out. There was no hope for it but to stand fast. He gazed down fiercely into his drink.

It didn't work. "Nice try, Marshall."

He looked up, pretending he didn't know what she meant. "Oh, hello."

She'd stopped just behind him. The young man halted obediently in her wake. He was gazing out over the bar, as if he were being conducted through it on a tour. "Denny," she said to him. "Why don't we have one more drink. Denny, this is Marshall."

"How you doing." Denny nodded at his own reflection in the mirror over the bar. Neither of them offered to shake hands.

"I'd like another scotch, please. Marshall," she explained, "is someone I used to sleep with."

"Two scotch and waters," said Denny. "How about you?"

"I'm OK, thanks." Up close, Denny looked even more fastidious and improbable. The hair was pinkish-blonde and fine, like some newly hatched creature's. Trish was smiling. Pleased with herself, no doubt. She was wearing one of her costumes. That was how he thought of them. A long dress of some smudged batik print. Enormous gold hoops in her ears. She looked edgy, glittering. Marshall wondered how much she'd been drinking. Her bright hair was twisted into a high braid, to go with the dress, he supposed, and the sleekness of her head and bare neck gave her a startled, expectant air.

"So how's every little thing, Marshall?"

"Peachy, thank you."

"You look a tad crisp around the edges. A bit frayed. That concerns me."

"It shouldn't."

"Oh, I know. You've made that clear enough." She sipped at her drink, and for a moment he thought she was going to launch into one of her bouts of sarcasm. Instead she lowered her glass and sighed.

"I always tried too hard with you, didn't I?"

"I wouldn't put it that way."

"Well I would. Fight the good fight. Once more into the breach. It seems to be the only trick I know."

Denny was still behind her, examining himself in the mirror, twisting his neck delicately inside his collar. Marshall wished she were with someone a little more proprietary.

"I expect you prefer them cool and unapproachable," she went on. "Or at least, you think you do. Is that what I should have been for you? Is that really what you like? They're so boring, Marshall, those Ice-Capade Queens. It would be boring even to pretend to be one for an afternoon. All that ritual homage they demand. Believe me, they keep track of it like parking meters. They know exactly what you get for your nickel. Maybe that's who you're mixed up with now. Some woman who goes tick tick tick."

"Don't be stupid, Trish."

"I know. None of my business. Still, I hope not. I keep thinking there are better things in you."

"What do you mean? What things?"

"Oh, I don't know." She seemed to be flagging even as she spoke. Her head drooped. "I guess I keep expecting you to be as crazy as I am. Never mind."

And what, Marshall wondered, should one say? Or do? He felt suddenly as if he'd reached some limit within himself, something flat, exhausted, failed. Could people ever understand each other? The room was noisy. Voices twined and drifted like smoke. The space where they stood seemed oddly sheltered, a pool of silence, or perhaps it was that she had moved closer without him noticing, waiting for him to speak. In spite of her jaunty braid and the gold swinging in her ears, she looked worn and even hopeless. To think that anyone should stand that way before him. That people should have such power over each other, and use it so badly. Ah Lord, he was tired of it all, these voices, his voice, saying nothing, tired of her certainly, but also of himself, his feeble dignity, his no doubt quite comical sullenness. "Look," he said. "Do you really want to talk about it? Here and now?"

"I'd like nothing better. Excuse me. That's hyperbolic. See, I'm trying, Marshall. I'm trying to be sensible for you." Her chin was working a little and when she looked up at him her eyelashes were already damp and matted. He felt the beginnings of a qualm, but muscled himself past it.

"All right," he said, keeping his voice low, though he doubted anyone else was listening. "Just what do you want from me, Trish? What do you expect? We've got nothing in common. Nothing. We can't go ten minutes without things blowing up in our faces. There's no future in it. Why keep pushing it?" It wasn't coming out right. It was too much like all the other voices, all the things he had ever said before. He tried again. "So why bother hating me just because I'm not what you want me to be?"

"What do I want from him," said Trish conversationally, as if to an onlooker. "He wants to know what I want from him." She made a quizzical mouth. Her eyes looked quite dry now. Had he only imagined tears? "I think what I want is to be every woman you ever make love to. Don't misunderstand me. Not the only woman. I'd want you to have lots of them. I'd want you to feel all the different things you could feel with each of them. And then I'd want to be all of them, all those women. How do you go about that, do you suppose? Make a pact with the devil? Go on a game show? Oh, what's the use. You don't know how I feel. You don't ever understand a word I say, do you?"

"You don't want to be understood. You just want to make a spectacle of yourself. Congratulations. You're managing nicely."

"All I ever wanted," she said sadly, "was for you to want me back."

Denny materialized at Trish's side, as if the tour were re-grouping. He held his empty glass.

"Another," said Trish, plucking it from his hand. Jaunty again. He couldn't decide which of her faces he mistrusted more.

Denny only shrugged. It looked to be a matter of perfect in-difference to him if he ever had another drink again. Marshall wondered if he was always this inertly distressed. The fellow ir-ritated him. So tell me, Marshall wanted to ask him. How is the shoe business nowadays?

"You're the one who plays tennis," said Denny suddenly.

"That's right." And you're the one with the hole in your face. What the hell else had Trish been telling him? Not that he gave a rat's ass what Denny thought. "Not as much as I used to. Back in school."

"I play sometimes," offered Denny. He managed to make even that statement sound petulant. "When I can fit it in. I'm pretty rusty."

"Easy to fall off your game."

"I'll say. You think about the pros, I mean, how much those guys have to work at it. Like somebody said, you don't practice for one day and you know it. Two days, maybe your wife knows it. Three days, the whole world."

"I think that was Heifetz."

"What?"

"The violinist. He's the one who said that."

"Oh yeah? A violinist, huh."

Marshall nodded. The conversation, which weighed less than a hair, nevertheless burdened him. Why was the fool talking to him anyway? They had nothing to say to each other about tennis or anything else. Trish was paying them no attention. She looked like any other woman bored at hearing men talk about sports. "Maybe," Denny was saying, "we could get up a game some-time."

"Sure."

"Although I bet you'd clobber me," said Denny, with un-called-for mournfulness. "I told you, I'm no great shakes."

"I wouldn't worry about it." In the unlikely event of a game between them, Marshall figured Denny for a hacker. Charging off in five directions at once, working up gallons of unnecessary pink sweat.

"I should take lessons," said Denny gloomily. "My funda-mentals are lousy."

The topic was apparently extinguished then, and they stood without speaking. Marshall felt himself sagging, as if the feeble conversational threat had supported him more than he'd realized. He should leave. He felt sour and hot from the drinking. It occurred to him that there was no reason, none at all, for the three of them to be standing here, pretending they had any common interest, connection or purpose for doing so, any liking or fellowship. How many times had he stood so, listening or speaking, with people he could no longer remember? He looked around the room and everywhere he seemed to see the same exhaustion, or perhaps it was only his own that filmed his eyes. All the faces seemed heavy with indifference or with the labor of displacing it. In none of them could he see pleasure, or ease, or delight in company. He could not seem to remember a time in his life when it had been any different. When he had felt any differently.

"Marshall?"

He'd closed his eyes and when he opened them Trish was looking up at him. Skeptically, he thought. "You all right?"

"Just tired."

"We should go somewhere else, the three of us. This place is stale. We should forge on into the night. What do you say, Den?"

"Sure. Let's forge."

Marshall shook his head. "Sorry. I was just going to head on home."

"One more stop," said Denny. The idea seemed to animate him. He beamed at Marshall, and his crest of hair quivered. "A last ride together. One for the ditch."

"Sorry. I really think I ought to pass."

"We shall quaff the stirrup-cup."

"It's no use," said Trish. "He won't come. He has spoken."

"Well shoot. What good is he."

"One wonders."

"We're all pals anyway, aren't we," said Denny. "The greatest word in the English language."

Denny was close to drunk, Marshall realized. They'd all been drinking rather fast. Now that he'd said he was going home, he was impatient to leave.

"If you could be any tennis player in the world," said Denny, "who would you be? Men's singles, I mean. Go on, pick somebody."

"Borg, I guess."

"I'd be Connors. People say he's past his prime. I say the hell with them."

"So take it easy, OK?" Marshall nodded to them and moved for the door.

"Wait for us. We're leaving right now." Trish began casting

about her for various evasive personal items and Marshall resigned himself to five minutes more of their company. It had been,
he decided, a truly wasted evening. Finally they emerged with
Marshall leading the way. The sudden darkness seemed to muffle
them; even Denny was silent. The air tasted thin after the bar and
they breathed it greedily. Marshall felt the drink rising in him as
a wave of heat that hummed and flared behind his eyes. Home.

He quickened his pace deliberately to leave them behind, and
when he reached his car he turned and waved. They appeared
not to have moved at all, but leaned against each other in a curious inert fashion, like inflatable toys from which air was escaping.
His vision was narrowed by the darkness, tunneled, so that their
figures in the faint starlike light from the streetlamps seemed infinitely far away. Even their clumsiness was miniature, harmless.
"Good-night," he shouted down the tunnel at them. One of them,
he couldn't tell which, called something back at him, but the
darkness blotted it out. He hadn't expected it to be that easy,
somehow.

He took extra care pulling out of the space. It was not, after
all, the first time he'd had to drive home with a snootful in him.
The important thing was to concentrate and to realize the machine would do nothing without you. You were the driver. None
of those intricately meshing and revolving parts would leap into
action of their own accord, no matter how cleverly engineered,
how well they mimicked animation. It was only a collection of steel
bones and dark oiled blood and electric heart. One had only to
direct it. So he was thinking, or rather, if he had been able to organize his sensations into words, they would have been something like that. He steered cautiously around a bank of parked cars.
Without warning, a white Camaro came roaring up the aisle behind him, just clearing him as he turned, and embedded itself in
the brick wall of the building. There was the first terrific crash and
then the sound of glass breaking over and over, like a waterfall.

Although the Camaro had missed him entirely, he had a sensation of such powerful and violent sickness that for a moment he
believed he'd actually been injured. The blackness around him was
absolute. He swam to its surface, opened the car door and stepped
out. He expected—he didn't know what. Crowds and sirens,
maybe. But nothing of the sort had yet materialized. It had only
been the briefest of seconds.

The Camaro's hood was peeled back and the front wheel clos-
est to Marshall had a cock-eyed look, as if the axle were broken.
There was a smell of smoke, or maybe it was only the heat of the
sheared metal, because there was no fire. A thumping noise was
coming from within the car. A door trying to open. By the time

Marshall reached them, a voice—Denny's—was saying, sorrow-fully, that the bastard was broken.

"What happened?" Marshall shouted. A stupid thing to say, but his voice was a booming mechanical thing, quite without con-nection to anything he meant.

"It's all out of line or something. Oh, balls."

"Are you hurt? Trish?"

Nuggets of glass were everywhere. A portion of the wind-shield was still in place. Light glittered and raced through the web of silvery cracks. "Trish?" He peered inside, could see nothing but a dark huddle which at first glance seemed to be composed of more than two bodies.

"I think I'm all right," said Trish. Her voice was small and indistinct. "If he'd just get his foot off my throat."

"Anybody hurt?" said a man behind Marshall. People had fi-nally emerged from the bar. It didn't take long for someone to be-gin giving orders and directions, then someone else. They shouldn't be moved. Or they should. Marshall listened, or tried to, but what they were saying skated and buzzed past him, a series of impor-tant-sounding noises. He wondered again if he had somehow been hurt himself. It was only fatigue and the alcohol receding. The door on the driver's side was impossibly jammed. Trish squirmed out of the passenger door without her shoes and stepped cautiously around the sparkling glass. One gold hoop had been torn through the lobe of her ear; she seemed not to have noticed it yet. Denny, still tangled on the front seat, complained that his head hurt. An ambulance had been called, and the police. The little group of spectators was beginning to drift and scatter. "I'll sue," said Denny from within the car. "I have whiplash."

When the police arrived, Marshall gave his name as a wit-ness. He would have very much liked not to. Then the ambulance came and Denny was borne away. Trish was leaning against Mar-shall's car when he walked back to it. Black smudges like wheel tracks showed on her neck and arm. Her braid of hair had begun to uncoil and she was trying to shake it loose. The long outlan-dish dress had wadded up around her knees. Her bare feet and torn ear gave her a queer, fierce aspect, both fantastic and awk-ward. He felt embarrassed for her. She didn't know how she looked.

"Would you take me home?" she asked as he came up to her.

"You should go to the hospital, you know." He looked around, but the ambulance had already left.

"I want to go home."

"Somebody should look at that ear."

She touched it vaguely. "It doesn't hurt."

"It will. Look, I'll go find the cops."

"No." She caught his arm. "Just stay here a minute, please?"

He turned and then she was pressed against him, her entire weight. It nearly threw him off balance. He put a tentative hand on her hair, patted it, and tried to think of something to say. Surely there was something he could say. She was rocking back and forth into his chest, noiselessly. She smelled singed, bitter, as if her skin too had been part of some violent collision which strained and disordered it, filled it with heat. She was sobbing but he couldn't hear it, only felt the struggling in her lungs. He sagged a little, holding her, and the sensation of love, of making love to her, was on him in an instant. Not as a memory, but as if he had suddenly awakened from sleep to find himself embracing her. He was so startled, it was so incongruous, that without willing it he dropped his arms and stepped back from her.

She stumbled but caught herself, leaning against the car. Her mouth was open and she looked up at him through her tumbling hair.

"You bastard," she said after a moment.

"I'm sorry. I didn't mean to." He was not sure himself just what had happened.

"You can't pretend to be human for a minute, can you?"

"It was an accident." It was all he could think of to say.

"Nothing," she said, "will ever ever happen to you."

After another moment he said he would drive her to the hospital if she wanted. She let him open the door for her. Carefully, she tucked her bare feet into the draggled hem of her dress. They didn't speak at all in the car. At the hospital it took some time to find out what had happened to Denny. He was still in emergency but was going to be admitted. He had a concussion and three broken ribs, they thought. The X rays weren't back yet.

"Drunks," said the doctor to Marshall. "They kill everybody but themselves. What kind of a jerk totals a car in a parking lot?"

For some reason the doctor had singled out Marshall. The doctor was a weary, middle-aged man with a stiff face, like folded paper. The two of them were standing outside one of the tiled cubicles. There was a long row of them and they reminded Marshall of bays in a garage. "I've got no sympathy for these jokers," the doctor went on. "None at all. I've seen too much of what they can do. Say, this guy isn't a friend of yours, is he?"

"No," said Marshall. "I was just there when it happened."

"I didn't think so. You don't look like you'd be mixed up in it."

Trish came back with her ear bandaged. "They stitched it," she said, before he could ask. "I've got to find Denny now."

Denny was propped up on a table in one of the cubicles. A green sheet was draped over his knees like a tent, and tape encased him from the armpits down. "Hey," he said to Marshall. "We may have to wait a little on that tennis game."

"You'll be fine. I bet you skunk me. Don't worry about it now."

"Borg versus Connors. Another comeback try."

"How are you feeling?" asked Trish.

"They tell me I don't feel too bad. That's a relief."

"Don't worry about anything, said Marshall. "Really. You shouldn't let it get you down."

"Borg is just a tennis machine. Everybody knows that. He's a snore."

"We should go now," said Trish. "You need to rest."

"Oh my God." Denny had begun to cry. His nose was running and he tried to maneuver the green sheeting towards his face. "I'm sorry. I'm sorry I'm nothing but a fool."

Marshall left the room and waited in the corridor until Trish came out. "He'll be OK, won't he?" he asked.

She looked up at him, startled, as if she'd forgotten about him. "Sure. Everything will be all right."

"I'll take you home, then."

"No," she said. "I don't think so."

He made his way past the receptionist's glass island, and the scattering of people in the waiting room. They looked up at him hungrily for a moment, as if he were bringing them news they'd been promised. Then they realized who he was, or rather, who he was not, and they ceased to see him. Outside it felt colder than it had before. His car was parked under a light and its smooth dark surface threw back egg-shaped patches of hazy gleam. Marshall got inside and put the key in the ignition but did not yet turn it. All he had to do was start it, as he had a thousand times before. All he had to do was turn the key and resume the life he had always known, but for a long time he could not.

OF HIS BONES ARE CORAL MADE

She was not, as a matter of principle, the kind of wife who pried. Who trespassed on things she felt to be private. Letters were, of course, private, one of those clearly marked checkerboard squares that you did not advance on. She stood at the end of the long gravel drive, weighing the envelope in her hand. It was postmarked Seattle where they, she at least, knew no one. The envelope was long and pale blue and the name in the corner was Lindberg. Nothing else. The handwriting too seemed deliberately noncommittal, a regular and sexless script. Then she shook her head, chiding herself. Silly, when that was the first thing you considered, whether or not it came from a woman. She wondered, briefly, what her husband would have thought had it been she who received such a letter. But that was even sillier, because she never did, and besides, he probably would not have given it any thought at all. She tucked the letter in the middle of the other mail and walked back up to the house. The autumn air was warm and perfectly still, a glassy warmth that made her slow her pace. The leaves of the red maples glowed like fruit. What flowers there were, the chrysanthemums in the garden or the wildflowers in the ragged grass along the road, nodded with heavy bloom. The world might have been sinking into its own ripeness.

"Anything interesting?" her husband asked, as he always did. She smiled and handed him the bundle. The bank statement and the insurance notice. Another of the endless appeals to good causes. Whole species faced extinction. People sickened and starved. Cruelties abounded. Without your generous contribution. It was unfortunate, but the cumulative dire effect of those appeals was to make you feel your generous contribution would be entirely futile. So she was thinking, carefully buttering a piece of toast, carefully watching and not watching her husband. He glanced at the letter, set it aside, and tended first to the other mail. Then he read the letter through once, his face not changing from its expression of steady attention, folded it, put it back in its envelope. "I'm off now," he said. "The list is all set?" For it was Saturday, he was going into town and she needed a few things. He put the list in his jacket pocket and kissed her good-bye. She saw the frilled edge of the envelope protruding also.

"Who was your letter from this morning?" she asked him that night. She was a little disappointed in herself, having spent all that effort in exhorting herself to virtue, but it was, she decided, a harmless enough curiosity. To pretend it didn't exist might be more unnatural than asking.

Her husband lifted his head to contemplate her. There was a fire in the fireplace, the first they'd had this season, and ribbons of flame laced and fluttered in the grate. "Funny," he said. "I was just thinking about that."

She looked up at him from her seat on the floor, waiting. "It was from an old friend, someone I hadn't heard from in years. Someone else we both knew—from college—died. Just last week."

She touched his knee. "I'm sorry."

"Oh well. It's not that I've been in touch with any of those people. Not for a long time. You know how that happens. But I guess you don't expect the friends of your youth to ever grow up, let alone die. Intimations of mortality and all that." He shrugged.

"What happened to—your friend?" It occurred to her that she did not know if it was a man or woman.

"An accident. He was only thirty-four."

She did not really expect him to go on but he did, in a slow judicious voice, as if he did not wish to embellish anything. "It was out in California somewhere. That's where he was living. He was walking on the beach. One of those places, a kind of rock inlet, where the tide comes in like fury. Dangerous as hell. Sometimes the waves carry in big logs the size of telephone poles and the things hit with about ten thousand pounds of pressure per inch. Well, that's what happened. Nothing you can do about it if you're in the way. Somebody else was there and saw it. Otherwise, nobody would have known what happened to him."

"What do you mean?"

"They don't always—find the people, you know. The tide's too strong. Listen, you shouldn't have to hear about all this."

"I don't mind. Really. Was he a close friend of yours?"

The flames rippled, lacing and unlacing. Her husband picked up his drink and cradled it in his hands. "I think maybe I don't feel like talking about it right now, if that's all right."

"Oh, sure. I'm sorry."

"It's not you. It's just how I feel right now."

"Listen, it's OK." She squeezed his hand, to show that she understood completely.

In fact, he was the one who brought it up again several days later. They were sitting that evening in a glossy and rather expensive bar. The bar was built on a pier and three sides of it were glass, for the spectacular view. But it was the end of the season and tonight the place was nearly empty. The small yellow lanterns that marked each table seemed to drift among their own reflections in the polished wood. The red-jacketed bartender leaned over a magazine. The ocean itself was flat and almost motionless in the smoky autumn dusk. She had dressed up a little and now she felt rather foolish. It was a disappointment to find the place so dead. Though neither of them had admitted it, they'd been looking forward to being among other people's laughter and voices, and now there was the faintest air of being trapped together. They smiled a little self-consciously and ducked their heads to drink. Perhaps it was the need to revive the evening that made her husband speak, the need to pretend they had sought out this intimacy rather than been consigned to it. Or perhaps it was the motionless water which reminded him of that other ocean, so different, a continent away.

"My friend, the one who had the accident," he began. "You remember me telling you?"

She nodded. "What was his name? You didn't say."

"Terry. Terry Warren. How come?"

"I was just wondering if I'd ever heard you speak of him."

"I doubt it. Not recently, at least."

"I guess I don't know many of your friends from back then."

"Well. It was a long time ago, you know." Her husband made a brisk little gesture, half-wave, dismissing it. "I've been thinking about him a lot, for some reason."

"That's only natural," she said. A little too helpfully.

"I suppose you don't have friends like that once you get older. Something about letting yourself be vulnerable. Or maybe not being quite sure of who you are yet, so you can be anyone you want to, you've got nothing to lose . . ."

She waited silently this time, watching her hands on the smooth surface of the wood. Their blurred reflection reached up to touch her fingertips. Her hands drawing these other hands up out of the wood.

"We had our first apartment together, Terry and I. You can imagine the place. Everybody's first apartment must be like it. Technicolor garbage. Nothing in the refrigerator but Velveeta cheese and a rusty fork. I don't think we owned a broom."

"That doesn't sound like you," she said. "Not at all."

/124/

"I was a young yahoo. You wouldn't have liked me."

"Yes I would have. I would have liked to know you."

"Terry was the one you would have liked. Everybody did. Isn't there always somebody like that, the one everybody else orbits around? They manage it without even trying. He was bright, too. He could have been anything. He was studying architecture." Her husband paused. "He used to say the University was like an elephant graveyard, where huge Georgian buildings came to die."

She smiled along with him, but of course she had never seen the school.

"I'm probably making him sound like one of those spoiled Golden Boys. All fake and charming and glib. I probably can't make you see him at all. I'm boring you."

"Of course you're not."

"I used to feel flattered that he'd chosen me for a friend, though I never would have admitted it back then. I wasn't anyone special. No, you don't have to look that way. I wasn't. Just another callow youth, working too hard at taking myself seriously. I used to wonder what Terry could ever want with me."

They were quiet a moment, looking out at the dull water. "So what happened?" she asked. For she could tell that something had happened.

Her husband shook his head. "Oh, it's hard to say. It was all so long ago. Remember back when it was the most natural thing in the world to stay up all night talking? For no reason at all. Lord, the things you can do to your body when you're young. Anyway, we used to do that a lot. We might be trying to study for tests, and we'd be drinking coffee that was strong enough to walk, and smoking five cigarettes at once, and then you start talking. By three a.m. you might as well be the only two people left in the world. I mean, you've redecorated the house with ashtrays and wet towels, the place is a ruin, and so are your chances of doing anything at all constructive the next day. But none of that matters, because you're alive and clicking like never before, you're being so ruthlessly brilliant and insightful. You're taking on all the problems of Western civilization at a mile a minute and solving them, you're speaking great Truths—"

Her husband smiled and turned his gaze once more to the water. It was black at the horizon, gunmetal closer to shore. Here and there a pool of color seemed to float on the surface, blue or violet, the last reflection of the western sky. "Did you get into an argument?" she asked.

"I suppose that's what you'd call it. It's hard to remember how those things happen. Nobody plans them. All of a sudden you reach those places in a conversation where people say things they don't mean. Or at least, things they shouldn't say. I don't know."

She waited, but when he spoke again, all he said was, "People can talk too much. That's what I've been doing."

"Oh no, really. I've been interested."

"Well." She could tell from the lightening of his voice that now he was through speaking, whatever else he might say. "It was just one of those things. It wasn't like we never spoke to each other again, but we'd soured on each other. That was senior year anyway, and school kept me pretty busy. Funny, Terry never got his degree. He didn't finish his course work. Started diddling around with this notion of interdisciplinary art. You know, everything's related to everything else, which finally boils down to nothing means anything. He was going to write his senior thesis on the architectural structure of *Ulysses,* if you can believe that. Of course he never started it. He went back home and got a job writing ad copy for a while. I guess these last few years he'd been trying to make it as a photographer, but without much luck. Sad."

"Sometimes that happens," she said. "There are people who reach their peak early. They seem like they can do almost everything well, but none of it well enough."

"I suppose you're right. Charming dilettantes. Something like that. Shall we go?"

She spent all the next day cleaning house. Her husband was at work and she was free to turn the rooms inside out, to fill the air with the smells of ammonia and scrubbed wood, to sing aloud in her shy breathy voice. Sometimes she'd only get as far as a phrase or two before she'd stop and grimace, as if apologizing to the empty house for the cracked little sounds she was making. It was while she was dusting that she came on the blue leather album in which her husband kept photographs. She pulled it out and sat down cross-legged on the floor. A small girl in cut-offs and an old T-shirt, blinking in a triangle of sunshine. Her light brown hair drooped around her face, its fringes nearly white in the sun.

Although she remembered her husband bringing the album out to show her, remembered him going through and explaining, carefully, who was who, and where, and when, all the people she did not know and never would, she found she did not remember the pictures themselves. The pages felt brittle. A brown wing-shaped stain, something spilled, appeared on each margin. The pictures were in no particular order, and she watched her husband age backwards and forwards. It was an odd sensation, as if he were endlessly eluding her, changing from merry little boy to man and then back again. There was a cluster of color snapshots and these she bent over closely, examining. She was certain they were from his school days—had he told her?—and that the one face was that of his friend who had died.

In the picture they stood together against an anonymous wall of white-painted boards. They might have just finished playing softball, or perhaps moving furniture for a friend. They wore the careless clothes that boys are most comfortable with, sagging shirts and jeans so faded as to be nearly colorless. The weather must have been warm; the white boards looked hot to the touch, and small, gnomelike shadows huddled at their feet. She recognized her husband's expression, the one he wore in all photographs, that air of being formally introduced to the camera. (So she saw him, even at this age, as her husband. As if he had already determined on it and was searching her out beyond the borders of the picture.) He looked both adolescent and precariously solemn, as if his older self was already attempting to struggle to the surface, as if he resented being preserved forever in this half-grown stage. His friend was extraordinarily good looking, the way boys can be at that age without either vanity or effort. His hair was the color of wheat and his skin a deep summer brown. They made an odd pair, for if her husband appeared to be pushing laboriously towards adulthood, his friend seemed entirely comfortable within his summer skin. The thin shirt he was wearing fell open at the neck, and she could not have said what it was about the frail architecture of his throat that moved her so. His arm was draped loosely around her husband's shoulders. The friend was laughing and his body was turned at such an angle that he seemed to be coaxing her husband forward, propelling him out of the wall. Here we are, he seemed to be saying. We will never be anything but young. This white afternoon, and our place in it, is as important as anything else in the world.

She supposed it was only what she knew that made the photograph seem melancholy, the knowledge that neither the friendship nor that boy's easy grace had long survived. Although she searched, she found just one more picture of his friend, and that a poor one. He appeared as a blurred figure behind a group of others, almost out of camera range, one hand raised, beckoning someone to follow him into that soft unfocussed region of the photograph. It was really a very bad picture, discolored and indistinct, but for some reason she was sure it was him. She wondered who had taken them.

She closed the album and replaced it, and finished the rest of her chores quickly. Outside she gathered the last bachelor's buttons, a few brass-colored chrysanthemums, orange hawkweed, milkweed pods, and twigs from the red maple. She spent some time arranging them in different vases and trying them in a number of spots around the house before she was satisfied. She took a long shower and washed her hair. She put on a blue dress she had always liked, and brushed her clean hair until it crackled.

When her husband got home he looked around him and smiled and patted her on the hip. "What's the occasion?"

"Nothing, really. No occasion at all."

"Everything looks great. You too."

They had drinks on the deck in back of the house, looking out over the hazy treetops. She served their dinner in the dining room with tall silver candlesticks and a bowl of flowers between them. Once or twice during the meal she caught her husband looking at her with an expression half amused, half ironic, as if trying to guess her mood. "You know," she said, when she'd cleared the plates and they sat again at the long table, "sometimes it's nice just to be by ourselves, isn't it?"

"Of course it is."

"What I meant was, it's nice to have a chance to really talk. To stay in touch."

He raised his wineglass to her. "Hear hear." There was a touch of wariness in his voice. It was simply his manner to speak so, with this mock courtliness. It was simply a habit.

"I never want us to start taking each other for granted. It's so easy just to go from day to day. Maybe we need to take time to— appreciate each other more." With the tips of her fingers, she traced the cool skin inside her sleeves. "Do you understand what I'm saying?"

"Hey, what brought all this on?" He smiled. "Are you upset about something?"

"No, not really." She tried again. "It's just that I want us to be everything we can be to each other. I want us to stay just as happy as we are right now."

"Well now. That would be some trick."

"Sometimes," she said deliberately, "I think you'd like it better if I could be different for you."

"What you talking about? Different? Don't be silly."

"You know. More—exciting, I guess. If I could be somebody more exciting for you."

The candles shimmered in her vision, as if the flames themselves were melting and softening, soft drops of fire falling and falling. Through them she saw her husband's face, his grave, concerned expression, and knew she had only succeeded in making him worry about her. She lowered her eyes so as not to see any more.

"Honey? What happened?"

She shook her head. The weight of her failure pressed on her.

"If there's something the matter, tell me."

"It's nothing. I'm just being silly."

"You're sure?"

Once, when she was a girl, she had fainted on the street. She remembered the faces peering down at her through layers of milky light. Concerned and avid at the same time, as if she had done something they found rather distasteful. "Really," she said. "Don't worry about me."

"Maybe this weekend we can get out somewhere. Would you like that? We could go to dinner at Godfrey's."

"Godfrey's. That sounds nice."

The phone rang in the hall and her husband pushed his chair away from the table. "Here, don't worry about it. I'll get it." He touched her shoulder as he passed behind her. She heard his brisk feet on the tiled floor, and the important-sounding phone, cut off in mid-ring. "Hello."

The candle flames had straightened. They purred steadily in the soft darkness. "What?" her husband said. "Who?"

She turned in her chair but his back was to her. His free hand clasped the other side of his head. "No, he isn't. Is this some kind of a joke? No. This is not. How did you get this number?"

He stood, both hands still pressed to his ears, as if he were holding two receivers to them, one she could not see. "No," he said finally. "Mr. Warren is deceased."

He hung up and she raised her face to him, questioning. "The damnedest thing," he said. "Somebody just called here for Terry Warren. You remember. My friend."

"Called here? Why? Who was it?"

"Somebody from an insurance company."

"Did he name you in a policy or something?"

"No. That's the hell of it." His eyes wandered over the table. He might have been looking for something in the smooth bare surface. "They didn't even know he was dead. They claim they had a message to call him here."

"Good Lord."

"Somebody's idea of a joke. Or some crazy screw-up. I can't imagine."

"What an awful thing to happen. You should call them back and complain."

He didn't answer, only stood gazing into the table.

"Did he ever get married, your friend?"

"What? Why do you ask?"

"I was just wondering if he left any family."

"No," said her husband. "He never married."

"That's sad. But then, maybe it's just as well. The way things turned out."

"What are you saying?" Her husband raised his head and stared at her sharply. His face looked almost ugly, the jaw gone heavy and square. "Why do you want to talk about it? Why can't you leave me alone?"

She heard his footsteps again, this time muffled by the carpeting of the stairs. She sat for a moment longer, then went into the kitchen to start the dishes.

"I'm sorry," he said later, when she came up to bed. He was on his back with his arms straight at his side. The sheet lay in smooth sculpted folds around him. He looked calm and tired. "I don't know what got into me."

"You were just upset. That's all."

She undressed quickly and got in beside him. The room was cool and his skin too was cool when she touched him. There was a heaviness about him; he was already half asleep. His mouth was soft underneath hers. She could not have said why she persisted or why she felt such a curious excitement. Her light, dragging fingers curled around his legs. He let out his breath in a sigh and she moved closer. She had never felt closer to him than she did now, stroking him out of sleep. She had never felt more tender or more exultant. "There now," she whispered, comforting him. "There now."

The air was layered blue and pink, cold colors like transparent ice, or the atmosphere of some fantastic planet. For a moment she stared, marveling, then it resolved itself into what she always saw, a square of morning sky framed by the familiar tailored drapes. She sat up, hugging the sheets to her, trying to retain her dream. But it had slipped away before she had a chance to claim it. Someone running, and gray rain-light coming in through a high window. And some emotion she could no longer even name, though she felt its weight still pressing in on her. She sat a moment longer. It had quite gone. It irritated her that the dream had been so full both of feeling and of quirky disconnections, that it had promised so much and given, finally, so little. Only the shape of its emptiness stayed with her, like a lost tooth the tongue keeps searching for. She closed her eyes and lay back again.

At breakfast her husband asked her if she slept well and she replied that she had. She was gazing at her plate of bacon and eggs, which she could not quite bring herself to eat. It was too highly colored, somehow, too plump and smug, like a magazine ad. "I had a dream," she said. "I think you were in it."

"I hope I wasn't doing anything—ah—indecorous." He smiled.

"Oh, don't you wish you were."

It was so much the sort of thing they always said that for a moment she wondered if she had actually spoken at all, or simply remembered herself speaking. But she must have, because here was her husband, smiling back at her. "So tell me," he said. "What was I doing?"

"I don't remember. No—" She found she did in fact remember. "You were running a race or something. You fell and hurt yourself."

"Thanks a lot. Sounds to me like some aggressive wish-fulfillment. Watch it, buddy."

Now it was becoming clearer to her all the while. "It was in this room, a gym or something." She saw again the long boards of blonde wood, and the high windows. "But there was something that didn't make sense in it, like dreams don't. The roof was open and rain was coming in. You fell and hurt yourself."

"I did that once, you know. Took a spill running track."

"Your knee. It was your knee you hurt."

"As a matter of fact," he said after a moment, "it was my knee."

She looked down at her plate, where the food had gone quite cold. She had the queer thought that the whole elaborate process of satisfying hunger might be regarded as a curiosity, if you felt no hunger yourself. So much effort, such a multitude of small rules and tasks and judgements necessary just to sit before this plate. She gazed at the eggs with their fat round yolk-eyes, as if to try and recall what they were for.

"There was something else in it too," she said. "Though I don't understand it. Like there was a piece of the dream missing, or else I've forgotten it. I was angry with you, for some reason. No, worse than that. Oh Christ." She stared at him across the table. "You'd done something terrible to me. You hurt me."

He smiled uncertainly, waiting for it to be a joke.

"You betrayed me."

"Hey now."

"You did," she insisted. "And then you tried to pretend it hadn't happened. You tried to laugh it off. Oh, that was the worst part. You knew how I felt, and you were going to ignore it. You were going to be—*tolerant*. Like it was all some embarrassment, something you'd be doing me a favor not to mention."

"What are you talking about?" he demanded. "Will you listen to yourself?"

"You betrayed me."

"I did something to you in a dream? What do you want me to do about it now?"

"I don't know." She shook her head so fast that the edges of her vision seemed to blur and soften, or perhaps it was the room itself slipping away.

"I'm sorry if it upset you," her husband was saying, "but you can hardly—"

"When you hurt your knee, it was cold outside."

"I don't remember. What does it matter?"

"It was cold, and there was this little boy, with a flag of some

/131/

sort. Oh, it was busy, and confused, too many people talking. And there was something—a radio playing too loud, and everyone was angry with it."

"What does that have to do with—"

"Wasn't there? The radio, and the boy with the flag. He was playing a game with stones. Throwing stones at something."

"At a tree."

"Yes. A tree."

They stared at each other. She was the one who broke it off. "How funny," she said. "I can't remember the last time I had such an odd dream."

She made a stack of the breakfast dishes. Since he was watching her she filled the sink right away and started in on them. Mounds of white suds rocked on the surface of the water. Spoons and forks and plates emerged from it gleaming with wet opal bubbles, like pirate treasure.

The weather turned damp, and a wind blew up, and overnight sad yellow leaves coated the ground. Every day leached a little more light from the sky. She looked out the windows at the silver wire of spiderwebs amazed by frost, or at the clear lemony sunsets that came after the rain, and sometimes she could not remember what these things were for. It was an odd sensation, like staring at yourself in a mirror for so long that you didn't recognize your own face. Then of course, you blinked or shook your head or smiled with one eyebrow raised, to show how ironical you were being, playing games with a mirror, and the world of common sense and habit reasserted itself. So it was at such times, standing before the window that muted all colors and sounds. Yes, weather, or yes, a sunset, she would say to herself at last, and remember that she should be fixing dinner.

"Do you ever want things to be different for us?" her husband asked her. They were in bed and the room was dark, but when she turned her head she thought she saw the liquid glimmer of his eyes.

"Different?"

"I mean, are you happy? I can't tell by watching you. If you'd only tell me, if there's anything you want me to do for you . . ."

"There's nothing," she said. "Nothing at all."

"If there's something I've been doing wrong, something you want changed. Please, don't be afraid to tell me."

She was so tired now. Sometimes it took her so long to understand what was being said to her, to pore over the words and turn them around into words of her own. Often by the time she'd done so things had moved on without her, as if she were lagging half a step behind and would never catch up. There was so much she had to puzzle over, to think through, and thinking was such an effort. She was always tired now.

"Please," her husband was saying, "please talk to me," and for a moment she could not remember words, why people strung them together like beads or hurled them at each other. She could not remember any of it. She struggled to sit up in bed, to see, but the room was only different textures of darkness, solid or filmy, like the rest of the world. Her husband's hand was stroking her face, and she felt the weight of it, and remembered the taste of him and their bodies moving together, but what was that for?

"Listen to me," her husband said. "You're going to be all right, I promise. We'll get help for you."

"I'm so tired," she said. How long had it taken her to speak?

"You have to trust me, though. You have to talk to me and tell me what's wrong."

And she would have liked to. But how could she say that someone had stolen away everything but the bare shapes of things? Voices reached her like echoes down a long tunnel. More and more often there were these moments in which she lacked both desire and understanding. I am afraid I'm losing my mind, she could say, but that would be almost funny. She had never imagined it could be so literally true. You lost things, like a pocket with a hole in it: feelings, hunger, words, meanings.

"What's that?" her husband said abruptly, and she realized she was humming, some scrap of a song. A slow tune with a catch to it, a single phrase, as if the notes had come to some obstruction and would not turn any further. It might have been an old hymn or a children's song, something that could neither be quite recognized nor quite forgotten. "Why are you doing that?" She shook her head, not wanting to interrupt the stream of music. It was so pleasant to have it coming out of its own accord, something she did not need to worry about. Her throat opened and she began to sing, delighting in the rich sound of it. "Of his bones are coral made," she sang. "Those are pearls that were his eyes."

His hand was cupping her chin, shaking the music to a stop. "Don't do that," he said.

"What?" She felt drowsy. She wondered if she had dozed off for a time. "What was I doing?"

"That song. It's— Why were you singing it?"

"I was singing? In my sleep?"

"You weren't asleep at all. You were just talking to me."

"Don't be silly." Another wave of drowsiness tugged at her. She yawned and reached for the pillow.

"Why were you singing that song?" her husband demanded, but she was already asleep.

It was several days later and they were walking on the beach, arm in arm like lovers or invalids. Her husband had arranged a vacation for them, a week at a seaside hotel that stayed open in the misguided hope of attracting late-year business. Besides themselves, the only other guests were a family of tourists who resembled nothing so much as a flock of migrating birds blown off course. One saw them huddling in the hotel's murky parlor, patiently working at a jigsaw puzzle (a brontosaurus rampant on a field of fern, three pieces missing), or on the beach trying to coax the meager, muddy sand into castles. The hotel itself was a fatigued structure of green-painted boards and low beamed ceilings and pervasive damp. Still, there was something hopeful and arousing about the rough clean sheets and the cold and the yellowing nautical maps on the walls, some novelty or promise of renewal that made them feel they had done the right thing in coming. The air itself might have been scrubbed clear for them, ready to be breathed for the first time.

The weather was somber but calm, and on this particular afternoon they walked for quite a long way on the shore. The ocean was dark jade with veins of dissolving foam. Sometimes they scrambled over ledge for as much as a quarter of a mile, sometimes they picked their way through the soft mud of tidal pools, and once a heron flew out of a tree above them, creaking and sawing at the air. They stopped at the edge of a cove where the land turned to marsh, and sat on a flat rock to rest.

"I'm glad we're here," said her husband. "I'm glad we could get away from things. We both needed it."

"We both needed it," she agreed. She was digging at the sand with a stick, trying to dislodge a dark blue mussel shell at her feet.

"Those shoes aren't made for climbing, you know. You could have hurt yourself."

"Well, but I didn't. They're fine."

"I want to tell you something. I want this to be a kind of a new start for us, right from this moment. Darling?"

She had succeeded in prying the shell up and now she was rubbing the sand from it, smoothing it with her fingers. "Do you think people can ever do that?"

"What?"

"You know. Start over. Do you think that's really possible?"

"Of course it is. If we want it to be, then it is."

She only smiled and looked out at the ocean, where a thin, cottony fog was just beginning to form at the horizon. "Darling?" he said. "What are you thinking of?"

"You really want to know?"

"Of course I do. I want to know everything that's important to you."

"Oh." She shrugged. "I was just thinking of the maps of the ocean they have back in the hotel. All the things they've charted, the numbers—soundings, I guess. There's not an inch of this coast they haven't marked. All those little curved lines look like fingerprints, don't they? And all the currents and banks and breakwaters. And—oh, it's silly."

"No," he urged her. "Go ahead, tell me."

"Just that it doesn't seem possible they could do that, I mean, mark everything so exactly."

"They have special equipment. Sonar and things."

"I suppose. But when you think of all the water in the world, how much there is. It's mostly water, isn't it? The earth's surface I mean. Like our bodies are. And it's the same water everywhere, really. If you dropped a bottle in the ocean, theoretically it could turn up anyplace, even on the other side of the world. Of course by then it wouldn't even look like a bottle any more. It'd be all barnacled, and maybe some strange sea-plant growing inside of it. Well anyway. That's what I was thinking."

From somewhere quite close, perhaps just beyond the far edge of the cove, a foghorn sounded. It boomed and echoed, deadening all other sounds. While it blew it was impossible to remember there had ever been such a thing as silence. A flock of herring gulls wheeled out to sea in alarm, but even their voices were pale by comparison.

"So I was wondering," she continued. "If there aren't some things you can't get away from, no matter where you go. Like the water. Like—things you've done or said."

"I think we should be getting back now," he said after a moment. "We have a long way to go."

"Let me sit and rest a minute longer. I'm still a little tired."

The foghorn sounded again. It was not only the tremendous booming noise of it that dismayed the ear, but the knowledge that it would continue to sound over and over, at the same interval and with the same exact voice.

"Listen," her husband said. "I've told you. I want things to change for us. I'm willing to change. I'll do everything I can to make you happy." He held out his hand but she did not take it.

"I'm tired."

"We can rest a little on the way. Let's get a move on, OK?"

Her eyes were closed and she clasped her knees as if protecting them. Her hair was lank from the damp air, and it did not move even in the wind.

"Do you really believe," he began, but the foghorn drowned him out. "Do you really believe there are things we can't undo? That we can't ever make right? Do you honestly, honestly believe that?"

She looked up for just long enough to speak. A lock of hair slid into the corner of her mouth. "Yes, I do."

"That's cruel," he said in a loud, hopeless voice. "It's cruel to feel that way. Or to say it, no matter how you feel."

"It's the truth."

"It's cruel," he repeated, looking around him at sky and bare rock and water, as if some help might yet come from them. "No matter what I've done, the worst thing is not to forgive. What is it you want? What do you want from me?"

"That's always what it comes down to for you, doesn't it? What people want from you. How much it will cost." Her voice turned suddenly breezy, affectionate. "Ah, poor old sport. People just won't ever shut up and behave themselves, will they? They're always getting messy on you."

"Don't," he said. "Don't talk like that."

"It's so hard for you, sport. It always was. You took yourself so damned seriously. You disapproved so much of anyone making a fool of themselves, well, I'm sorry. I guess I was a fool, by anyone's lights. But you made me ashamed. I wasn't ashamed of myself until I saw how you felt."

"Stop talking like that," he commanded, but she put a finger to her lips mischievously. Her knees were still drawn up to her chest and she rocked back and forth, smiling with some private amusement. The fog was rolling towards them, indeed, seemed to have already crept up behind them and was tangling itself in the thick brush. "Who are you?"

"You would not love me back."

"Terry?"

"You would not love me."

"I *couldn't*. I couldn't feel that way for you. It was wrong, we would have both been sorry. Can't you see that? What should I have done?"

"You would not love me."

"Please," he said desperately. "Please come away." But they were on an island of colorless rock in a white cloud sea, and the horn sounded again and again, without mercy.

THE BEST
IT COULD BE

Larrabee was a city boy, and had been all his life, but the city did not really seem his until he began to make money. He worked in an investment firm. The ways in which money could be prodded and coaxed into multiplying itself delighted him. He was twenty-six and it seemed a very good age. His face, when he contemplated it after shaving, would not always be this young, this pink and fragrant, unmarked by anything but expectation. He knew this, but he settled for reminding himself of it occasionally rather than believing it. There were some mornings, the best and most hopeful of times, when he stood on a street corner and felt he could have seized a coil of sparkling air in his hands and snapped it in two. And surely money would spurt out like a fountain or a pulse; money was everywhere, pushing and whispering at him. Larrabee would not have said that money was the most important thing to him. But he was gratified at how easy it made all the other things. Money, and sometimes the lack of money, he decided, was the smell of the city: of cars in the street, and new clothes, and pale-carpeted rooms and the women who lived in them. Poverty smelled of damp newspapers, or whiffs of hot frying food that reminded you of your own hunger. There were certain sidewalks, certain dark underpasses where the lack of money smelled so violently it choked you. Larrabee had known such places without knowing exactly why they made him sweat and sicken and feel as if his very life was about to spill out onto the soiled ground. Now he understood it as the fear of dying without ever having known just what it was you longed for, the fear that the richness of the world was not meant for you. Sometimes he felt, superstitiously, that things might never again be quite as good for him as they were right now.

He sat in the bar of a large hotel, a place of such theatrical elegance that he found it difficult at first to feel anything but amusement. Such carnivorous-looking potted plants, such an abundance of brass and wine-colored suede, such tender and beatific waitresses: could one really take such a place seriously? He had come with a friend from work. They were friends without being intimates. Their conversation had a pleasing courtesy to it, a deference they both enjoyed. Larrabee weighed the moment as he did the thick dimpled glass in his hand, and asked himself, as he often did, if this was the best it could be. And the answer came back no, not quite, not yet. He would have liked to have a woman with him, for one thing. And he was always a little uncomfortable with such extravagance as this. He tried to spend himself freely, out of respect to whatever generous god or luck had brought him this far, but some more cautious part of his nature refused to let go entirely. Still, he thought, nodding at the halos of soft pink light on the ceiling, it was not bad. It was not bad at all.

"You know what I've been thinking?" his friend said suddenly. "I've been thinking about fishing. Up in Canada someplace. One of those blue lakes with forty miles of pine forest around it. For breakfast every morning you have fresh trout cooked with cornmeal and bacon, and fried potatoes, and coffee. Have you ever been in a canoe? Is it hard to learn that stuff?"

Larrabee said that he never had, but he imagined it wasn't too hard to learn. "That would be the life," the man said. "That would be the ticket." His friend sank back into his chair with an air of grievance, as if the taste of that morning trout was an inheritance to be forever and unjustly denied him. But Larrabee thought of the wealth of possible dreams and visions, and how one need never worry about exhausting them.

At the next table, a man in an improbable gray velvet jacket was saying, "A plague on both your houses. Give me scope. Give me music. I want to scratch where I itch." His arm swung outward and the drink in his hand showered over Larrabee's neck.

The coldness and the drenching smell of Bourbon distracted him from everything else. He was aware of chairs scraping, and a waitress dabbing at him with a towel, and a woman's drawling voice: "Give you *elbow* room, sweetheart." Larrabee heard himself saying there was no harm done, and there wasn't really, except for the brief submerging of his dignity. The man in the velvet jacket proved to be tall. He peered down at Larrabee with the precarious, hostile concentration of the near-drunk. "Oh balls," he announced distinctly. Larrabee saw that a number of possibilities shimmered in the air: he might hit the other man, or the man hit him, or it might all be shrugged off, or what actually happened, that he would be invited to sit with them.

There were five or six of them at the table. He found himself immediately in their midst, as if his immersion had been a tribal rite of initiation. Someone thumped him on the back; someone else ordered a drink for him. Larrabee looked around for his friend, but he'd slipped away. A woman, perhaps the same one who had spoken before, said "What else can we do for you? Set fire to your tie, perhaps?"

"We usually save the tie flambé for birthdays," said a man across from Larrabee. "But what the hell. Just this once."

Larrabee smiled and accepted the new drink and tried to sort them out individually. All he could manage was a collective impression of cigarette smoke and faces nodding at him with mild good will. The man who had spilled his drink was seated to Larrabee's right. "I bet you think I'm a real oaf," he said moodily. "I bet you think I go around squirting people with seltzer bottles or something."

"Of course not," said Larrabee. He recognized the signs of mixed belligerence and apology. "I did the same thing myself once, but to a woman. Dumped a whole piña colada down the front of her dress. She went off like a siren." In fact, he had only sloshed a little of the drink, and the woman had laughed and put her hand on her breast where the wetness had soaked through. He had watched that hand and its soft probing and knew at that moment he could have her if he wanted, and indeed that was the way it happened. The truth made a better story then the one he had invented, but it was not a story he could tell to strangers.

The man nodded and his fierceness seemed to lose focus. Larrabee decided he resembled a ruined cathedral, or some such grand decay. Age had given his rather preposterous good looks a historical or guidebook status. It was a massive, exaggerated face, sullen in repose, a face weary with the effort of accepting attention. Now he turned to Larrabee and extended his hand. "Franklin Bowie."

"Franklin Roosevelt Bowie," someone corrected, as Larrabee too announced himself. "He'll tell you that sooner or later. That and his Djuna Barnes story."

"It's a good story," retorted Franklin Bowie. "Your waspish presence would only spoil it."

Larrabee did not know who Djuna Barnes was and it seemed that he would not be enlightened at present. He wondered who these people were, so glib, so pleased with themselves and their surroundings. The women were all formidably dressed and embellished, so intricately composed of scent and polish and colors that Larrabee found it difficult to tell if they were really beautiful or not. They were all older too, he decided, by which he meant older than himself. Bowie was the only one of the group who looked unequivocally middle-aged. Larrabee guessed him to be forty-five, although he realized he was the sort of man who might have looked forty-five for the last ten years.

"Tell me," said one of the women, leaning towards Larrabee and presenting him with such quantities of teeth and bosom and jewelry that he actually had to blink his eyes in order to hear properly. "Tell me something about yourself that will amuse and delight me."

She was beautiful, Larrabee decided. Her hair was red and smooth and it swung heavily against her throat like a bell. "I love red hair," he said, and she laughed and said he should tell her more. The low neck of her dress had silver and gold threads woven through it and when she squeezed her shoulders together, the light rippled and swam. Larrabee had an impulse to rest his forehead against her and let the spangles wash over him.

Franklin Bowie, on his right, dropped a hand to Larrabee's shoulder. Once in place the hand seemed immovable, a permanent fixture. "My young friend," he said. "May I call you that? May I presume? Let's have a serious conversation. Let us drink deep and swear mighty oaths. Fie upon this quiet life. We should live intensely and with a wild poetry."

"He always talks like this," said the red-haired woman. "Don't mind him."

"Beneath my histrionics, I am a deeply discontented man. No shit."

The red-haired woman gave the impression of elbowing Bowie aside, though she had really only shifted in her chair. "Do you like this bar? Sometimes I think it's a little stuffy."

Larrabee considered. "It makes me think of Disneyland. Or something in a museum. American Interior, Late Twentieth Century. It's not quite real."

She laughed, then drew her eyebrows together to show that she was being serious. "Why?" she demanded.

"Oh, I don't know," he began lamely, but the others were listening and he amended himself. "Because it's all so perfect. Nothing could ever really be this perfect. Everyone looks happy. It's always five o'clock on a Friday afternoon, and no one will ever have to drink alone. That's how it makes you feel, at least. And we can sit here and feel benevolent about life. We can afford to. That's what a place like this does for you."

He waved his hand to encompass the room's mellow light and accumulated glossy and plush surfaces. He was tempted to go on and talk about himself, how unlikely it was for him to be there in the first place amid the elaborate trappings of affluence. It was not so long ago that he lived with his family in rooms that seemed to shrink each time you entered them. He still remembered, indeed was unable to forget, the smell and texture of the brown soap they had used down to its last unyielding sliver. He wanted to tell them this and more. He recognized it as the liquor cresting within him, and besides, he was afraid he'd already broken their good humor, speaking too seriously. But their faces were grave and soft, contented with this agreeable melancholy.

"We have here," said Franklin Bowie to the other, "the child Jesus in the temple. Speaking wisdom to the elders."

"Let's adopt him."

"We'll give him everything we never had."

"We'll be fair but firm with him."

They decided to go to another bar after that. Larrabee sat in the back seat of a cab between Bowie and another man. He felt somewhat cramped, but also enclosed, supported by them. He was a little drunker than he liked to be. Bowie was talking about flying. Larrabee was not at all sure why. He seemed to have rather lost track of things. "When I dream of flying," Bowie was saying, "I never imagine myself as a bird. I'm still human, but more compact, somehow, and infinitely more graceful. None of this silly arm-flapping business. Everything below me is like a storybook landscape, tidy and exquisite. And I never, ever dream I'm falling. No Icarus. What do you suppose that means?"

"You're too full of hot air," suggested the man on Larrabee's other side. He was munching a ham sandwich he'd sent the waitress out for, and he offered Larrabee half. "I think it means," said Bowie, inclining his formidable head, "that I'm immortal. Possibly omnipotent. Such a comfort."

Larrabee wondered where they were going. He hoped the new place would feature gangsters or perhaps leopards on leashes, something unimaginably exotic. He peered out the black windows at the strange refracted streets, everything flattened by darkness and the layer of shining glass, lights overlaid with lights, all of it streaming effortlessly past them, and he tried to decide why he was so happy. There seemed to be no particular reason he could point to, no mathematical proof for it. The evening was a pure gift; he had not earned it. But after all, what right had one to anything? To this body encased in shining skin, its warmth and strength and singing nerves? What right to sit in pleasant rooms and think well of other people and have them think well of you, what right to the luxuries of emotion? Life, he thought mazily, life, but he could push his thought no further. He felt as if anything could happen, anything at all, and he would welcome it. He had only to wait for it. He had only to be unafraid. At that moment the cab made a strange, digestionlike noise, and slid into the curb. The tires scraped hard.

"Are we there?" asked the man with the sandwich, and Larrabee replied that they did not seem to be anywhere. The streets had stopped their smooth motion. The cab had come to rest in a neighborhood, if it could be called that, of blind anonymous structures, warehouses, he guessed. His stomach folded softly in on itself. It was not, he knew, a place one would have chosen to have a breakdown. The streetlights' angry pink glare made the shadows of doorways and corners shimmer, as if they contained other, more amorphous and menacing darknesses. Not another car was in sight.

They all began talking at once, in rather high and foolish voices. "What's the matter?" "Where are we?" "I say, Ollie, this is another fine mess you've gotten us into." The driver said nothing. He was an impassive, elderly black man whose silence was somehow more disquieting. Now he cranked the ignition with the stolidity of the mechanically ignorant, until the starter began to bark and gasoline perfumed the air. The driver's name, Larrabee read, was Augustine Bethune. He had given up on grinding the starter and was sitting very straight and helpless behind the wheel. Larrabee did not know where they had been going, so he could not judge why they were in such a place. But it seemed unlikely it was on the way to anywhere at all. The cab had simply broken down before they'd had a chance to get thoroughly lost.

"I say," Franklin Bowie repeated, more plaintively now. "What seems to be the problem?"

Augustine opened the cab door and got out. The sudden flood of light revealed his dark, mutely sorrowing face and graying close-cropped hair. He did not look like a man who took misfortunes lightly. They watched him tug at the hood, which would not open, and carefully examine the tires wedged against the curb. Then he got back inside. "Cab broke," he announced.

"Well, fix cab," said the man with the sandwich. He had produced a bottle of dark beer from one pocket and an opener from the other and was busy working on the cap. But the driver was conferring with the radio. The three in the back seat listened.

"What language do you suppose he's speaking?"

"Druid. All the new drivers are Druids these days."

"Do you suppose they understand him?"

"I hope so," Larrabee said. A barrage of static came out of the dashboard.

"I'll bet he's straight from the islands. I'll bet he just learned how to *drive*, for Christ's sake," said Franklin Bowie. He leaned forward and tapped the man on the shoulder. *"Alors. Qu'est-ce que se passe?"*

The driver only raised mournful, bruised-looking eyes to the mirror. It was difficult to tell if this paralytic gloom was his normal state, or if the situation had reduced him to it. They felt obliged to console him, as if for some personal loss.

"I say, old man, it wasn't your fault."

"Really, they won't blame you for it. These things happen."

Augustine shook his head, but it was impossible to say if he were disagreeing with them, or only expressing a general negativity. Being deprived of his native speech, whatever that was, seemed to invest his silence with a portentous quality. He wore a lumpy brown suitcoat that gave off a faint but permanent smell of closet. Now his shoulder blades moved in the same eloquent, untranslatable gesture. To live is but to suffer, he might have been saying, or, As flies to wanton boys are we to the gods.

"So now what do we do?"

"Stand fast. Smokem if you gotem."

"Where in East Jesus are we, anyway?"

Larrabee found that he did not know, exactly, although he prided himself on never getting lost. The street was long and unadorned by signs. The sky was pink and impermeable. Far ahead he saw what might have been the motion of traffic, like fish glinting dimly in an aquarium. He felt the need to urinate, mild at first, then increasing in geometrical proportion.

Ten minutes or so passed. The situation reminded Larrabee of children playing at travel with lines of kitchen chairs. "Look," he said. "I don't care what's out there. It's better than waiting."

The others agreed. "But what about him?" said Bowie, indicating the front seat.

"I guess he has to stay here. The captain going down with his ship and all that. We should ask him, though."

Bowie opened the back door and cautiously unfolded himself. *"Allons,"* they heard him say. *"Vamanos."* The driver did not move.

Larrabee and the other man emerged. The night air was cold and smelled chemical and unclean. Larrabee looked behind him at the hollow, infinitely receding shadows. Nothing. He was spooking himself. Pussy. Nya nya. Show a little spunk. "Goodbye," Bowie was saying. *"Reservoir. Chevrolet."*

They began walking, single file in an untidy marching fashion. Larrabee, who was last, looked back at the cab's hulk. There was something unexpectedly forlorn and derelict about it. He was reminded of the abandoned dead on a battlefield. He pumped his arms to try and warm himself, and trudged on. They had not gone half a block when the cab door slammed and Augustine emerged. They halted and watched him approach. He appeared to be trying to run, but in a jerky, stiff legged fashion that resembled a water bird on land.

"H'lo," Franklin Bowie called to him. "Coming along, are you?"

/143/

Augustine stopped an arm's length away from them, wheezing. The air was cold enough so that his breath was visible, pink-tinted puffs of frost that diminished gradually until he was able to speak. "Eight dollar," he said.

"He wants a *fare?*" said the man with the sandwich. "For getting lost and trashing the cab, he wants money?"

"Eight dollar," repeated Augustine, though less insistently. Pink sweat was beading along his forehead. Standing next to them, he seemed more insubstantial than ever, a heap of clothing loosely wired together.

Franklin Bowie shook his head. "Sorry. Service has not been rendered. Unfortunate for us all."

Augustine dropped to his knees on the sidewalk. Or so one would have said his intention was. He more resembled a man entering the too-hot water of a bathtub. The effort was considerable, and involved much repositioning of trousers and heels. Only when everything else was in place did he arrange his hands as in prayer, and gaze up at them. His face was docile, even expectant, but his hands knotted and clenched. He might have been trying to wring speech out of them. You see, his hands might have been saying, you see what a pass one can come to.

Somebody coughed. The temperature dropped another notch, and their pink breaths churned around them like their embarrassment made visible. Finally Larrabee reached for his wallet. The folded bills looked snug and plump, like birds in a nest.

"It's a hustle," warned the man with the sandwich. "He dresses up like a pitiful old man and makes a dozen trips over here a night."

The thought had in fact occurred to Larrabee, but he had decided it didn't really matter. He was merely purchasing a clean conscience. He was merely being a consumer. He drew out a handful of bills without counting. There were several tens among them. All of a sudden, he felt foolish. "Here," he said, thrusting the money forward. "Here, for God's sake, get up."

They heard the old man's breath leaking from his chest, heard his knees popping. Larrabee could not remember when he had felt more uncomfortable. "Here," he repeated, and mashed the bills into Augustine's hand. It was a thin and unprotesting hand, light as a wing. "Try not to get mugged, OK?"

They watched Augustine go through a rapid facial pantomime, hooding his eyes and exhaling pinkly. It was less gratitude than shame, and less shame than caution. The hand that held the money clenched tighter. He ducked his head and loped back to the cab.

"Watch," said the man with the sandwich. "He'll start the damned thing up and drive away."

But nothing on the street moved. It was impossible, at this distance, to see beyond the cab's gleaming windows. They stared after it, feeling disappointed, though they would have found it difficult to say why. Bowie put a hand once more on Larrabee's shoulder. "A quixotic gesture," he said approvingly.

"It's only money," said Larrabee.

"You know those experiments where they rig electrodes to the pleasure centers of rats' brains?" Franklin Bowie was saying. "And the little beasts exhaust themselves with leaping at the stimulus buttons? That's me. The rat in bliss. Aren't we having a wonderful time?"

"Wonderful," said Larrabee promptly. He was eating scrambled eggs and sausage and hash browns. He couldn't remember food tasting better. They were sitting at the counter of an all-night restaurant, Breakfast Anytime, and drinking coffee from thick china mugs. The third man had left in another cab. They'd shaken hands and wished him Godspeed. "One more traveler to that distant bourne from which some travelers don't return," the man had said, regarding the cab with some wariness. "Oh well. Hi ho."

Bowie motioned to the waitress for more coffee. She hurried towards him with the dazzling impatience usually seen in lovers reuniting in airports, and Bowie smiled engagingly at her as she poured. Larrabee sensed that he was always thus wooing people, always coaxing their attention towards himself. It came almost too easily for him. He would do it involuntarily, a little perversely even, for what could one do with such quantities of attention, such wasteful portions of it, besides push it away eventually in a fit of impatience? The waitress's face, seen through the rising column of steam, was demure, and when she turned away from them her walk had grown indolent. But Bowie was already swinging around on his stool. "It would be nice to be sober," he said, "because then we could start drinking all over again."

Larrabee agreed. He no longer really felt drunk, though he knew inductively he must be. He felt like a TV screen between channels, all fizzing static. He was surprised to see that it was only one o'clock. There were hours and hours left for them to disport in, should they so desire, and the thought suddenly wearied him. Maybe he should go home. Leave them while they're laughing. As if he'd sensed Larrabee's thought, and wanted to distract him, Bowie leaned towards him confidentially. "Have you ever done anything illegal?"

"Huh?"

"Have you ever broken any laws. I mean something flamboyant. Downright criminal."

Larrabee considered. "No felonies," he admitted. "How come?"

/145/

"Just curious. Just making conversation. It seems like an important thing to know about somebody."

"Oh. Well, what about you?"

"Mail fraud," said Franklin Bowie. "But that was a long time ago."

"Sure."

"If I had it to do all over again, I'd choose highway robbery. It has more panache."

"There's a lot to be said for highway robbery," agreed Larrabee.

"Now we know all each others' secrets. Now we're blood brothers."

"Sure."

"We're blood brothers," Bowie informed a passing waitress. "We went to Camp Winnemucca together. I taught him how to spit."

"Sure," said the waitress.

"What else can we talk about. Let's keep talking. Let's go do something illegal. The important thing in life is to experience everything. Aren't we having an outrageous good time?"

"Outrageous," agreed Larrabee.

"You think I drink too much, don't you. Everybody does."

"I wouldn't know, really."

"You don't have to be polite. I drink too much."

"You drink too much, Bowie."

"I like drinking too much. I like all forms of wretched excess. Ah, my young friend. I know how I seem. A capering old drunk. But it's one way of convincing yourself you're still alive. You get to that point, you know? You wouldn't know. You start wondering if you've used everything up already, people, words, feelings, so you have to keep going out and finding more. Amen. I'm only being maudlin. Drink up, drink up."

Although it was only coffee, Larrabee drank obediently. When he looked up again, Bowie seemed to have recovered his cheerfulness. He looked as he had all evening, worn and even a little battered, as if being a fading beauty was an effort, something one had to work at aggressively. And work and work. Wretched excess. The fatigue which had only nudged at Larrabee before swept over him in a wave.

Bowie too drained his coffee and rose to his feet, sighing. "Well, enough of all that. I suppose now I have to take you home for Alicia."

"What," said Larrabee, but Bowie was already striding away towards the door, where he turned and beckoned. Take him where? Larrabee's feet were unsteady beneath him when he stood. Who was Alicia, and why was one compelled to procure people for her? Perhaps he had not heard correctly. It sounded too predatory.

"Listen," he said when he'd caught up with Bowie on the sidewalk. "I'd love to keep this up. It'd be terrific. But I really have to be getting home."

"Of course you do," Bowie reassured him. He was scanning the street, and his arm shot up to hail a taxi. "Just a quick stop, that's all we'll make. It's on your way."

"You don't know where I live," said Larrabee, but when confronted with the open door of the cab, he was too tired to protest further. He felt like a domestic animal artfully herded. "Who's Alicia?" he asked, but Bowie was instructing the driver and did not answer. Larrabee closed his eyes. The seat cushions were well sprung and infinitely yielding. The cab began to move. The back seat spun slowly. Once more he was being borne away. Franklin Bowie was humming. Larrabee recognized it as "On, Wisconsin." Some time later he opened his eyes and looked blearily about him. Revolving shadows flickered over his face, and in the front the driver was a hunched shadow silhouetted in the green glow from the dash. Bowie noticed him and nodded. "Resting up a bit," he said. "Very wise."

"Who's Alicia?" asked Larrabee, but Bowie had begun to hum again, beating time with his hand flat on the seat between them. Larrabee closed his eyes once more.

When he opened them, the cab was stopped in front of a gray, castle-like structure. It was only a townhouse on a city street, he realized a moment later, but his first impression was one of turrets and casements, floating lights and oaken doors. It looked, unsurprisingly, expensive. Bowie's head appeared at the open door of the cab. "*Nous sommes arrivé.* I claim this sidewalk in the name of the Emperor. C'mon."

"Where are we?" asked Larrabee, but by this time he did not really expect an answer.

The front door opened into a foyer whose black-and-white tiled floor strobed and swam beneath him. A light burned down a far corridor, but the rest of the house was in cavelike shadow. He was vaguely aware of stairs before him, and other corridors branching off. Bowie had preceded him, thrusting the door open carelessly, as if it had not been locked at all. "Hup, hup, hup." Now, when Larrabee looked around, Bowie had disappeared. "Bowie?" His voice bounced foolishly off the tiles, alarming him. He wondered who else lived here. It occurred to him that Bowie himself might not even live here.

Sweat bloomed under his arms. "Bowie," he called again, but softly this time. Elaborate paranoia seized him. For a moment he breathed as if through layers of gauze. He remembered their silly talk about doing something criminal. It was a burglary. A practical joke. It was a set-up, part of some monstrous con job. The foyer had a high table on which were displayed some bits of Oriental pottery. They were no doubt valuable antiques, Larrabee thought, and so strong was his confusion and imagined guilt that he fingered one of them as if he would indeed thrust it into a pocket.

But the house remained silent, and his head cleared a little. The front door still hung open on the frosty night. The cab had gone. Larrabee closed the door. The reasonable thing would be to find out where he was and call another cab, or otherwise make his way home. He walked cautiously down the hallway towards the lighted room. He felt calmer and more purposeful, but the impression he'd had of the house as a castle returned to him. He thought of secret rooms and winding stairs, of enchantments and magical tokens, or rather, he thought of none of these things, only a vague storybook memory brought on by darkness and fatigue.

The room he came to was ordinary enough, and empty. Two lamps and a chandelier blazed in the silence. The furniture was upholstered in apricot silk, conversational groupings of couches and chairs. There was gilt, and brass, and glass, and a variety of other textures susceptible to polishing. It appeared to be one of those extraneous rooms found in the homes of the rich, who can afford to maintain rooms in which one does nothing. There was a little desk against one wall, but it was as blank and burnished as the rest of the furniture and gave no clue of where he was.

Although he had heard no sound, he turned. In the doorway stood a tall old lady in an Oriental robe of midnight blue and silver. "A nice cup of tea," she said coaxingly. "How does that sound."

"Excuse me. . . . I came with ah . . ." He was unable to remember Bowie's name.

The old lady shook her head. Her hair was long and sparse and white, and it floated for a moment after she had stopped, like a dandelion gone to seed. "A nice cup of tea," she repeated, and motioned for Larrabee to follow her.

He bumped hard against the walls of the corridor this time. The old lady was a blur of darkness and silver ahead of him, and though she appeared far away, like a figure seen through the wrong end of a telescope, at one point he tripped over the hem of her robe. "Sorry," he said, but by then she was already far away again. He thought he heard her laugh.

They emerged into a small kitchen with a kettle already purring on the electric stove, and a bamboo tray beside it holding a Japanese tea set. "Lapsang souchong," she said.

"Huh?"

"It's Lapsang souchong tea. Do you like it? Some people don't care for the smoky taste, I know."

"S'fine," said Larrabee. He felt hilariously relieved to find that she was in fact speaking something comprehensible. There was a stool before him and he sat on it, but retaining his balance was so difficult that he stood again. "Where's Bowie?" he asked.

"You needn't worry about him. I've locked him in the bathroom."

"Beg pardon?"

"He's perfectly all right in there. Really. There's even a radio."

"Yes, but—"

"You could go say good-night to him, but I wouldn't advise it. Those are the only times he really hurts himself, when he tries to get out."

He could not decide if she was Bowie's wife or his mother. Her face was soft and shapeless, as if age had tugged it in one direction and she, resisting, in another, and the skin had given up entirely during the struggle. Deep ruddled lines extended from her nose to her jaw. She smiled at him over the tea tray. Her teeth were long and bluish. "Sugar?"

"No thank you." He watched her fold back the sleeve of her kimono to pour, a gesture that was both coquettish and antique. The cups had no handles; he scalded his palms. He disliked tea intensely, and this tasted thin and burnt. He put the cup down. "I really feel I ought to explain."

"Don't." Again she smiled bluely at him. "Don't even tell me your name. I assure you, it's not at all important."

"We were riding in a cab together, Franklin and I," (but hadn't that been much earlier?), "and the cab broke down. An accident."

"There are no such things as accidents," she informed him. "We do not live in a random universe."

Larrabee had to pee again.

"Nothing is without purpose. Nothing is meaningless. It took me years to learn that. I tell it to you now, as a gift."

"Thank you," said Larrabee.

"It took me years to learn to accept the physical body and its weaknesses. I had always attempted to transcend it. But now I can celebrate even the most degrading animal processes. I think of our lives as prisms, splitting sunlight into rainbows, and each band of color is necessary for the Whole."

She had closed her eyes to speak. Her shaggy eyebrows lifted and her voice grew flutey. He thought it best to humor her. "That's very interesting."

/149/

"You're humoring me," the old lady said. "Don't patronize me, you son of a bitch. I don't have to put up with it. I could have your head on a plate if I wanted. I could have you eaten up and spit out."

Somehow, he found the front door. The house was dense with silence, but as he stumbled he imagined screams exploding in the blind space around him, alarms going off, pits opening beneath his feet. He leaped for the sidewalk and it rose to meet him.

He felt cold air along his spine, and discovered that his jacket had split down the back. One ankle throbbed like a drum. Larrabee picked himself up and gave a good imitation of a man briskly setting himself to rights in case anyone was watching. But the house behind him was as closed and indifferent to him as its neighbors were. The sky was still stained pink, although now it was the sun that colored it, rolling over a horizon he could not see. He set out walking east.

He would find his way home somehow, and sleep, and send his jacket out to be mended. He would try and tell his friends about this evening, he supposed, but he knew he would never get it all right. The sun was visible now, a bulb of milky radiance. Windows in its path turned to sudden gold, a shifting and liquid brilliance as if the light were rolling about on a plate. The houses Larrabee trudged past wrapped him in long blue shadows. Within them, he wanted to believe, were lives as unimaginable as his own. He would never be able to tell it all right. There was simply too much. There was always too much. He felt a crowding in his chest, as if a multitude of hearts had come to roost there, as if they would lift him up by their beating to startle the sooty pigeons on the roofs. He turned his head from one side to the other, blinded by watery gold. For a moment he saw the world before him as God might, shimmering within a single perfect teardrop, finite and containable. But the sun's angle shifted and the light receded and in another instant it had all quite gone.

DANNY'S CHICK

is this skinny white girl called Tina. Not pretty. Danny's friends give him some shit at first. How she so plain, plain as cement sidewalk. Plain as bread crust. But they freeze that talk now when Danny come around, he won't hear it. Don't know about that boy. That boy in love he think. Think he going to live on love. What his friends say to each other when they fill up the afternoons with talk about money, mostly, and women some, filling up rooms with TV noise and floating smoke and sandwich wrappers. Shaking their heads. Think he in love, oh my.

is one of those girls you see slouching along on the street, one of those thin sullen acned tubercular girls in jeans gone nearly white around the seams from wear, and boots and a shirt meant to look tough and a head of hair that's all wrong somehow, like they found it growing on another head. You see a girl like that and you sigh, *oh yes*, you know all about such girls and their purses full of cigarettes and staling drugstore candy, their heads full of trashy songs or maybe it's that they live inside the songs, who can tell which. They always look a little unclean, such girls, like you could run them through a car wash and they'd still come out looking less than clean. It's the skin that defeats them, that damp pale patchy skin. Oh yes, you've seen these girls before, you've read about them in the Sunday newspaper magazine section, their furtive rebellious pre-delinquent lives, their contributions to the alarming rise in illiteracy/illegitimacy/drug abuse/venereal disease. You think you know all about them but you don't. You wouldn't know Tina, who at least has nice hair, bright yellow-brown and long. And who doesn't get high, doesn't drink anything but sometimes rum-and-coke and once a margarita but she didn't like it.

What's more, she comes from a home that is not only respectable, but prosperous. She had to work at looking like the child of unemployed urban Appalachian-transplant trash, had to study the clothes and the walk and the tough bored face. (Such girls examine themselves critically in mirrors. And there are times when they can stand or smile a certain way and decide they look exactly right. Something you wouldn't know about them, watching them on the street, that they're carrying in their head a shadowy image of themselves looking exactly right.) It all drives her parents crazy. The clothes and the cigarettes and the music have sprouted like the symptoms of a disease, and nothing has been able to prevent it, not years of roast beef dinners or enriched cultural background. Nothing immunizes children against adolescence. The way she looks is bad enough but the boys are worse. The parents know they're worse because they never see them. There are only phone calls and cars roaring out of the driveway like derelict rockets and her stories about where she's been that they don't believe a word of. All boys are bad but the ones you don't see are the worst, they feel instinctively, and you'd have to say they're right, at least about Danny.

Who's black as a hat. Blacker than his own shadow. Not one of your light bright boys, not a cup of coffee with half a cup of cream, but black. Tina's father tells this joke to company:

Why did the nigger wear a tuxedo to his vasectomy?

Because the doctor told him he was going to be impotent, and he wanted to look impotent.

Which is really a good one if you think about it. What else can you say. Those jokes are another thing we think we know all about. We either tell them or we don't. What you couldn't know is how Tina felt the first time Danny's head pushed against her chest. Scared. Something gone wrong. It felt rough and wirey, like some strange new animal. *This is crazy,* she thought, and she tried to push him away. Crazy, to be frightened of hair. There's a joke in there somewhere. Hair jokes lip jokes nose jokes watermelon jokes. Sambo jokes coon jokes dark meat light meat jokes. Every nigger joke she's ever heard, trying to push her off that bed where she'd thought she'd wanted to be. *Crazy,* and then just in time she made herself stop thinking.

Danny's got his own flat. A dump, but they like it just fine. Sometimes the two of them, him and Tina, spend all day just sleeping and waking up and sleeping again and listening to the box and Tina cooks things like pork chops and eggs. They like it just fine. Even the smell of it seems good to them, a smell of laundry, sex, furnace, smoke, and sweet hair oil. It's their own smell after all, their own place and they can do whatever they want. Which is usually going to bed but not today. Today they're trying to decide what to do about Claude.

Danny's sitting on the couch, Tina's in the beanbag chair. The color TV is on, one of the soaps, and the actors swim through bands of distortion that tint their skins violent orange or green. Tina says, Well, you could at least go talk to him again. Danny shakes his head. He's wearing a pair of old gray sweatpants and no shirt and it makes him look sort of fat though he isn't really. Shoot, he says. You been listening to me? No point talking to that nigger. He tell you anything you want to hear. Talk don't cost him nothing.

Claude's this friend of Danny owes him two hundred twenty dollars. It gets complicated. Claude said just til next payday but then he got himself fired. Then he says how his car needs fixing. That's some weak shit. Everybody's seen Claude's car on the streets, who'd miss it. Black-and-silver Oldsmobile Cutlass with the bad muffler. Imagine trying to sneak around town in a ride like that. So everybody knows Claude's full of it. And now Danny's rent's late, and the phone's already out, and the light-and-gas going any time, and Claude poor-mouthing all over town while he slides around in his big loud black-and-silver trashmobile. Some weak shit.

Something's got to be done. But right now Danny and Tina are watching the soaps and thinking, if you've got to have problems, they wish they had interesting sexy problems like these orange-and-green folks on the tube. Their problem is mostly Claude, but part of it's the two of them, and if they talk much it turns into a fight. So it's easiest just to watch TV. Danny's staring at the Crisco commercial. Orange fried chicken held in green hands. His stomach makes a noise like shifting gravel. Well maybe he is a little fat. He pulls at the waist of his sweatpants and counts three folds of belly piling up. It doesn't help his mood. He ought to be out running and shooting some hoop. Ought to clean up the crib so your bare feet don't stick to the floor. Look at this trash. Ought to get the phone back in. Ought to go see Claude. Everything's ought. He settles back into the couch, mad bored disgusted with it all, and Tina better not start in again. No ma'am. Just better not.

Claude's no good. That's what Tina thinks, and what she's said maybe a couple times too often. No good, you can tell just by looking at him. Little yellow-skinned monkeyish dude with sly bright eyes and a crooked smile. Maybe it's not his fault how he looks. Maybe some people are just born looking illegal. But he acts no good too, always either bragging or complaining, talking big or talking mean. Rolling his yellow eyes back in his head like he's got jokes too good to share, and Tina can just guess the sort of things he says behind her back, anyway, the very last person you'd ever lend money. Anybody'd see that in a minute. She can't understand why Danny's let it go on this long. If he gets kicked out of his place and has to move in with his mother what's going to happen to the two of them, and does he care at all? Look at him. Just plants himself on the couch all the livelong day, sometimes he makes her so mad she could just she doesn't know what.

She flips her hair back over her shoulders, a nervous habit. Every so often she finds herself chewing on damp strands without knowing how they got into her mouth. Danny and Claude. She shakes her head and more hair floats loose, beginning to get mussed. She doesn't understand those guys. Any of Danny's friends, it's something she can't get inside of. How they can sit and gossip and bullshit about each other, ten times worse than girls, or forget promises or even get into fights, and still it works out that they're friends. They fuss and carry on and just when you'd think they'd done something absolutely unforgivable, it's over like it never was. There's something in it that bothers her if she thinks about it too much. About why they stay friends. She can't decide if it's because they're all men, or because they're all black, like those are the really important things, the things he won't ever betray, and either way she's not a part of it. Can't ever be. Maybe you can learn *black*, at least the easy things like talk and music, but how could you ever learn *man*? Sometimes she thinks Danny's life, his real life must be something he does when he's away from her: loyalties and feuds and history and things happening all the time that she's not a part of. Jokes she can't understand, looks that turn into secrets. His real life is everything she's not. What he can always go back to, what draws the line. Man and woman? Black and white? She doesn't know. Such a lonesome feeling, and sometimes it makes her so blue that Danny says, like he does now, What's the matter with you?

Nothing.

So what's the *matter*?

He sounds mad but he's worried, mostly, she knows it, and she says Oh . . . and shrugs. She really can't explain it so he'd understand, it's all too sad, so she comes up with the easiest and the worst thing to say: It's just this business with Claude.

Danny says something that sounds like Hump, and pretends to watch TV again. He's thinking, she's got this attitude. He's thinking, it's not that simple. Nothing's ever as simple as Tina thinks it is. So Claude's sort of worthless. A friend's still a friend. Besides, it feels good to lend money. That's the part you don't always admit to. How it felt good to count off eleven new twenty dollar bills like you did it every day of the week. Here you go. Who'd ever think paper could feel and smell that good but it does, all cool and stiff and clean. There's nothing cleaner than new money. And Claude said Hey you done saved my ass, Danny, that's straight up, and Danny said It's cool, and they both had a beer and sat there feeling good about each other. So it's not just money, it's feeling, or maybe it's money that makes for feeling.

Tina wouldn't understand, he knows it. Money's just money to her. Something you spend or keep, something you have or haven't got. It's not that simple. She doesn't know how money can turn itself into anything it wants to, anything in the world, friend enemy mother lover hope no hope good or bad weather. The taste you get in your mouth just before you put food in it. A hand filled with its own reaching. All that's money. If he tried to explain she'd think he was just talking about greed, which is way different than talking about money. He tells himself she can't understand because she's young, but sometimes he thinks she'll never be any older. She won't have to be. She's a rich girl who can afford to look poor. A white girl who can pretend to be black, maybe color too comes down to money. And because he doesn't like thinking this way he says Come on. Let's get out of here.

Oh where we going, asks Tina, but he doesn't know himself so he doesn't say. Just heaves himself off the couch and starts padding around looking for clothes. Tina's ready to go before he is, as usual, and she stands by the door with her coat on. Automatically her eyes stray to the television. A blonde lady cries big blonde tears. Tina couldn't tell you what she's been crying about, though she's been watching the show all along. Maybe because she's orange and in love with somebody green? Tina's getting impatient waiting for Danny, who's always late, impatient to get out of the apartment. It seems suddenly overheated, and full of arguments waiting to happen. Sometimes it's better to be out on the street, even though she has to watch out for her parents, even when people yell Hey salt and pepper or worse. Sometimes that's better than what you don't say to each other.

Outside it's March and still cold. Thin trees and thin sunlight, frozen, Popsicle-blue sky. A winter's worth of beat-down trash in the gutters. Danny's car won't start at first. That's no surprise. Tina's father, he'd know with one look that he wouldn't want his daughter in this car. Old green Plymouth, half rust and half Bondo, one mashed front fender, one window taped together, a big wide fat low bumper-dragging wreck of a car with nigger music blasting from speakers in the back seat. Watch out, that car says. Here comes a load of bad-ass spades looking to rape knife shoot somebody or at least drive reckless and cause accidents or at the very least talk too loud and make a mess at the table next to yours in the Steak 'n' Shake. Watch out.

Danny pokes around under the hood while Tina waits inside

the car. She knows he'll fix it. He can fix lots of things with wires and parts and plugs. She likes that. She likes it when he gets all serious about fixing something, she even almost likes it when he ignores her at such times. She watches him frowning into the engine. He's got his coat unbuttoned and no hat or gloves and she can just imagine how cold he's getting. She's thinking he looks good out there. She thinks it's how a man ought to look, standing out in the cold and being serious about fixing something. Well, that's silly, but she knows what she means. Danny gets back in and cranks it up and the engine makes a sound like something trying very hard to remain dead and turns over. They're both glad. Not just about the car but because Danny fixed it, something he did and did right and they feel good about. Their quarrel hasn't entirely gone away, but the weight of it lifts a little.

Three o'clock in the afternoon. No place to go. The Plymouth leaves a trail of dark blue smoke and jazz, and somebody watching from the air would see it crossing and recrossing its own path, past gas stations and the Seven-Eleven and the metal-and-glass hutches selling cheap food. This is their country, if they have one. They are citizens of the afternoon fast-food strip, a territory of traffic and loose change. Anyone can walk into Burger King or Long John Silver's or Kentucky Fried, anyone and everyone does, coming and going, temporary, anonymous, always strangers. Nobody really belongs there, and Danny and Tina don't not belong much worse than anyone else. They fit in just as well as the fake fishnets and anchors hung on a wall a thousand miles away from ocean, or the sombreros and cactus of the taco stand. Today it's a steak house and cowboys.

Danny walks slow and Tina fast, so she has to do a little backwards dance to keep them together. It takes him a long time deciding on his food too. He frowns at the photographs of pink rubber steaks. Two forty-nine for a six-ounce rib-eye, two ninety-nine for the platter. Special dollar seventy-five ham-and-cheese with medium soft drink. Somewhere in there, he knows, is the best deal. A way to get more than they want you to. You just have to figure it out.

Help you?

Pimply white boy behind the counter in a red bandana and cowboy hat. Danny watches him pretending not to watch. He can tell. How the kid's mouth squeezes shut, like he's saving up something good to tell somebody later. Tina acts like none of it bothers her. Danny can't decide if it really doesn't or if she just never knows what's going on. She's standing with one hip stuck out stiff, like a picture she must have seen someplace, smiling about nothing. She wants— Oh, just a salad. And giggles. White boy's staring at her crotch. Danny moves up behind her, makes the kid drop his eyes. Nobody stares at Danny for long.

They get a different kind of look from the black girl who serves up the drinks, and another from the old man at the cash register. So what's your problem, bitch? And what's yours, old peckerwood, it's a prejudiced store and that's no lie. By the time they sit down to their food he's got such a face on him it's Tina's turn to ask: What's the matter?

This place, Danny says. It gets on my nerves.

It's not that bad, she says. She's busy putting red stuff on her salad.

You think you know what you're talkin about but you don't.

Cabbage, says Tina. I can't believe they put cabbage in this thing. Barf. You mean people looking. Big deal.

Is a big deal to some.

If you let it be. Hey this is not news.

News you don't never seem to learn, girl.

So we're supposed to go around apologizing to the world or something?

You a trip, says Danny. He's thinking it's times like this he can't decide if she's very brave or very dumb or both. Tina asks him what that's supposed to mean, but he just shakes his head. You a trip, he says again, and she can tell it's something all right.

I like that shirt on you, you know? says Tina, and she waves a forkful of wet white lettuce for emphasis. It makes you look tough. Like a lumberjack or something.

Quit throwing food. Lumberjack? Some dude who climbs trees?

I'm just telling you. It makes you look tough.

Finish eating that stuff, says Danny, and that's all he'll say. A trip. He's watching her lean across the table top to be serious, watching her light eyes and pretty hair and the thin silver rings on her little hands that are always cold, always moving, always trying to explain things so they come out right.

He met her three months ago at a bar she was way too young to be in. Tina and two of her girlfriends, all of them nervous and dressed up and drinking their fancy drinks too fast, little girls looking for trouble. Every ten seconds they'd check out the scene, put their heads together and laugh about nothing. That's what he saw of her first, her thin little neck arching around the room. She wore her hair up that night, trying to look older, maybe, and she had on these earrings. First thing he ever said to her. Hey mamma, some fancy hoops. And she giggled and looked scared and said thank you. Looking for trouble and here it is. He asked if she wanted another drink and she said yes. And did she want to dance and she did and it was all just about that easy.

Looking for trouble. Leading her up his stairs the first time he wondered: Are all white girls this dumb? He still doesn't know. It's like she never knows what anything's worth, what things cost, herself included. Dumb or brave? She kept making it easy. She held onto his arm going up the stairs and she wasn't really that drunk but she pretended she was. Oh my, she said when they got inside. I hope you're not somebody mean, you don't look mean. You have nice eyes. He wonders what it's like to be born that trustful. It's got to be something you're born into, a luxury. He knows that never in a hundred lives could he learn to be that careless, spending yourself that easy. More like he can't unlearn what he knows. Caution. Watching your back. People out to do you dirt. Something he's stuck with as sure as his color. He looks across the table at her playing with her food. She never eats anything. Little breasts he weighs with his mouth. Little girl hands with the nails she can't keep from chewing, pretty hair, peppermint lips. Oh, he's crazy about her, or maybe just plain crazy, but sometimes, like now, he feels they're part of a very old story, him and her, one that's happened too many times before and he already knows how it ends up and there's nothing he can do or say to change it. There's one last bite of fatty meat on his plate and he swallows it without tasting, getting his money's worth.

He's right, Tina doesn't mind people staring, at least not like he minds, and here's why: It makes them together against everybody else. It makes her more of a part of what he is. Him and her. She pokes at her salad like she wants to make sure it's going to lie still. She's seventeen years old and she's in love. Those are the really important things to know about her. Black and white? She believes in equality and all that, but mostly she believes in love and how it makes everything all right. How it's what really matters. She wonders what her parents would do if they knew about Danny. Kick her out of the house or more likely lock her up in it. She and Danny would have to run off together and Danny'd get into fights for her and win or even lose and maybe they'd both end up dying together. Well, not that, but anyway something beautiful and sad. She's in love. She fusses with her tray until Danny looks up.

You through wasting food?

I'm done, if that's what you want to know.

Let's go then.

Danny walks ahead this time and Tina watches him. She likes his big hands and his heavy shoulders and even the way he walks, slow and sort of mean looking. He's not one bit mean. That's something else she likes about him. Not one bit, not like the white boys her own age who have nothing better to do than see how much snot can come out of their mouths, how much meanness they can invent. Danny's twenty-two and he's a serious person. He has a real job too, a hard job, lifting and moving things at a factory. She'd like to brag about that a little if there was anyone to tell. There's something valuable she thinks, in having a real, adult life, even having important problems like money and jobs. She thinks there's something less than real about her own life, that gossip and school and parents are just taking up space because there's nothing more important to fill it. It's a life where you keep waiting for something to happen, as if everything's been promised but nobody says when it's coming. Sometimes she gets so sick of it all, sick of herself too, like she'll never grow up, never know anything. She gets very stern with herself, tells herself she's spoiled, all she's good for is complaining about nothing, saying the wrong thing, laughing too much, look at her, bowlegged, big-ass, everything wrong. *Danny*, she wants to ask him sometimes, *tell me what you like about me, tell me about me, I don't know anything.* She catches up with Danny and slips her hand through the crook of his arm and Danny sort of scowls. Just like a man, she thinks, wanting to pretend he doesn't know you until you get behind closed doors. Just like a man, she says to herself, finding some comfort in it, as if she knew exactly what that meant.

The car lumbers backward out of the parking space and Tina rests her forehead against the window. The glass is smudged and thick and it makes everything she sees waver a little, lightpoles and buses coughing up dirty smoke and people waiting on corners looking cold. If she squeezes her eyes almost shut everything runs together, melting. Mashed bus, tilting sky, bodies swallowed up by soft curbs. She wishes they could drive forever. Just the two of them and the music cranked up all the way and nothing else to worry about. And Danny would take care of the car and she could make him laugh about things and whenever they got hungry they'd stop and eat. Just the two of them. She sighs and makes a few more blocks worth of ugly scenery melt with her eyes but it won't go away and neither will anything else and sooner or later she'll have to go home. Her parents' house is large and small at the same time. Big rooms they fill up with quarrels and their narrow faces watching her til there's no space to breathe. And the hundred questions they throw at her, trying to trip her up. Who are you, that's what all the questions come down to. Who are you, and they don't know one real thing about her and never will. She sighs again and turns away from the window.

Danny, she says, if we were older—if I was older, mostly—do you think we'd live together?

Well you ain't older, are you.

But I'm asking. Would we?

Danny shrugs. He has all the usual cautious male instincts. He says, How am I supposed to know?

Well haven't you even thought about it?

I don't know. I guess. I mean, I got too much else to think about.

Yes or no?

Yes or no what?

I'm just asking. Would you want to? It'd be so nice. We could fix the place up, everything.

Uh huh.

So what does that mean. It means you don't want to.

Did I say that? I said, why worry about it right now. Worry about something you don't have to make up. So what's the matter with you now?

Nothing, says Tina, meaning, Everything.

Oh man, says Danny. Oh man. You for real?

I'd get a job, says Tina. It's not like I'm saying you'd have to support me or anything. Oh never mind.

The Plymouth rolls and rolls, the tailpipe belching argument now, radio noise too loud and everything else too quiet. Danny looking like thunder. Tina looking like rain. A very old story. Maybe every fight comes down to this sooner or later, a man thinking: She wants too much from me. A woman afraid he won't want enough of her. Just like a man. Just like a woman, and how does anybody get along with anybody?

You can get pretty good mileage from arguments, keep things rolling as long as you want. But look here. Something up ahead in the road. Danny sees it first.

Damn if that ain't Claude, he says, and hits the gas.

Tina sits up now, with dignity, remembering she's still mad, but damn if that ain't Claude. Black-and-silver Cutlass cruising up ahead. OK Claude. Danny catches up to him and honks. Funny how much you can tell sometimes from the back of somebody's head. How Claude sees them in the mirror, wishes he hadn't, waves, ducks, speeds up, slows down, aw shit. No way out of it. OK Claude.

Watching from the air, you'd see both cars rumble into the parking lot of an empty Tastee-Freeze, see Danny get out and go over to lean against Claude's car. They stand there awhile, just talking, because of course nothing's going to be as simple as Claude reaching in his pocket and handing over money, everybody knows that, even Tina. Finally Danny gets back in the Plymouth, and both cars start up again.

It's over to Claude's flat now. Tina wants to wait in the car. It's almost a fight. She knows she can't come in, and she doesn't want to go home. She says she wants to find out what happens, which is true enough. Old deadbeat Claude, she says, and Danny tells her that's about enough. Maybe he'd say more, but there's Claude waiting for him, pretending not to watch. Claude doesn't miss much. He has all the instincts of the natural gossip.

Damn, this door about broke, says Claude, who's having trouble with his key. Danny looks back at Tina, sitting across the street in the Plymouth. He can just see her through the cloudy windshield. She's combing her hair, letting it hang down long. She's got the radio on, he can see her mouth pouting along with the music. *Damn*. He wishes she wasn't here. It shames him somehow, having her sit there waiting for him, like she knows he made a mistake. The part he doesn't want to admit about Claude is how it felt good to lend money. Big shot. Now he has to go back on it. Like that feeling good was a fool's feeling, and generosity is something not allowed him. Almost he'd rather be Claude. It would be easier, just pay or can't pay. How is it all so mixed up with Tina, why does he feel she's making him do this, sending him in here to collect money for her? Why does she think everything's so simple, white girls can afford to be dumb, what does she want him to do? Almost he'd rather be Claude.

Once they get inside Claude goes over to the box, switches things on and off. Music squawks and growls. Neither of them starts in about the money yet. They're friends. They know what's what. No point in rushing. They know how it gets complicated, measuring out the demands of hospitality, gratitude, dignity, how it all takes time.

Danny sighs, getting comfortable. He says You got any pop or anything, and Claude fetches them some.

Me and Al went out last night and drank up all the beer in the world, offers Claude.

Yeah? says Danny, mildly interested. Where at?

I know where we started out at. I can't even lie to you, I don't know where we ended up.

That so? says Danny. Both of you trouble.

It's all just talk that doesn't cost anything. Just passing time. So Claude's sort of worthless, but he knows all the good stories. He can make you laugh like crazy once he gets to carrying on: Then Al, he just yells out, Damn bitch, how much? And then don't things get wild. You should see it.

Yeah? says Danny again, and Women, he says, as if this is what they've been talking about all along, and he shakes his head.

More trouble than they worth, says Claude. They have this conversation all the time, he knows what to say.

What is it they want from you. It's always something they're after from you.

Well I'll tell you Danny, says Claude, and he winks. He looks just exactly like a monkey. I'll tell you, what they want is what they ain't got. The equipment, you know?

Outside it's clouding over, with a taste of something warm and damp in the air. Tina's still waiting. She knows how to wait for Danny. He never shows up when she thinks he ought to. It's like algebra: when he gets there = when she thinks he ought to get there + x. So she plays the radio a little. She sorts through her purse. She knows she has to wait in the car. Danny has to go in and take care of business. Talking man, talking black. She knows she has to wait.

She thinks that there will always be times when one of them, her or Danny, will have to wait in the car.

She wonders sometimes if she wants to be black.

She wonders sometimes if she wants to be anything as long as it's not herself.

She has this feeling that somebody somewhere's looking at her and Danny down the barrel of a gun. She believes in love, but other people don't. Somebody somewhere, maybe God Almighty himself getting ready to squeeze off a shot. She thinks it will sneak up on them, something quick, something they'll amost see coming. And when it's over they'll lie there quiet together, both hearts open like flowers bleeding red, one color.

You think you know all about those girls, those little white girls who go out with the black boys, but maybe you don't.

The clouds are low and warm and purple, like the sky changes sometimes between winter and spring. It's after five now. Even without a watch you could tell time from the way the streets change, wheels sounding heavier, everything faster. Tina closes her eyes and listens. She thinks she can hear the world in the streets the way you hear the ocean in a seashell. The world sounds confused, she thinks, like a hundred voices all talking at once. She tries to hear just one at a time. Her eyes are closed and maybe she falls asleep listening, because here's Danny getting in the car at last.

He reaches over and tugs at her hair and she can tell by looking at him that it's something all right. Oh Danny, she says. I knew you'd fix things up.

Shoot, says Danny. Didn't I tell you?

What he doesn't tell her is Claude only gave him a hundred and seventy-five, but that's OK. Its all right for now. He listens to the Plymouth's engine stutter and heave and then finally catch. It's all right for now.

I bet Claude was scared to death when he saw you. I bet he was scared as shit.

Huh, says Danny, just to be saying something.

You know I'm thinking, says Tina, once they're driving again. (She sounds dreamy, like she's still listening to the voices outside. Like she's listening to herself too.) I'm thinking when I'm just a little older I could get a job. A good job too. I could sell clothes. I could wait tables or mix drinks.

Don't want you working behind no bar.

Well something. And first thing I'll do is move out. The very first thing.

Danny's waiting for her to say more but she's chewing on her hair. There's one voice for black, she's thinking, and one for white, and another for black-and-white.

Well, says Danny after a minute. Maybe we can think about us getting a place together. That's all I'm saying for now. We can think about it.

Later, when they're back at Danny's, it starts to rain. A warm rain, they can smell it through the open window. They lie in each others' arms in the dark and listen to the winter melting. They're pretending this roof is the roof of the world and nothing can ever get in.

Their breath is a warm wind. Their hands are Africa and Spain, almost touching. Outside, the rain is soaking into the soft earth. It rains and rains, like God's suddenly bored with dryness and with making things too easy. Water builds into streams, into floods. Everything is coming loose in the pounding water, everything begins to move and change its shape. Everything turns into something else. They can no longer tell sky from water. When they close their eyes to sleep, they float in a current filled with darkness and other people's unquiet dreams. No matter. This room is the world, their skin is its roof. Nothing will get in tonight.

Jean Thompson is the author, most recently, of *My Wisdom*, a novel about life in America in the 1960s, and of *The Gasoline Wars*, a widely acclaimed collection of short stories. Among the magazines that have published her stories are *Mademoiselle, Ploughshares, Chicago, Southwest Review* and *Kansas Quarterly*; two of her stories were included in the 1979 *Best American Short Stories* and *The Random Review* (1982). In 1984 Ms. Thompson received a Guggenheim Fellowship and the John H. McGinnis Memorial Award from *Southwest Review* for her story "Naomi Counting Time."

A graduate of the University of Illinois, she holds an M.F.A. in creative writing from Bowling Green State University. She lives in Urbana, Illinois, where she is associate professor of English at the University of Illinois and where she has taught fiction writing since 1973. Jean Thompson's second novel, *The Woman Driver*, will be published in 1985.